She didn't know the humans had named her Star.

Nor did she know that she was in a five-acre penned area deep inside the Flat Tops Wilderness near Sweetwater, Colorado.

Star was the alpha female of the pack of six wolves, in many respects more important to the pack's survival than the alpha male. She and her companions had been captured months before, thousands of miles away in northern Canada, shipped south in a series of terrifying enclosures, allowed to grow accustomed to these alien, drier southern mountains. Initial terror had faded to acceptance, and the faraway tundra receded in the pack's collective consciousness. This was home now, as it was meant to be.

The day was cool and clear, the aspen trees swaths of bright gold on the mountainside. Star sniffed the air: today something was different.

The gate to the pen was open.

Star's senses spoke to her of danger, although she could not yet be sure of its form. She was going to find out, though, and it would walk on two legs and reek of hatred for her and her pack.

UPON A
MIDNIGHT
CLEAR
Lynn Erickson

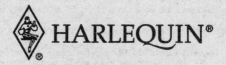

HARLEQUIN®

TORONTO • NEW YORK • LONDON
AMSTERDAM • PARIS • SYDNEY • HAMBURG
STOCKHOLM • ATHENS • TOKYO • MILAN • MADRID
PRAGUE • WARSAW • BUDAPEST • AUCKLAND

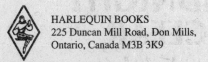

HARLEQUIN BOOKS
225 Duncan Mill Road, Don Mills,
Ontario, Canada M3B 3K9

ISBN 0-373-65313-1

UPON A MIDNIGHT CLEAR

LYNN ERICKSON

When writing together, after fifty-plus books, Molly Swanton and Carla Peltonen are truly one voice—that of Lynn Erickson. They met in the sixties in Aspen, Colorado, and still live in the beautiful mountain resort with their husbands, Erik and Terry Lynn. Get it? Lynn Erickson?

The ladies began writing when their children were babies—now the kids are long gone, not too far from middle-age and the moms get to visit them in New York, Seattle and Sydney, Australia. When they aren't plotting their next book, Carla horseback rides and skis and Molly is still trying to break ninety in her golf game.

Please address questions and book requests to:
Harlequin Reader Service
U.S.: 3010 Walden Ave., P.O. Box 1325, Buffalo, NY 14269
Canadian: P.O. Box 609, Fort Erie, Ont. L2A 5X3

PROLOGUE

SHE DIDN'T KNOW the humans had named her Star because of her white coat of fur. Nor did she know that she was in a five-acre penned area erected exclusively for her and her companions. The area was at the end of a dirt road deep inside the Flat Tops Wilderness near Sweetwater, Colorado. Her reality was first scent, then hearing, then sight, then fear and age-old instinct.

Star was the alpha female of the pack of six wolves, in many respects more important to the pack's survival than Silverfoot, the alpha male. It was fall now, and in the winter to come they would mate, or so the humans hoped, and next spring there would be pups.

The wolves were all fat on game they hadn't chased or caught, game that had miraculously appeared at regular intervals. Star ate the game, but something inside her seethed with unease, remembering her previous life as a huntress.

She and her companions had been captured months before, thousands of miles away in northern Canada, shipped south in a series of terrifying enclosures, then let loose in this area of safety, watched over by humans, allowed to grow accustomed to these alien, drier southern mountains. Initial terror had faded to acceptance, and the faraway tundra receded in the pack's collective consciousness. This was home now, as it was meant to be.

The day was cool and clear, the Colorado sky uniquely, piercingly blue, the aspen trees swathes of bright gold on the mountainside, the spruce and pine trees black in contrast. Star sniffed the air: humans, yes, but something was different.

The gate to the pen was opened.

Warily Star approached and sniffed. Silverfoot stood as still as a statue, testing the air for danger. The others crowded behind, the beta female's muzzle on Star's flank.

Their eyes darted nervously, but they proceeded forward, tails tucked, hackles raised, into the wilderness that was to be their home. They moved in a wolf's typical loose, cycling motion, so that it appeared as if their bodies floated over their long, spindly legs, a somewhat feline movement, totally unlike dogs. Their pace was slow and cautious now, but they could accelerate to forty miles an hour in the hunt.

Star gathered in the scents: the accustomed human ones that were behind them now, familiar ones of stone and dust, mice droppings, dead leaves, unfamiliar ones that were new types of plants, strange birds and shrubs.

Silverfoot led the pack to a stand of colorful aspen trees, and they disappeared into its dappled shade. He asserted himself, growling at an omega male, marking a tree with his scent.

The pack moved on, up into the mountains. A squirrel chattered angrily at them, resenting these intruders, but how could the squirrel remember the last time a wolf had passed below its tree some sixty years before?

An abrupt crashing sound—a terrified white-tailed deer bounded away through the undergrowth, but the pack was not hungry, only intent on exploring this new land. Star stopped short, ears cocked, one foot raised, and listened. Miles away a bull elk bugled. It was rutting season. A good sound. Familiar.

The pack moved on, tense, anxious. Ancient instincts needed time to adjust to the alien environment, but the instincts were there and had allowed the wolf to survive for hundreds of thousands of years in this location, through drought and blizzard and ice age, through the extinction of the woolly mammoth and the arrival of the recent but most dangerous predator, man.

Star's shoulder muscles bunched and her flanks quivered as she moved higher, away from the smell and sound of her natural enemy. Her senses spoke to her of danger in this foreign place, although she could not yet be sure of its form. She was going to find out, though, and it would walk on two legs and reek of hatred for her and her pack.

CHAPTER ONE

One Year Later

STEVE SLATER HUNKERED down on his heels beside the remains of one of his calves, thumbed his Stetson off his forehead and whistled in frustration.

Another dead calf. That was two in ten days; four, no, five in the past year. Those damn wolves were getting bolder, killing for a lark now that they'd figured out what an easy mark cattle were. Hell, it was only November. They couldn't be that hungry now, but they were coming down here anyway to hunt, right on the home fields where the stock had been moved for the winter.

He didn't touch the carcass; he'd call the U.S. Fish and Wildlife Service in Denver. Again. The good old USFWS. Pretty hard to convince them that wolves were vicious predators who threatened ranchers' livelihoods when the service itself had made the decision to reintroduce the wolves into Colorado. They'd made the decision despite years of controversy, after public meetings and studies and high-flown speeches, protests and sit-ins. Well, they'd made their goddamn stupid decision, and this half-eaten calf was the result.

Anger burned in Steve, a slow burn. He straightened up and studied the ground. It was dry, no snow yet, the grass brown and mostly trampled by his herd of cattle, but he could sure see quite a few paw prints in the soft dry soil between the hillocks of bunch grass. Yeah, wolves.

Steve stood there and looked off into the distance toward the jagged, snow-topped mountains that rose from his ranchland, as if he could see the wolves, the six of them that made up the pack that had been released not twenty miles from his home. Twenty miles was nothing to a wolf; he could lope along for five or six miles then speed up for the chase.

Endangered species. Steve gave a grunt of disgust. Protected by federal law. What about him? What about the small rancher and farmer? Wasn't he an endangered species? He'd sure like to see the day Washington helped *him* out.

Steve took one more look around, checked the number on the dead calf's ear tag, whistled to his two dogs and walked back to his muddy pickup. He waited for the dogs to jump in the bed, then patted them on their heads. "Wish you could talk," he said, "because I know you could tell those dumb Fish and Wildlife agents exactly what happened here. They sure won't believe me." Then he closed the tailgate, climbed into the cab and drove across the five-hundred-acre ranch toward home.

Everyone used the side door of the house, the one that opened onto the mudroom. The front door faced the carefully tended lawn, Leslie's pride and joy, which she'd watered and fertilized for years. But the front door was only used for guests, of which there weren't many lately. The long driveway and the easiest place to park was near the side door. Steve stopped the truck in its usual spot and crossed the drive, the irrigation ditch, the patch of autumn brown grass, and went inside.

The Slater house had been built in the twenties by Steve's grandfather, replacing the original log ranch house. It was a traditional two-story building, roomy and comfortable, with siding painted blue and the entire front faced with river rock. The floors were wide-planked wood, there was a big fireplace in the living room and there was a view of the mountains from the many-paned front windows.

He strode in, angry still, tossed his hat onto the kitchen counter, adding to the clutter, and picked up the phone. He knew the Denver number by heart, knew the extension, too: Hal Franklin, 336. Drumming his fingers impatiently, Steve waited for Hal to answer. Goddamn, but he hated to be under the thumb of agencies and bureaucracies. He worked for himself, as his father had before him, and his father, back to the first Slaters who'd settled here in the 1870s. None of them had asked for or received help from the government when they'd settled this land. They'd made it safe and productive for people, and if they'd eradicated the wolves, well, that's what they'd had to do to survive.

Today he was at the mercy of Fish and Wildlife and a thousand federal laws. It was a felony to kill a wolf now, for God's sake, when not too long ago the self-same government had paid a bounty to exterminate them!

There was a click in his ear, then a voice came on—a recording. Agent Hal Franklin wasn't in, but if you'd leave a message…

"Steve Slater here. Sweetwater. We've got another dead calf, Hal. You better get on up here and take a look-see. Paw prints, the works. And what's the status on the one from ten days ago? Call me." Then he slammed down the phone, hoping Hal's voice mail picked up the noise.

He made a couple more phone calls—one to his neighbor Ben Garrett, another to Brad Milligan. "Yeah, another calf. This has gotta stop. I know it. I've got a call in to Hal Franklin in Denver. Yeah, I know. A lotta good that does."

Same old conversation, same old worries. And no way to protect themselves. Their grandfathers had simply poisoned or trapped or shot predators who killed stock, but now it was against the law. Wolves were right in there with the spotted owl and that weird kind of salamander. Endangered species. He gritted his teeth in frustration.

Hal Franklin finally returned his call just after four o'clock.

"Another calf, Steve?" he asked.

"That's right. Paw prints all over the place. They're coming in closer and the kills are at shorter intervals."

"We're still not convinced it's the wolves doing it, Steve," Hal said cautiously. "You know that. I got the autopsy report on the last calf, and there's some doubt...."

Steve gave a short laugh. "So you think aliens are doing it? Land in some spaceship, kill a calf, take off. Come on."

"It could be dogs, wild dogs, or those wolf-dog hybrids."

"Hal, no one around here's ever seen a wild dog or a hybrid. There aren't any."

"Look, Steve, I really feel for you guys up there, you know that. All of us here are real concerned. We're trying our best to figure out who—what's killing your stock. You know it's as bad for us as it is for you if the wolf reintroduction doesn't work out. We've both got a lot at stake. And I'll tell you, Steve, we just aren't sure wolves are killing your stock."

"For God's sake, Hal, who's doing it, then?"

Hal sighed. "When we find out, you'll be the first to know."

"I expect you up here, Hal. I need to put in a claim for the calf."

"I'll be up tomorrow. But you know all the claims are on hold until we have proof it's a wolf kill."

"Proof! What more do you want? You want a nice, tidy video of the wolf smiling into the camera and saying he did it? No one can catch those animals—they're too smart. We never see them."

"I know, I know."

"What good is the law if it just isn't practical? Sure, I can shoot a wolf if I catch him in the act of killing stock, but when's the last time that happened? And this fund that's supposed to reimburse ranchers for stock is on hold. Some help that is. You guys better figure out what to do or you'll have one of those sagebrush rebellions on your hands."

"Steve, don't go off half-cocked. Tell your friends. Don't do anything crazy. We're going to settle this thing."

"Time's running out."

"Look, I'll be up tomorrow. See you then. Believe me, Steve, we're working on this problem. We've got ideas. Things are in motion. Trust me."

"Right," Steve said, and he hung up.

When he turned around he saw that his two daughters had gotten home from school and had come in so quietly he hadn't heard them. But they'd heard him.

"Dad," Heather said. "You were yelling."

He took a deep breath and tried to calm himself down. "I was just trying to make a point."

Jeannie just stood there, her lower lip trembling. She was extremely sensitive. At twelve she hadn't yet grown a protective facade; maybe she never would. And he'd upset her.

"Now Jeannie's going to cry and I've got to listen to all that stuff about wolves again. Gee, Dad, it's getting awful old," Heather said scornfully.

"I am not," Jeannie said, but her eyes glistened with unshed tears.

"Come here," Steve said to his younger daughter. "I'm sorry, honey. Come on." She hung her head and moved toward him, and he patted her shoulder awkwardly. "I'm sorry," he repeated. He knew Leslie would have hugged Jeannie, a big, tight hug, and maybe shed a few tears with her daughter, but he couldn't do that. Men didn't show that kind of emotion.

"What happened?" Heather asked.

"Another calf."

"I thought so." She cocked her head and eyed him. "What're you going to do?"

Steve ran his fingers through his straight dark hair. "What *can* I do? My hands are tied—you know that."

"I'm glad," Jeannie said in a small voice.

"Jeannie, you know what's going on here. It's our survival. It's a roof over your head, shoes, gas for the truck. We don't live in a petting zoo." He kept trying to explain it to her, but his youngest daughter had such a soft heart, she was utterly without defenses.

"I know," she whispered, "but—"

"Oh, Dad," Heather interrupted, "don't waste your breath. We've both heard it all before."

"Well, I guess you haven't understood it, then," Steve said.

"I understand," Heather said in that defiant, quasimature way she'd developed. Where her sister was too sensitive, Heather had buried all her feelings under a hostile teenage veneer. They were both hard to deal with, Steve thought. And he just didn't seem to have the parenting skills to do it very well.

Parenting skills. Psychobabble. He loved his girls, what else did they need? But he knew what they needed, and he couldn't provide it. A mother.

"I've heard both sides," Heather was saying. "We've had debates at school. The trouble is, you old-fashioned ranchers can't see the world is different. Miss Timroth says man has to take responsibility for the bad things he's done in the past and try to correct his mistakes. The environment…"

Steve held up a hand. "Please, honey, spare me the ecological-disaster speech. I have a dead calf. Tom Morehead had one ten days ago. There were three last summer. I may be old-fashioned, but something's got to be done, and soon.''

"Oh, Dad.''

"Please don't hurt the wolves,'' Jeannie said. "Please, Dad.''

He said nothing. Those damn wolves, plastered all over the newspapers, on TV, in *Time* magazine. They were famous. People had even named them: Star, Silverfoot, Auntie Mame. As if they were pets. Every rancher around Sweetwater knew what kind of press they'd get if they touched a hair on the head of one of those precious beasts. It'd be World War III.

He saw Jeannie's misery and relented. "Aw, honey, I'm not going to do anything right now. That's why I called Hal in Denver. The Fish and Wildlife Service put the wolves here, and I guess they'll have to take them away again.''

"And let them loose somewhere else?'' Jeannie asked.

"Sure, someplace where there's no cattle for them to eat. Far away.''

Jeannie smiled. "I guess that'd be okay.''

Steve noted Heather rolling her eyes in derision behind her sister's back. At least, he thought thankfully, it was silent derision. This time.

"So, girls, how about some help with dinner? I've got more chores to do. There's some hamburger meat in the freezer. How about you get it out and…''

"Spaghetti, hamburgers or meat loaf,'' Heather said dryly.

"Pick one,'' Steve said. "Your choice.''

"Meat loaf,'' Jeannie said. "I like the way it squishes in my hands when I mix it.''

"Gross,'' Heather remarked.

"Just wash your hands first,'' Steve said. "And mashed potatoes?''

"Sure."

"You kids have homework?"

"Of course, Dad."

He shrugged on his jean jacket, plucked his hat from the counter and went out. He still had to drive hay out to the west pasture to feed the yearlings. Backing the truck up to the stacked bales of hay, he wrestled a dozen onto his truck, whistled for the dogs, who jumped on top of the load, and drove down the bumpy dirt road. He hopped out to undo the wire gate, drove through and started dropping bales at intervals in the field. It took a lot of starting and stopping for one person to do the job, and it had to be done every day from November through May, when he drove the herds up into the high country, onto BLM, Bureau of Land Management, land for the summer. He paid $1.61 per cow per month for grazing rights on four hundred acres, the same way most ranchers did. A few ranchers owned enough acreage outright to graze all their stock on their own land, but they were the exception.

A lot of work, but that's what a rancher did. At least he was his own boss. He had a guy who came to help five days a week, but this was one of his days off, so Steve worked alone, climbing onto the truck bed, cutting the baling string and spreading the hay on the ground. If you just tossed it off in a pile, the stock would fight over it.

His black-and-white dog, Shep, loved to herd. He jumped off the truck and dodged around, nipping at the yearlings' heels, growling ferociously. Shep could scare a calf if he kept after it, but the big bulls merely turned their huge white faces toward him and refused to budge, far more intent on eating.

Boots, the old shepherd mix, kept guard on the truck, watching everything with his great serious brown eyes.

It was dark before Steve got back to the house. He was sweaty and dirty, hay stuck in his hair. He smelled meat loaf cooking, saw his girls' heads bent over schoolbooks at the kitchen table.

Heather looked up. "Aunt Naomi called."

"Do I need to call her back?" Steve asked.

"No, we both talked to her. She was just seeing how we are. They're coming for Thanksgiving."

"I know. And Grandma's okay?" Steve's mother lived with his sister in New Castle, about an hour away.

"She's fine."

"I'm going up to take a shower, okay, kids?"

"Take your time. Jeannie cut up the potatoes and put them in the pot, then she forgot to turn the stove on. It'll be a while."

"Shut up, Heather," Jeannie cried.

"I won't help you with your spelling, Jeannie-weenie. Be nice."

"Don't. See if I care."

Steve left them arguing. Whenever he tried to referee, their spats got worse. He didn't quite know what to say or how to settle their fights. Well, they always made up eventually. He guessed if you loved your kids, things would turn out all right. It was just that it was hard for him to show his love. Leslie had been the one who hugged and dried tears and gushed over crayon pictures from school.

He showered and dressed in clean jeans and a denim shirt. His jaw was shadowed with whiskers, and he rubbed a callused hand over his chin. No sense shaving again. He'd do it in the morning.

Downstairs, Heather was drilling Jeannie on her spelling. Inwardly Steve sighed with relief. "I'll finish asking her," he said to Heather. "Then we'll set the table."

Evening routine. It was okay now. It'd been difficult at first, with the girls so young, but it was okay now. They ate a lot of boxed macaroni-and-cheese, and spaghetti, but they managed. The girls loved it when Grandma or Aunt

Naomi visited, because both women cooked up a storm while they were there, making casseroles and thick, hearty soups and freezing them in neatly labeled freezer bags so that the poor Slaters didn't starve to death or come down with beriberi, whatever that was.

The phone rang as Steve was laying out napkins and forks.

Heather answered it. "Dad, it's for you."

It was Tom Morehead, one of the valley's ranchers. "I heard about the calf from Ben," Tom said. "This is bad, Steve."

"Sure is. Brad's going to call a meeting. We've got to present a united front, Tom. Let's make sure we do this whole thing legally. No vigilante justice. I spoke to Hal Franklin in Denver. He'll be here tomorrow."

"Hal Franklin," Tom said angrily. "He's just one of them head-in-the-clouds tree-huggers. What's he gonna do?"

"He said they're working on it. He assured me they were as worried as we are. Said they have as much at stake."

"Bull cookies!"

"Yeah, well, I'll talk to him tomorrow. Maybe we can set up a meeting with him."

"Well, all I can say is, I carry my rifle with me all the time now. I see one of them critters on my land, I'm gonna blast him to kingdom come."

"I know how you feel, Tom."

"Have you talked to Brad?"

"Yeah, I called him earlier." Brad Milligan was president of the local chapter of the Colorado Cattlemen's Association. So far the association hadn't issued an official opinion on the wolf introduction, but the Sweetwater local chapter sure had. "Brad said he'd call a meeting."

"We've had meetings till they're coming out our ears," Tom said. "When're we going to do something concrete?"

"I don't know, Tom. I just don't know."

When he hung up, the girls were already at the table, waiting for him.

"Sorry," he said, sitting down.

"This is getting boring, Dad," Heather said in her newly honed superior manner.

He shot her a glance from under straight black brows. "Maybe to you, kiddo."

"You know what Mrs. Farley said at school today?" Jeannie interrupted, trying to head off a disagreement.

"What'd she say?" Steve asked.

"That winter's coming early, because the caterpillars are real woolly."

"Hey, I'll keep that in mind. Think I have enough hay to last?" He was glad for the change of subject, glad his younger daughter wasn't as prickly and difficult as her sister.

"You have enough," Jeannie said, smiling her sweet, shy smile.

After dinner he helped the girls do the dishes. They were pretty darn good about doing their chores. The house stuff, anyway. Naomi and his mother were always scandalized at the mess, but he kind of liked the homey clutter of the old house. He and the girls kept the kitchen and bathrooms cleaned, did the laundry, vacuumed once a week or so. It was fine.

The girls finished up some homework after the table was cleared, and Steve went into the den to watch the news on TV. He was dog tired and sank into the old armchair with a sigh, put his stocking feet on the footrest, clicked the remote to CNN.

He found it hard to relax, though. Anxiety gnawed at him. What if the wolves kept killing stock? In his case— in the case of a lot of small ranchers—a couple of calves could make the difference between profit and loss. He watched the screen, but his mind didn't register a thing. Somebody had to do something about the situation—there had to be a solution, some compromise between the ranchers and the government. There had to be, but he sure as hell couldn't come up with it.

Heather appeared in the living room doorway. "Is it okay if I go out Saturday night? A group of us are going to the movie in Eagle."

"How're you getting there?" he asked.

"Nan's mom will drive. She's got a class that night."

"Sure, honey. That's fine."

"Jeannie's gone up to bed."

"Okay. I'll go up in a minute. Uh, Heather…"

"Mmm?"

"Go easy on Jeannie. You know how sensitive she is." Heather made a face. "She's such a baby."

"It's been hard for her."

"Oh, it's been so easy for me."

"I didn't mean that, Heather. You know that. It's hard for all of us." He couldn't say anything right when it came to his older daughter.

"You meant it. Just because I'm older…" She was sulking.

"Yes, you're older, and I depend on you. I always thought you were sorta proud of that. Your mother sure would have been…."

"Don't talk about her! She's gone, that's all. So don't keep bringing her up, Dad!"

He couldn't bear the pain in Heather's voice. The anger. Somewhere in his brain he knew he should talk this out with Heather, but it was too painful and he didn't know where to start. He'd only make it worse.

"Okay, honey. Take it easy."

"You take it easy. You're so uptight," she said. "Oh, I give up. I'm going to bed."

"Sweet dreams, kiddo."

"Yeah, sure." She tossed her thick dark hair and ran up the stairs.

Steve leaned his head on his hand, elbow on the arm of his chair. He massaged the bridge of his nose. God, you had to be careful with her. You had to walk on eggshells every moment. A word, a gesture, anything would set her off. All that hostility. He so badly wanted his kids to be happy, but he couldn't seem to manage it. They needed a mother. They needed Leslie.

He waited a minute until he knew Heather was safely in her room, then he trudged upstairs to say good-night to Jeannie, a nightly ritual she seemed to relish. Of course, Heather had outgrown it, or at least she said she had.

He knocked once on Jeannie's door, then went in. "Hey, Jeannie, how's it going?"

"Fine, Dad. I know all my spelling words and I wrote a story about the trip we took to Denver last summer."

"Good work." He sat on the edge of her bed and smiled down at her small, earnest face. Her hair was brown, not as dark as Heather's or his own, but a rich brown, and her eyes were blue, like Leslie's. Oh, she was her mother's child, all right, just as Heather took after him. Maybe that was why he got along with Jeannie better and clashed with Heather. He loved them both equally, but one was tough to love and the other was easy.

He leaned over and kissed Jeannie on the forehead. "Sleep tight," he said, "and don't..."

"Let the bedbugs bite," his daughter finished.

Back downstairs, watching the Denver weather report, Steve couldn't help remembering the framed photographs on Jeannie's dresser: One was of two of those blasted wolves taken last year when the pack had been released from the pen into the Flat Tops Wilderness. Published in *Time*, the photo was famous all over the country. The white wolf, Star, with the other one, the alpha male, nuzzling her neck. Real cute.

The other picture on Jeannie's dresser was of his wife, Leslie. She was smiling, looking into the camera, her hair blowing in the breeze. Jeannie kept the picture in her room, but Heather kept no such reminders of her mother. Posters adorned her walls: Brad Pitt, Pearl Jam and Bon Jovi.

Leslie. He didn't talk much about her, despite Heather's remark to the contrary. He tended to keep his feelings to himself. Oh, he had feelings, all right, but he'd been raised to consider it a weakness in a man to display them. A man took it on the chin and kept his cool, kept his dignity. No weeping or wailing or gushing. Women could do that, but not men. All his life Steve Slater had accepted those rules of behavior without analyzing them, but lately he'd begun to think that the reason men weren't supposed to show emotion came not from strength, which was what he'd always assumed, but from weakness. Because if he ever gave in to his emotions, he might lose control for good. It was, he sometimes thought, as if he were hanging on to a rope strung over an abyss. And, by God, even though his arms were being pulled out of their sockets and he was in terrible pain, if he let go... Well, then he'd be a goner.

But when the house was quiet, like now, when his mind wasn't on everyday concerns, he thought about Leslie. They'd had a good marriage. They'd loved each other. The future had stretched ahead of them: raising their children, growing old together, grandchildren. And then Leslie had been thrown from that horse—a freak accident—and broken her neck and died. Just like that.

He wasn't good at dealing with pain. He didn't deal with it at all, to tell the truth. He buried it, refused to acknowledge it. For three years he'd suffered silently, the first sharp agony only now fading to loneliness.

Steve rose from his chair, turned off the television set

and went through his nightly routine. Let the dogs in, give old Boots an extra pat. Turn off the lights. He never locked the door. Hell, not here. Not like in the city. The dogs would warn him if anyone came close to the house, anyway.

He made his way through the shadows to the stairs. The cold moonlight streamed through the front windows, laying silver squares on the floor. Up to his bedroom, the fifth stair squeaking as usual.

Night after solitary night he went through the same routine. He'd always done it, but there'd been Leslie waiting for him in bed for so many of those years. Now he went into his bedroom, flicked on the light and it was empty. No warm body in his bed, no one to greet him with a smile, a hug, a kiss.

Steve began to undress. He was only forty-two years old, and he could live a real long time. That was a lot of years ahead of him, and it looked like he was going to spend them alone.

Better get used to it.

CHAPTER TWO

THE GREEN-AND-WHITE interstate sign read Exit 133, two miles. No town names, no route number. Nonetheless, Brigitte Hartman knew what lay ahead on that high country road—a couple of tiny ranching communities, little towns with names few people in Colorado had ever heard: Burns, McCoy, Toponas. And there was Sweetwater. Not even on the main road, but east of it, at the base of the White River National Forest and the Flat Tops Wilderness area. She'd been in Sweetwater a few times last year, and she recalled the couple of blocks of scattered businesses that served the ranching community. Oh, yes, she'd been to Sweetwater.

Brigitte switched on her turn signal and slowed for the exit. She'd been bursting with confidence and optimism, anticipating this assignment. But now, to be honest with herself, she was feeling the tiniest seed of doubt germinating. There was an awful lot at stake here. What if she blew it?

The rutted road twisted along a river valley that was brushed with a palette of Rocky Mountain autumn hues: yellow, gold, ocher. The colors were intense down here on the valley floor, but they faded as the mountains rose, until the bare-branched aspens gave way to spruce and pine and snow.

In Denver, Brigitte had been able to drive her Cherokee sport utility with the window down. It had been a bright, warm November day, but up here it was cooler. Up here she could believe winter was at hand. The sky was still a deep, perfect blue, though, and the snow-capped peaks were glorious.

"Not bad," she said aloud. She was glad to be in the mountains again, felt her spirits lift to familiar heights at the sight of the majestic range that split the continent in two. This country was, after all, more of a home to her than the city ever would be. Too bad this wasn't an ordinary assignment. Or a vacation.

It must have been fifteen miles before she turned east onto another road that would lead her to Sweetwater. To both her left and right there were ranches, cattle country that spanned the river valley and rose into the aspen-dotted hills beyond. The air smelled crisp and pure, faintly dusty. Hard to believe that two days ago an early storm had rushed across Colorado and dumped three inches of snow in Denver. More up here probably, but it had melted.

She remembered the day of the storm with clarity; it was the day the great idea had come to her, the oh-so-clever impulsive notion that had led her here.

She'd left her apartment that morning as usual, driven to work and marched into the office of her boss, the head of the Denver division of the U.S. Fish and Wildlife Service. And she'd laid her plan on the table.

"I'm going to Sweetwater, Mac, and I'm going to find out what's killing the cattle up there."

He'd looked up from the pile of paperwork scattered on his desktop. "Oh," he'd said.

"Seriously." Brigitte had pulled a chair up and propped her elbows on his desk. "I'll just casually scout around, meet a few of the locals, keep my eyes and ears open."

"Uh-huh." Mac McCarthy had pointed to the sign on his door. "Does that read CIA, or am I in the wrong office here?"

"Listen to me...."

"You're a biologist, Brigitte. You're a field biologist. Not a spy."

"Both you and I know it's got to be the ranchers doing the killing up there."

"We don't know that. The autopsies on the carcasses have been inconclusive. Read them."

"I have." She sighed. "I'm only talking a few weeks here, Mac. I'm not on assignment right now, and I've got the time. It's my responsibility to see to it that the wolf pack survives this reintroduction. For Lord's sake, Mac, I've put five years into this pack. I was with them the whole way. I know every single one of them...."

"You're too emotionally involved."

"Not true. And you forget, I come from a town in Montana that could be a clone of Sweetwater. I know these ranchers. I speak their language. I know how they feel about the reintroduction, even if I think they're dead wrong. Mac, I can relate to them."

"I don't know."

"I've talked to Hal Franklin. He's been dealing with the ranchers all year. They're getting impatient, Mac, and he doesn't know what to do. There was another calf killed, and they're getting pretty insistent."

"I know. It's a hell of a mess."

"You know what Hal thinks. You've seen his reports."

"Yeah, I've seen them."

"He agrees with me that ranchers, some or one or all of them, are killing their own stock and blaming it on the wolves. And if someone doesn't prove it real soon, the reintroduction is going to fail."

Mac had sat back in his chair and tapped a pencil against his teeth, staring at her. After a long minute, he'd said, "They aren't going to open up to a stranger. No one's going to come up to you and say, 'Hey, guess what? I killed one of my neighbor's calves last week.' "

"God, Mac, I know that. But something might turn up. I could hear some town gossip. I could overhear some saloon bragging. It's worth a shot. We've got nothing to lose here."

"Well," he'd said, hesitating, still chewing things over, "won't the locals think it's kind of strange, a single young woman suddenly nosing around town? A stranger?"

"First off, Mac, I'm thirty-two. That ain't young. And as for nosing around, well, it's hunting season. Maybe I can get some sort of job, you know, something part-time while the town's filled up with hunters and fishermen. I don't know. I'll play it by ear."

"I don't like this," he'd said, but the skepticism in his voice was evaporating. "People don't move to small towns, they move away from them."

This had taken Brigitte a moment to think through. Then she'd said, "If anyone asks, I'll say I'm leaving the city behind—I got mugged or something, and I've had it. I'm looking for a spot in Colorado where I can feel safe. There's nothing hard to swallow about that."

It had taken another ten minutes to persuade Mac to let her go, but in the end he'd agreed.

"All right, all right," he'd said. "Go. Three weeks. A month. I'll spare you for that long. But that's it. And for God's sake, stay in touch and don't go getting into any trouble. You aren't Mata Hari. Just nose around a little."

"I will, really. I'll be fine, Mac." She'd jumped to her feet. "This is going to work."

"Uh-huh," Mac had said.

She'd been raring to go, a woman on fire. But that had been then, in the safe confines of Mac's office. Right now doubt was clawing at her. She wasn't a spy or a detective or an investigator. She wasn't even a good liar. People—decent, innocent people—were going to ask her all sorts of questions, and how was she going to answer them? With lies. She cringed inwardly at the thought.

On the other hand, she knew she was about to confront small-town narrow-mindedness, and very likely violently opinionated people who were breaking the law. It was the same shortsighted point of view she'd fled from years ago when she'd gotten her wildlife biologist's degree from the University of Montana. She did fieldwork—plenty of it—but she lived in the city where, if you didn't like one person's point of view, all you had to do was turn to someone else. Variety. Mental stimulation. That's what she craved. To heck with these small-town bigots who were trying to ruin the wolf introduction with their own lies and deceit.

And yet... Brigitte took a breath and looked at the countryside. Absolutely breathtaking. Despite herself, her heart swelled. She lived in the city by choice, but she'd always love the land that had spawned her and the creatures who lived on it. That's why she did fieldwork. That's why she'd always return to the wilderness. It was in her blood.

She arrived in Sweetwater shortly after one that afternoon and drove through its few streets. Step one was having to be able to find a comfortable spot in which to spend the next few weeks. Mac had budgeted a thousand dollars for her *field*work. Surely that was plenty.

She picked the Whispering Pines Motel at the edge of town. It was a clean-looking place, with an office and fifteen or so separate log-cabin bungalows. If any of the bungalows had a small kitchen unit, it would be perfect.

"Hi," Brigitte said at the desk. "Have you got any cabins open?"

The friendly woman who appeared to be about Brigitte's age smiled. "Sure do."

"Any with a kitchen?"

"Just one right now."

"Great. And what are your weekly rates?"

"Well, during hunting season, like now, it's thirty-eight a night. But for weekly, we can let you have it for two-twenty."

"Sounds fine," Brigitte said. "I'll take it for two weeks to begin with."

And then the inevitable question came. "You a hunter or something?"

Brigitte was prepared. "Oh, no," she said, smiling. "Just needed to get out of the city for a while."

"I hear you," the woman said. She introduced herself as Edie and told Brigitte if she needed anything to just ask.

It occurred to Brigitte, as she gave the cabin a quick look, that she needed a better cover story, at least a more complete one. Yes, she'd have to think about that.

After putting her clothes away, she locked the cabin door and walked into town. Sweetwater was picturesque, the small downtown featuring false-front Western-style buildings left over from Victorian times. She counted three restaurants and a hardware store housed in a charming brick building with a portico and turned wooden posts. There was a feed store around the corner from that. There were several other motels, a few saloons, two gas stations with adjoining groceries and general merchandise sections. There was a bank, the post office and a real-estate office shared with an insurance agency. There was a barbershop-beauty salon. Down one street from Main was a big brick building—the Elks Lodge. Down another was city hall. The hardware store was bigger.

Brigitte decided that all in all the town of Sweetwater was doing okay. Not one closed-down building. A healthy sign. Of course, there was no superstore at the edge of town killing off the local businesses, either.

Sweetwater, Brigitte thought. A nice friendly place. But behind that facade she knew how truly closed the community was. They talked a different talk than folks from the city. Walked a different walk. And Brigitte could plead her case for the wolf reintroduction till she was blue in the face, and it wouldn't make an iota of difference. Given the chance, most of these people would slaughter the pack in the blink of an eye.

She bought a bagful of groceries at one of the gas station minimarts and strolled back toward her cabin. Down one of the sidestreets off Main was a brick school, obviously just getting out. Kids rushed from doors, laughing, running, the older ones too mature for that, walking slowly, the girls' heads together, the boys looking cool. Brigitte remembered her own high school years fondly. Her school hadn't been much bigger. In a small town like this where the kids weren't bused off, you knew everyone. It was like one big family. But then she thought: one big closed family.

Back at the cabin she fixed herself a sandwich and called the office in Denver, using her credit card rather than billing it to the room—an added precaution. It was four o'clock, and she just caught Mac.

"Hi, I'm here, in Sweetwater, all settled in," she began.

"God, am I glad you called," he said. "I tried to catch you before you left. There was another one. Yesterday."

"Another…? Oh, Lord, another dead cow."

"That's right. And the rancher, ah, Slater, Steve Slater, is demanding action. I got a second call just this morning from the Cattlemen's Association president up there—he's swearing they'll get rid of the pack themselves if we don't take some action."

"Oh, boy." Brigitte let out a breath.

"Hal went to pick up the carcass early this morning. Anyway, he's back in Denver, and the carcass is being examined even as we speak."

"It can't have been the wolves, Mac. There's so much wild game up here that—"

"I know your opinion. Believe me, I've heard it all before. But until we can prove it's the ranchers behind these killings, we're on the hot seat. Next thing you know, I'll get a call from some damn senator in Washington telling me to destroy the pack.''

"Don't say that. Don't even think it, Mac."

"I'm being realistic."

Brigitte stared at her untouched sandwich. "I'll get to the bottom of this, Mac. I swear I will."

"Well, good luck. I only hope you don't find out it really is the wolf pack killing livestock."

"That isn't even funny."

"I didn't mean it to be. Now, you stay in close touch."

"I will. I'll call to find out about the autopsy results in a few days. What was that rancher's name?"

"Slater. Steve Slater."

"Okay. I got it."

When she was off the phone, she went outside and sat on the tiny porch in front of her cabin, hugging herself in her jacket despite the warm sun. She looked up toward the Flat Tops Wilderness and sighed. Somewhere up in those vast mountains the wolf pack roamed.

It was terribly important to Brigitte, this reintroduction. Mac had been right—she *was* emotionally involved. To Brigitte, it was a sad commentary that of all the flora and fauna found in the Rocky Mountain wilderness when Europeans first set foot on this land, only the wolf was extinct. She was trying her best to remedy the situation. The reintroduction was part of her job, but it was also her passion.

She tried to imagine what the pack would be doing right now, and she pictured each individual wolf as if they were friends.

There was Star and big old Silverfoot, the alpha male, Auntie Mame and Uncle Joe, the beta female and male. And also two young males who were not quite ready to strike out on their own. The idea was to eventually introduce several more wolves from Canada to the Flat Tops area so that the young males could form new, viable packs. There was more than enough territory and more than enough game for hundreds of wolves.

Brigitte was real curious as to whether Star and Silverfoot had had pups this past spring. She sure hoped so. That was the whole point: to repopulate the wilderness naturally. But these wolves had not been fitted with radio collars, the first reintroduced wolves not to have them, so the pack was on its own, and nobody knew if there were pups or if all the adults had survived.

Brigitte's mind was roaming the mountainside with the pack when the hunters began to arrive back at the cabins. First one pickup pulled in, then another. Soon a Jeep arrived, and three men got out. They were all decked out in Day-Glo orange, rifles slung over shoulders. A couple of the guys smiled and nodded at her. She smiled back, lifted her hand and waved. Hunters didn't bother her, though she'd never hunt herself. Without hunters to cull the herds of deer and elk, the winter kill would be astronomical. Animals that starved to death suffered for such a long time that Brigitte couldn't bear to think about it. Better a clean shot from a rifle than a long, lingering death.

In actuality, the herds of deer and elk in Colorado had grown enormous, even with the hunting season: 200,000 elk and at least as many deer. As a matter of fact, the Flat Tops were home to the largest deer herd in North America.

Hunters did some good, but they tended to kill the strongest animals, the trophy ones. Wolves, on the other hand, preyed on the weak, making the herds healthier, and Brigitte was convinced that wolves would restore a more natural balance.

That's all she was trying to do—to restore the environment to its optimum condition.

Of course, there were plenty of people who disagreed

with her, who hated wolves with a passion, the descendants of those who'd slaughtered every last one in the country. Never mind that mountain lions and grizzly bears killed people routinely and that wolves did no such thing. To Brigitte the hate was irrational, but it had to be dealt with.

She remembered clearly an incident at Red Lodge, Montana, in 1995. A hunter had shot a big male wolf on the Fourth of July. Brandishing his kill, he rode a horse in a parade through a town near Yellowstone National Park, and he was wearing a T-shirt that read Northern Rockies Wolf Reduction Project.

Of course, the man had been arrested and convicted of killing a wolf under the Endangered Species Act. But apparently he refueled a lot of sentiment against the wolves. Suddenly all sorts of ranchers were sporting T-shirts with slogans. Wolf Management Team was a popular one. Another showed a wolf's head in a rifle sight, and read: Shoot, Shovel And Shut Up.

Cute, Brigitte thought as another truck pulled in, churning up dust. But these guys were legitimate hunters, probably city folk. Some or all would be supporters of reintroduction programs. The problem lay mostly with ranchers.

Looking around this small, quiet town, she felt an even greater urgency to get to the bottom of these cattle slayings. The trouble was that she had to get on the inside, which was no easy task. She had to be in a position to hear things, to ask questions without arousing suspicion.

BRIGITTE SLEPT reasonably well that night, and the next morning she took another stroll around town. What she needed was some sort of job in a place that had lots of local traffic flow—maybe the hardware store or something. But when she checked with the manager at the Ace Hardware she learned he'd just hired a cashier last week. Didn't need anyone else right now.

She walked on, checking out other prospects. Nothing.

She was walking past one of the minimart gas stations when she spotted it—a sign reading Help Wanted, Inquire Within. She walked in, looked around. The place sold everything: food, gas, sporting goods, hunting licenses. She took a breath and walked up to the woman behind the counter. A believable cover story for her presence in Sweetwater, a job like this one, and who knew—maybe a closed door would begin to open.

"Hi," she began. "I saw your sign...."

TWO-THOUSAND FEET above Sweetwater, thin rays of morning light spread across Deadhorse Gulch in the Flat Tops Wilderness. A squirrel chattered from a tall spindly pine; deep in the forest another answered. There was a light cold breeze, and the few remaining golden aspen leaves danced as they fluttered to the earth.

Star raised her head and sniffed the air, then went back to the doe the pack had brought down just past dawn. Beside her were Silverfoot and Uncle Joe. Auntie Mame sat off to the side, panting.

The pack fed with little urgency; game was plentiful. And a full-grown wolf could eat one quarter of his body weight—twenty pounds—at one meal, then go for a prolonged time without eating. The pups, indulged by all the adults, were the greediest. One snapped at another, growled, then leapt away from the carcass, intimidated by his own nerve.

One of the young males looked up at the ravens that perched on branches all around them. He watched them warily, because sometimes the big black birds would dive-bomb and peck at a wolf who appeared submissive. Ravens were always present at a kill, as if they had a special relationship with the wolf, and their hoarse croaks alerted the rest of the animals.

Once the pack left, the ravens would descend and partake of the feast. Martens and fishers would come soon, and foxes and coyotes. Then eagles, naked-headed turkey vultures and woodpeckers. And lastly the chickadees and nuthatches and Canada jays.

It was, truly, a feast for all.

A raven ruffled its wing feathers, patient, observing the wolves. Then Star lifted her head. Something had changed; the air was displaced. She sniffed, listened. Then Auntie Mame clicked her jaws shut, her head also lifting, alert. Even the pups quieted abruptly.

Now it could be heard clearly throughout the valley, a low, mechanical grinding, the engine of a Jeep.

Noses twitched, testing the air. Ears perked. There was the distinct odor of exhaust, a sign of danger, and Star's left ear turned toward the mounting whine of the car's engine.

Silverfoot yipped softly at the pack. It was time to go. Star led the way, her long legs eating up the distance between her and the approaching noise. Behind her the pack spread out in low brush, the six-month-old pups tripping, a bit confused, but moving nevertheless into the forest. After a few minutes, Silverfoot, who guarded the rear, stopped and turned, staring behind through golden, almond-shaped eyes. He raised his head and howled while the pack moved on ahead in a tireless lope, deep into the wilderness, where no human had set foot.

CHAPTER THREE

BRIGITTE HAD BEEN in Sweetwater a week. She'd worked for five days at the gas station-minimart, which was aptly called Locals Corner. Her hours varied, and it was a surprisingly pleasant job, selling mostly gasoline, candy bars, pop, newspapers and magazines. Lots of coffee, too.

The store's owner was a middle-aged woman named Bess Cantrell. Brigitte found her to be easy to work for, gossipy, with an inexhaustible supply of dry wit. Bess was plump and blond, and Brigitte guessed she'd been a real wild child in her younger days. She had a husband named Stan who ran the local road crew for the county, and two grown children who lived in Denver.

And, most importantly, Bess knew everyone in town.

After only one afternoon at her new job, Brigitte was sure she couldn't have picked a better person for her purposes. The only sticky part came on the first day, when Bess had asked her a lot of questions about where she was from, what she did, why she left. But Brigitte had been prepared.

"Oh, I worked in an office, you know, for a, um, car parts wholesaler. Typing, filing." Brigitte had shrugged. "The usual stuff."

"So why'd you leave?"

"The city was getting to me. I got mugged last week. Scared me to death. And all those drive-by shootings. Denver's not all ritzy Cherry Creek and trendy LoDo. I decided to take a leave of absence and to get out for a while."

"How long you planning on staying?" Bess had pointed a warning finger at Brigitte. "I can't hire you and train you and see you leave before the hunting season's over."

"Oh, I'll be here that long. At least till Christmas. I promise."

"Where you living?"

"At the Whispering Pines cabins."

Bess had nodded. "Edie Zimmer's place. I'll talk to her, and maybe she'll give you a long-term rate."

"Oh, thanks. That'd be great."

Brigitte had waited three days before starting to ask Bess questions about the Sweetwater valley, not wanting to appear too curious. And Bess was smart as a whip; if anyone would get suspicious, Bess Cantrell would.

Brigitte had started by asking general questions about the population of the town, the businesses, what the people did for a living, and Bess was a gold mine. Brigitte was sure Bess knew everyone's bank account to the penny, even their kids' grades in school.

"Basically," Bess had explained, running the day's credit-card receipts, "the town services the ranchers in the valley. No one's rich and no one's real poor. The ranchers—there're seven big ones, with over five hundred acres—have fat years and lean years. I keep telling 'em to grow bean sprouts, because beef consumption's been going down, but they're too stubborn to change. Once a rancher, always a rancher." Bess had gathered the receipts and torn off the read-out from the cash register, deftly folded and rubber-banded them together.

"They're cattle ranchers, right?" Brigitte had asked.

"Yeah, mostly. There's one small sheep ranch, but he mostly raises them for wool, and there's that hippie kook who raises llamas, but they hardly count in our local economy. And there's hunting season, like now, and in the summer we get lots of tourists—hikers and such."

"Have I met any of the ranchers here?"

"Yeah, sure. Tom Morehead was in this morning. Filled his diesel pickup. Skinny, dark guy. Sale was $35.27."

Brigitte had gaped at her. "You remember the amount of every sale?"

Bess had pointed to her forehead with a finger. "It's all in here, honey, every penny. I only use a cash register in case the IRS gets after me."

"I'm impressed," Brigitte had said.

"And the first day you worked, there was a heavyset guy my age. Big gut but good-looking. Fancy snakeskin hatband. That was Ben Garrett."

"Hmm, I'm not sure I remember."

"I'll start introducing you. Pretty young single girl like you should get lots of attention here. There're more men than women, and the single guys are hard up. Not that I mean they'd have to be hard up to ask you out...."

"No offense taken." Brigitte had laughed.

That night she'd gone back to her cabin and started her list: Morehead, Garrett. Two of the seven ranching families. She also called Mac in Denver and got the names of those ranchers who'd reported stock killed by wolves and added their names. Morehead and Garrett were already on the list, and so was Steve Slater. Then there was a Brad Milligan. That was four out of seven. The four most outspoken against the wolves.

And the next morning, she'd met another rancher, Calvin Robertson, who stopped by for coffee and gasoline. Two to go.

Sweetwater was a friendly town, a lot like the place where she'd grown up. Lots of people stopped in every day just to chat with Bess, and after school lots of the kids paraded in to buy junk food. Then, later, the hunters came in to fill up their campers and Jeeps and buy six-packs of beer and odds and ends.

Brigitte had met lots of the people in town by the end of the week. She kept a sharp eye out for names on credit cards, in case any of the ranchers she hadn't met came in, but so far neither Slater nor Milligan had shown up.

And, thank heavens, no more cattle had been killed.

It snowed that night, a light, dry snow with wind that blew it sideways. Brigitte walked home after closing up by herself for the first time, and she had to hug her arms around her jacket in the wind. She'd have to change to winter gear, she guessed. Well, it was almost Thanksgiving.

It was late, there was nothing urgent, so she waited until morning to check in with Mac.

"Anything new?" he asked.

"No. Listen, Mac, it's a small town and I have to be real careful. If I start asking questions, it'll be all over before it starts. Give me some time."

"No one's said a word?"

"Not to me. Not yet. But I know it'll happen sooner or later. I'm meeting people. I'm getting a handle on this town. The guys who come into the store flirt with me."

"Hallelujah, Brigitte. Now you've made me happy. They flirt with you."

"You know what I mean," Brigitte said defensively.

"While I'm on the receiving end of all kinds of flak, you're flirting."

"It's the means to an end."

"Have you met any of the ranchers who've had stock killed?"

"A couple, very casually."

"Mata Hari you are not."

"Come on, Mac, I need more time."

"Until Christmas," he said.

"I'll find out, really I will."

When Brigitte hung up, she sighed. She may have sounded confident to Mac, but she was feeling pretty doubtful about her ability to ferret out what she needed to know. If anyone really was killing his own cattle and blaming it on the wolves, either that person was working alone and no one here suspected what he was doing or the whole damn town was in on it and they were all protecting one another.

What she needed was an opening, just a crack to get her foot in the door. A reason to bring up the subject of wolf reintroduction to gauge people's feelings. The trouble was, living in town made it hard to meet the ranching families, and Brigitte just couldn't figure out how to solve that problem. But, she told herself, she'd get her break sooner or later.

Meanwhile, she fretted about how the wolves were doing. Had they bred? Were they finding enough game to fatten themselves up for the winter? Were they adapting to this new ecological system? Maybe they should have been fitted with radio collars; at least then she'd know if they were alive. She'd argued against the idea at the time, but what if she'd been wrong?

Brigitte would give anything to see the pack once more. She'd come to know them so well. But it was unlikely she'd ever see them again. Wolves were extremely shy of people, unlike coyotes and bears, and people almost never saw them in the wild, only their paw prints, which were distinguishable by their size—sometimes six inches in length.

She longed to see them, check on their condition, hear them howl, as she'd heard them in the enclosure, before their release. She shivered just thinking about the sound, the long, wavering, mournful song that had been absent from the American West for so many decades.

She went to work at three that afternoon, and Bess left her to handle things alone for a few hours.

"Watch those kids," Bess told her. "There's been stuff missing lately. You know, candy bars and chips and stuff."

The supplier's truck pulled up outside just as the junior high let out, and Brigitte was busy checking invoices when a bunch of kids piled into the store, talking and laughing. One by one, they paid for their ice cream sandwiches or candy bars, most of them plunking down the exact change.

Brigitte saw the girls out of the corner of her eye as she rang up a bag of chips. They were walking toward the front door casually, too casually, one right behind the other. There was something about them....

"Just a sec, girls," Brigitte called out, and all the kids who were lined up at the register swiveled their heads toward the two girls, who kept walking as if they hadn't heard.

"Hold on," Brigitte said, coming around the counter, heading the two off.

"What?" the first girl asked rather rudely, a pretty girl, with dark hair and dark eyes.

"Did you, uh, need to pay for something?" Brigitte asked.

"No. Come on, Nancy," the girl said to her friend.

Uh-oh. Brigitte put out a hand to detain the girl, who jerked her arm away. "Come on, I know you have something. Hey, it's only a small thing, but all your friends paid for theirs," she said.

"I don't have anything," the girl muttered.

"Sure you do. And, believe me, it won't taste any better 'cause you snagged it when I wasn't looking."

"Come on, Nancy," the girl said again.

"Sorry," Brigitte said. "Not until I see what's in your backpacks."

"Heather," the girl called Nancy said fearfully.

"She can't do that," Heather told her friend.

"Watch me," Brigitte fired back. "Hand it over."

The kids who'd been at the register made themselves scarce, and Brigitte was alone with the two girls. She was torn between anger and the anxious feeling that perhaps she wasn't handling this right. But it was too late to back down now.

"Girls," she said, "you've been caught. Give in gracefully."

"How dare you..." Heather said.

But Nancy was almost crying. "Here," she said, thrusting her backpack at Brigitte. "I'm sorry, I'm really sorry."

"Yours, too," Brigitte said to Heather.

"Oh, take it. Here!" Heather said.

Cupcakes. That's all the girls had. Chocolate cupcakes with white frosting across the top. Brigitte held them up. "These are lousy for you, girls. You'll get all pimply. And your teeth will rot. If you're going to steal, at least have some class about it," she said dryly.

Nancy sobbed. Heather glowered.

"Okay, I'm not going to call the police or anything, not this time. But I would like your names. I'm going to have to call your parents."

"Oh, no!" Nancy cried.

Heather was silent, her arms folded across her chest, her cheeks red with anger.

"I have to, kids. You know that. Now, what are your last names and phone numbers?"

"Nancy Ramsey," the girl sobbed. "555-5924."

"Okay, Nancy. You know, if you tell your mom before I call, it'll go better for you."

"She'll kill me," Nancy wailed.

"Heather Slater," the other girl said tightly. "555-6248."

Brigitte wrote the names and numbers down. "I'm sorry this happened," she said. "Please don't do it again."

"Don't worry," Heather said coldly, "I'll never come in here again. Ever!"

"Tell your mom," Brigitte advised. "Honestly."

The girl named Heather drew herself up. "My mom is dead, for your information, so I can't tell her!" Then she turned and ran out of the store, Nancy behind her.

Oh, God, Brigitte thought. She'd done it now. Said the worst possible thing. Poor kid. But how could she have known? No mom. That was probably half her problem right there. Now she wished she'd gone easier on the girls. Bess would have known the girls and their families, would have known that Heather Slater didn't have a mother.

Brigitte ran her hand through her short hair and made it stand up in spikes in front. Damn. Well, she wasn't Bess, and she'd done the best she could, and tonight when she phoned Heather's father, she'd apologize. Poor kid.

Slater. Wait a minute. Wasn't that one of the names on her list? Yes. Slater, Steve. And he was also the one who'd had a calf killed the morning before she'd arrived in Sweetwater.

Wow! The break had come at last. A blessing in disguise.

That evening, after she ate, Brigitte took a deep breath and got out the scrap of paper with the girls' numbers. Ramsey first. She leaned on her kitchen counter with her elbows and wound the telephone wire around her fingers as the phone rang.

Mrs. Ramsey answered. Brigitte plunged right in, telling the story to Nancy's mother. But Kathy Ramsey already knew.

"Yes, she told me," Kathy said. "And she's very upset. She'll be punished, don't worry. I really appreciate the way you handled it, Miss Hartman."

"Brigitte, please. I'm glad she told you before I called. I could see she was upset. I bet she learned a lesson today."

"I hope so. And, you know, I really think Heather led

her into this. I don't mean to make excuses for my daughter, but Heather's been a problem…well, since her mother died, and I think she's sort of a bad influence on some of the girls.''

"Yes, she told me about her mother. I'm afraid I suggested she tell her mom about the incident this afternoon, and…''

"I can just imagine. Her dad, Steve, well, he's a good man, but he's having a hard time raising those girls alone, and Heather's at that age…''

"I remember it well," Brigitte said.

"Are you going to call Steve Slater?" Kathy Ramsey asked.

"Absolutely. I said I would.''

"He's a real proud man. He, uh… Well, I guess what I mean is, I'd be careful of what I said if I were you.''

"I understand," Brigitte told her. "I'll be careful. Thanks." Then she added, "I hope I meet you in person sometime. If you ever come by Locals Corner, look for me.''

"I stop by once in a while, sure. I'll say hello next time I'm in town.''

"I'm so glad you weren't mad about this thing with Nancy. When I was a kid, I wasn't always an angel, either. My mom had it tough at times.''

"Kids aren't easy. Do you have any of your own?''

"No, I have to find a man first, but I sure hope I have them someday.''

"Uh, listen, don't mention to Steve Slater I said Heather was a ringleader, okay?''

"I wouldn't dream of it. Bye now.''

Well, that had gone all right. Somehow Brigitte had the feeling that the next call wasn't going to be quite as easy.

Steve Slater. Widower, rancher, single father, outspoken

critic of the wolf reintroduction plan. Hmm. She dialed the number.

A young girl answered—not Heather. A younger sister, Brigitte guessed. "Is your dad home?" she asked, then heard the girl yelling, "Daddy! Dad! Phone!"

A moment later there was a click as another extension was picked up. "Hello?"

"Mr. Slater?"

"Yes."

"My name is Brigitte Hartman. I work for Bess Cantrell at Locals Corner."

"Uh-huh."

She drew in a breath. Heather had obviously not told her father. "Well, today I was working when your daughter came in."

"You mean Heather?"

"Yes. She was with Nancy Ramsey. And they, uh, well, they had taken some things and I...I guess you'd have to say I caught them at it."

Dead silence.

"Mr. Slater?"

"Yeah, I'm here."

"I told Heather I was going to call you. I've already spoken to Kathy Ramsey...."

"Wait a minute. You caught Heather...stealing?"

"Actually, more like shoplifting, Mr. Slater. It was just, I mean, cupcakes."

"You're sure it was Heather?"

"She gave me her name and number."

Silence.

"Mr. Slater? I really felt I had to carry through, you know, since I told the girls I would, and I really feel it's important to do that. With kids." She was babbling. "Mr. Slater?"

"Uh, yeah, I'm here. I just... You're sure it was Heather?"

"I'm afraid so."

"Good God."

"She hasn't said anything to you about it?"

"No." A pause. "Who did you say you were?"

"Brigitte Hartman. I just moved here. I work for Bess Cantrell."

"Do I know you?"

"No, I don't think so. Unless you paid me for gas in the past week."

"Well, I don't quite know what to say. Heather's a good girl, but lately she's been, sort of, uh, hard to understand. For me, that is. I just don't..." His voice trailed off.

"Listen, Mr. Slater, it's not such a big deal. I thought you should know, that's all. You might want to talk to Heather about it."

"Talk to her..."

"Sure, discuss it. Ask her why she did it."

"She's not easy to talk to these days."

"Hmm..."

"Damn it! I can't believe she'd do that. She knows better."

"I'm sure she does." Brigitte wondered how frank she could be with this man. Parents were notoriously touchy where their kids were concerned, and she didn't want to antagonize him. That's not what she was here for. "She, well, she seemed to be a pretty angry young lady today. She's not going to like you hearing about this from me."

"You got that right."

"And, Mr. Slater, I have to tell you, I told both the girls it would be better if they informed their moms about the incident before I called. And Heather said..."

"I can pretty well imagine what she said."

"I wanted to apologize to her. I didn't know about her

mother. It must still be very painful for her, for all of you. I'm really sorry.''

"Yeah, we're all sorry."

"Well, I thought you should know."

More silence.

Brigitte chewed on her bottom lip. This man was obviously having a hard time with his daughter. He didn't have a clue how to approach this whole thing. Did she dare try to help? Would he accept help if she offered? Or would he be mortally offended? Kathy Ramsey had said he was a proud man. "Look, Mr. Slater, I'm no shrink or anything, but I've been where Heather is right now. I really don't want to intrude, but I could give you some advice on how to handle difficult teenage girls. We could meet, say, at Rosie's for breakfast tomorrow and talk. If you have time. I mean, if you want to."

Silence again. Oh, God, she'd really put her foot in her mouth this time. Made an enemy of one of the ranchers she needed to get to know. "Um, I'm really sorry if I sound nosy. I mean, maybe you've got a friend who could help, someone who knows Heather better. After all, I just met her today."

"Breakfast?"

"Sure, if you can, if you want to...."

"I could make breakfast."

Brigitte's heart thumped. Got him. "When? What time, I mean?"

"Eight-thirty. I'll drop the girls at school first."

"Eight-thirty's fine. I'm looking forward to meeting you. Heather is a beautiful girl. I know she'll outgrow this stage."

"When?"

"What?"

"When'll she outgrow it?"

"Oh, goodness, I don't know. A year or two. Or three."

"God."

"Talk to her, Mr. Slater. I'll see you tomorrow."

She hung up, palms sweating, and rubbed them on her jeans-clad thighs. Whew. That was tough. She couldn't believe she'd actually done it, made plans to meet a man she didn't know on this pretext. Maybe this was her in to the ranchers around here, at last. And, then again, maybe it wasn't. Maybe it would lead nowhere. She had to try, though, and Mr. Slater needed help with Heather, that was for sure.

Well, everyone always told Brigitte her strength was the way she confronted situations head-on and made things work with her positive attitude. So what was the big deal? She could handle this Steve Slater. Before she was through with him, he'd spill his guts and she'd find out everything she needed. No problem.

STEVE HUNG UP the phone and rubbed his eyes wearily. He couldn't believe it. Stealing. He didn't know whether he was disappointed, angry or humiliated. Maybe all of the above. He'd have to talk to Heather, but his mind balked. What could he say? She'd just get angry and defensive, and then the whole situation would snowball into ugliness. He simply didn't know how to reach her or show how much he cared or ask what was really bothering her.

He sat there at his desk and tried to think, but nothing useful came to him. This lady who'd called, Brigitte Hartman, sounded like she knew what to say, and she might have some ideas to help him, but he still couldn't believe he'd agreed to meet her. Lay out his personal problems to a stranger, expose his family's dirty laundry. What in hell had gotten into him?

Maybe he wouldn't bother going in the morning. Maybe he'd just blow it off.

Heather. No wonder she'd been so quiet at dinner. His

heart squeezed in his chest at the thought of confronting her. He was so tired of the constant tension between them that he couldn't even get up the energy to be really angry at her.

Slowly Steve rose from his desk and climbed the stairs. Damn, he felt a million years old. He knocked on Heather's door once, then went in. It was like climbing out of a foxhole onto a battlefield.

She was on her bed, feet up, a schoolbook propped on her knees. Music came from her CD player, and he went over and turned it down.

"Heather," he said.

She watched him with his own dark eyes, full of hostility. "I suppose she called you, didn't she?"

He stood there looking down at her. "Yeah, she called."

"And I suppose you're going to think up some awful, unfair punishment to torture me with."

"Honey, you did something wrong. You know that."

"Big deal. It was just a stupid cupcake," she said, sulking.

"Stealing is stealing. It's wrong. What I can't figure out is why you did it."

She shrugged.

"I'm doing my best here, Heather, but I'd like to understand you better. I really don't get this."

"Just give me my punishment and leave me alone."

"No." He shook his head. "That's too easy. I think I'll let you decide on a punishment. You figure it out and let me know, because I'll tell you, honey, I'm just about at the end of my rope here. I don't want you punished, I want you sorry for what you did."

"Can I finish my homework now?" she asked sullenly.

"Goddamn it, Heather, who are you trying to punish— me or somebody out there I don't know about, or yourself?

This is crazy, the way you've been. There's no reason for it.''

She turned her face away.

"Okay, I'm going. I have that Cattlemen's Association meeting. But you be thinking about how you should be punished.''

He went back downstairs, cursing under his breath. He just didn't know what to do. He found Jeannie watching television in the living room and told her he was going into town for the meeting.

"What's the matter with Heather?" Jeannie asked.

"She got into a little trouble today.''

"What trouble?''

"Uh, you better ask her.''

"Is she going to jail?''

"No, kiddo, no jail time for your sister.''

"She's such a jerk sometimes, Dad.''

"Yeah, we all are sometimes.''

"Not as much as Heather.''

"Listen, you get to bed on time and don't bother your sister. She's not in a good mood,'' he said.

"I know that.''

"See you in the morning, Jeannie.''

All the way into town in the muddy pickup truck, Steve thought about his older daughter. He felt so useless. What had happened to the cheerful little kid he remembered? He needed Leslie. God, he needed her. She'd know how to handle Heather. A spark of anger ignited in him—futile, childish anger at his dead wife. *Why did you leave us to struggle on without you? Damn you, Leslie.*

The meeting was in the council room of city hall. All the valley ranchers were there, along with the mayor, a few interested citizens and a newspaper reporter from Glenwood Springs, forty-some miles away, who was keeping tabs on the wolf-reintroduction program.

Steve sat on one of the uncomfortable folding chairs, rested an ankle on the other knee, laid his hat on the resulting platform and crossed his arms over his chest.

Brad Milligan, the chapter president, opened the meeting with a rundown of the stock killed most recently—Tom Morehead's and Steve's. He repeated what Hal Franklin had told Steve, that the autopsies had been inconclusive and their claims were on hold until the USFWS knew what was killing their cattle.

Angry voices rose in the stuffy room, everyone trying to get in his own two cents' worth. The reporter scribbled furiously.

Ben Garrett stood, hat in hand, his forehead baby smooth and white over his weathered face. He held up a hand and quieted the room. "Look," he said. "Those government types will never understand what we need here. They'll never agree with our point of view. They went and dumped those wolves on us without listening to our legitimate concerns. Anyone with half a brain can see that cattle and wolves don't mix. For God's sake, we got rid of cockroaches, didn't we? Anyone in Washington say we gotta have them reintroduced? Hell, no! Wolves don't belong here. We don't need 'em, we don't want 'em. They're gonna put us out of business."

Brad pointed to another rancher, who stood and spoke. "Us small ranchers are just as much an endangered species as those darned wolves." There was applause. "We need to make the government listen to us. I mean, they say there's plenty of land for the wolves and us both. They swore up and down the pack would stay up in the Flat Tops, but look what's happened. Five dead calves since they let 'em loose. Nobody can control where those wolves wander. They go where there's easy food."

Steve raised his hand and stood. "I know we all agree on the problem here, but what we have to decide is how to solve it. If we go off half-cocked, do something crazy or illegal, it's going to be worse for us. We have to be rational. Smart. We need to figure out how to convince the USFWS that we should have more control over our own land. We don't want Washington running our lives. They're using our tax dollars to pay for this reintroduction plan against our will. We have to remember that. They're violating our rights. The question is, what's the best way to get them to pay attention to us?''

"Shoot the goddamn wolves!" someone yelled. Then there was a babble of voices and some laughter.

Steve sat down, shaking his head. Sometimes he thought these guys acted a little like Heather, totally unreasonable.

Bill Ramsey stood. "Listen, you guys, I don't like Washington any better than you, but I gotta tell you, I can see the future, and we're gonna have to share this land with lots of creatures from now on. There's no going back. We have to face the fact we're in the minority.''

"We have our rights!" Tom Morehead yelled.

"Sure we do, but only when they don't rub up against someone else's," Bill said. "I agree with Steve—we gotta do things nice and legal. Get our senators on our side, something like that.''

"The hell with those sleazebag politicians! I say shoot, shovel and shut up, and that's what I'm gonna do. And my boys all agree with me," Ben Garrett said, eyeing his oldest, Chris.

"Take it easy, Ben," Brad Milligan put in.

"Take it easy? I'd like to get a posse together this minute, go after that pack before there's too much snow, set traps, put out poison. Shoot 'em. Whatever it takes.''

Steve had heard it all before. No one seemed to come up with any answers. They just went round and round. Bill Ramsey on the calm end, Ben Garrett at the other extreme.

Steve himself was somewhere in the middle. But that could change if he had many more calves killed.

After the meeting, the men stood around the coffee urn and drank the foul stuff. They muttered and threatened, the usual talk, and Steve wondered when one of them was going to be pushed too far, get desperate and do something drastic. He wondered whether that would come sooner or later, but he had a feeling it would indeed come. It was a goddamned shame it would have to happen, he thought, but no one was listening to the ranchers. Well, maybe then they would.

He drove home through the dark night, thinking. It was pitch-black out, no moon, no stars showing, the sky clouded over. Snow was forecast. Well, it was time for snow. A dry winter was bad for everyone because the farmers and ranchers needed the spring snowmelt in the rivers for irrigation.

He thought about Heather and the wolf problem. His mind circled uselessly. And that woman, that Brigitte Hartman, whose voice had seemed so full of concern. Should he meet her for breakfast? What a dumb thing, letting himself get trapped into meeting her for "advice." What advice could she offer? She wasn't Heather's mother.

He pulled up in his usual place and parked. The dogs came, tails wagging, to greet him. The girls' lights were out. Good. He yawned, letting the dogs in, automatically turning off lights and checking everything.

He went upstairs, peeked in his daughters' bedrooms, closed the doors with quiet snicks. Flicking the light on in his room, Steve undressed, down to his boxers and T-shirt, the way he always slept. He sat on the edge of his bed and scrubbed his head with both hands, then swung his legs around, sliding them between the cold sheets.

CHAPTER FOUR

"EXCUSE ME, ma'am," Steve Slater said, and Brigitte looked up, "but are you Miss Hartman? Brigitte Hartman?"

Brigitte felt her hands tighten around the coffee mug. "That's me," she said, clearing her throat. "And you must be Mr. Slater."

"Steve," he said, shaking her hand as he slid into the booth across from her. "Seems like this might be easier if you just call me Steve."

"And I'm Brigitte. Glad to meet you."

He put his Stetson on the red plastic seat beside him and unconsciously smoothed his dark hair. "Have you ordered?"

She shook her head. "I thought I'd wait for you."

She couldn't stop staring. In no way, shape or form was Steve Slater anything like she'd expected. Actually, she couldn't quite say what she'd expected, but this wasn't it.

"Ready to order?" the waitress asked, pen poised above her pad.

"Ah, I'll have two eggs, over easy, wheat toast, potatoes."

"That's a number three." The woman wrote, then turned to Steve. "And you, Steve? The usual?"

He closed the menu and nodded. To Brigitte he said, "I read it every time, but I always order the same. Habit, I guess."

Brigitte took a sip of coffee and smiled.

They must have talked about something for the next few minutes, although Brigitte would never recall exactly what either of them said. All she was aware of was Steve, Steve Slater, cowboy rancher. He was straight out of a Marlboro cigarette ad, right from his worn barn jacket and Stetson to his green-and-black plaid wool shirt to his faded jeans and scuffed boots.

He was inordinately handsome. Not pretty handsome, but rugged and strong. She guessed his height at just under six feet. Everything about him was dark: his thick black-brown hair with a widow's peak, his straight black brows, black, black eyes with long, dark lashes. His nose was generous and straight, with flaring nostrils. His mouth was wonderful, sexy, with a full lower lip and deep male dimples. His skin coloring was surprisingly fair, the summer tan fading, and a dark beard had begun to shadow his face, despite his having obviously shaved earlier that morning.

Brigitte remembered to put her paper napkin in her lap when the food came, but she was having an awful lot of trouble doing the most ordinary things—such as talking.

It seemed it was just as difficult for him. Of course, he had an excuse. He was on the defensive, needing to protect his child while at the same time faced with having to discipline her. He poured syrup on his pancakes, ate two eggs with a ranching man's gusto and said practically nothing. Rarely did his glance meet hers.

"Nice restaurant," Brigitte offered. "Real busy."

"Mmm," he said. "It's like this every morning."

The waitress poured them more coffee, and for the first time she could feel his gaze rest on her before he looked back at his plate.

Awkward was the only word that came to her mind. They were total strangers who had nothing whatsoever in common.

She tried again to thaw the chill. "Your ranch far from town?"

"Mmm," he said. "Few miles northwest."

"Oh," she said, "that's not so far." What was wrong with her? She was good with people—open, cheerful. This was absurd. She ate and let her mind drift and realized what a stupid idea this breakfast had been.

"I'm real sorry about the trouble you had with Heather," he finally blurted out, and Brigitte had to drag her thoughts back to the real issue, why they were sitting there together. His daughter, the shoplifting. Right.

"I wouldn't call it trouble," she said. "Stuff like that happens all the time. I mean, didn't you swipe something at least once when you were growing up?"

He looked at her and cocked his head. "I don't... Well, maybe I did. Yeah, maybe Bruce Pfister and I took something...." He was thinking. "Sure," he said. "We snitched this penknife from the old hardware store. It was where the Ace is now. I remember. My dad found it and asked where I got it. Took a while, but I finally had to 'fess up. He made me walk all the way into town and give it back."

"It's a pretty common thing with kids," Brigitte said.

"That doesn't make it right." His big hands were clasped around his coffee mug, and he was looking down, his whole body tensed.

"No, it doesn't," she said, "but it makes it understandable." She phrased the next questions carefully. "You want a suggestion?"

He shrugged his broad shoulders.

"Tell her about what happened to you."

"Lotta good that'll do."

"It'll help. Really. She'll feel you trust her enough to confide in her. And then ask her what she thinks would be a fair punishment. Maybe suggest *she* walk into town and tell Bess the truth."

He looked out of the window of the restaurant, his profile to her. He finally replied. "Yeah, I did tell her she should think of her own punishment. But it sure won't be apologizing. She'd never do that."

"You might be surprised."

He looked at her quizzically.

Brigitte laughed. "Okay. So I confess. I stole this candy bar at our local store, and my mom drove me right back and made me pay the owner and apologize. I hated it. I thought I was going to faint. But I did it. And believe me, Heather couldn't hold a candle to how sassy and defiant I was. It's a stage. Girls go through it. Boys, too, of course, but they aren't half as sneaky."

And then Brigitte ventured a little further. "It's got to be the hardest thing on earth to be a single parent," she said softly.

He nodded; everyone in the valley knew his situation. Even this stranger.

She went on. "My mom raised me and my older sister pretty much alone. My father left when I was nine." She shrugged as if it meant nothing. But in reality it was a pain she knew she'd live with her whole life. She felt for Heather. "And, see, I turned out okay. My mom and I get along fine now."

He was having a hard time meeting her gaze. He took a swallow of his coffee, and she saw the movement of his Adam's apple in his throat. He said nothing.

She leaned across the table, elbows on either side of her plate. "I hope you don't think I'm being too pushy, but I see an awful lot of myself as a teenager in Heather. You know, it would help if there was something she really, really wanted and you could do it with her, or for her. I mean, as long as it wasn't dangerous or illegal or anything."

He frowned into his coffee.

"Is there anything like that?"

He hesitated. "She wants to drive. She's been pestering me about it. I keep telling her she's too young."

"Do you think you could teach her? On your ranch? She wouldn't have to go on the highway."

"I suppose."

"Look, it's almost impossible to talk to kids when they're like that, but if you do something like teaching her to drive... It shows them you care, and it'd give you time with her."

"I guess I could do that," he said. "I'll have to think about it."

Brigitte smiled, trying to lighten the mood. Steve Slater wasn't easy to talk to, that was for sure. "You know," she said, "I was kind of surprised you showed up this morning."

He gave her an assessing look, and the barest hint of a smile pulled at his lip. "I almost didn't."

Brigitte pushed her plate aside and looked at her watch. "Oh, darn," she said. "Work. I'm going to be late if I don't hurry."

Steve was reaching for the check.

"Oh," Brigitte said. "I didn't mean for you to..."

He gave her a swift look. "Least I can do." Then he said, "Thanks," and it seemed to have taken a very great effort.

"Hey, anytime," she said.

They both got up and walked to the door, and Brigitte felt that dozens of questions had been left unanswered.

He held the door open for her. "Need a lift to Locals Corner?"

"Ah, no," Brigitte said. "I like to walk. Well, maybe I'll see you at the store or something," she tried, realizing that she was supposed to be cozying up to these locals, trying to dig up information. This wasn't working, though, not one bit.

"Could be" was all he replied, and he tipped his hat, strode toward a mud-spattered pickup truck where two big dogs sat in the bed waiting, tails wagging.

"Bye," Brigitte mouthed, and she waved when he gave her a last glance before backing onto Main Street.

She headed toward work and thought that at least she might have been able to help the man through a hard time with his kid. It had been difficult, though, the breakfast a study in why you don't go out on blind dates. Especially with men like Slater. He was your typical cowboy type. Strong and silent. A shame, a seemingly nice man like that raising two teenagers by himself. It was a wonder every single woman in the county wasn't trying to nab him. Of course, maybe they were, but Steve Slater didn't seem to be on the market.

Bess greeted her at the store then took off to run errands. "When the Coke delivery man gets here, tell him that cooler's on the blink again, would you?" Brigitte nodded. "Oh, and the gas delivery truck's due about eleven. He's always late. Anyway, tell him the storage tank under aisle two—the superunleaded—couldn't have been filled all the way last month. 'Course, they billed me like it was. Just tell him to quit rushing the job."

"I will," Brigitte said, and then Bess was off on her usual routine.

Brigitte really did enjoy running the store. It was easy and usually busy enough to keep her from getting bored. She was meeting more and more folks, too. Some even called her by her first name. That was nice. And the old lady next door, who bought something every day, always told her how pleasant and cheery she was. That was nice, too. What wasn't so nice was the fact that the days were drifting by and she wasn't any closer to finding out what was going on with those livestock killings. She might as well have been in Denver for all she'd learned.

Everything changed that afternoon. It was Brigitte who finally broached the wolf subject with Bess, but it was Bess who opened up.

"The wolf pack that was let go up here last year?" Bess answered. "I'll tell you what happened to them. Far as I know, nothing. They're still up there. Every once in a while someone sees their tracks. You know they've got huge paws. Easy to spot. Seems to me one of my husband's fishing buddies said he saw pup tracks, too, last summer, I recall."

"Pups?" Brigitte couldn't help her delight.

"Oh, sure, why not? Everyone 'round here knows all about them. The big honcho male... What're they called?"

"Alpha males," Brigitte dared to reply.

"That's it. And the female. They're the only ones who mate in the pack, I guess."

"Hmm," Brigitte said. Pups.

"Those two were on the cover of *Time,* you know? Star and Silverfoot. Everyone knows them. Hell, they put Sweetwater on the map. We get tourists now, too. Not hunters, but folks who just come up here to hike and try to get a glimpse of the wolves. Puts money in my cash register, I'll tell you."

"I'll bet," Brigitte replied. Then she pushed a bit. "Didn't I recall not too long ago in the *Denver Post* that some rancher's calf got killed by wolves?"

"Oh, yeah, that sure did happen." Bess opened a carton of potato chips and began restocking a shelf. "You know," she went on, "it's more like a half a dozen dead calves now."

Five, actually, Brigitte thought.

"'Course, the ranchers are blaming the wolves. You have no idea, honey, how much those cowboys hate that wolf pack. Fact is—" Bess stood and put a hand on the small of her back "—I wouldn't put it past some of them to be killing their own stock just to blame it on the wolves."

Brigitte tried to cover her amazement at this brutally frank statement; she was surprised that Bess would even consider it possible. In reply, she said, "No way. They wouldn't go that far, would they?"

"I told you, they hate those wolves, honey, and these old Western dudes would go to any length to get rid of them."

"Wow" was Brigitte's last word before dropping the subject.

She worked and thought a lot about the names on her list: Milligan, Garrett, Morehead, Ramsey, Robertson, Hecht and, of course, Slater. Steve Slater. He'd had a calf killed. And recently. Did he really believe the wolf pack was responsible or did he know better? And she remembered, too, what her boss, Mac, had said before she'd left for Sweetwater: it *could* be the wolf pack. In Brigitte's mind those odds were very slim; still, there was always a chance. And that chance made her hair rise on the back of her neck.

It was actually Bess's idea that Brigitte get out on the town at night. "What on earth do you do, honey, sit and watch TV all night alone in that cabin?" she asked when Brigitte was putting on her jacket, her shift done.

Brigitte smiled ruefully. "It's pretty boring," she admitted.

"Well, if you're thinking about starting a new life," Bess said, "you better get out and meet some folks. Now, of course, there's the ladies' auxiliary at the Elks Lodge. But most of them are old married gals, like me. Pretty dull. There's a church group, but they kind of do sewing and baking projects. You won't meet a nice young man that way. That is, if you're even interested."

"Oh," Brigitte said, "I'm not out of the market. If I meet someone, that's fine. If I don't, well, I'll live."

"It's Friday night," Bess went on, "and the Yampa Tavern's got live music and dancing. Country-western, natch. But most of the singles head on over there on Fridays. Nice crowd. No local-yokel drunks or anything."

Brigitte smiled. "They're probably all younger."

"Younger nothing. There's lots of thirty-something singles around here. Why don't you give it a try?"

"Well," Brigitte said, thinking. "Maybe."

"Ah, don't be so shy. Go out and meet the natives."

By the time Brigitte got back to her cabin, the idea of the Yampa Tavern was sounding better and better. And if singles went there, well, what the heck? She sure was single. She even recalled telling Mac that she might overhear gossip or bragging in a bar. She guessed it was high time she gave it a shot.

As was becoming routine, Brigitte telephoned Mac that evening.

"We got the autopsy results back on the last dead calf," Mac was quick to tell her. "There's good news and bad news."

"Better give me the bad first." Brigitte sat on the edge of the double bed and twirled the phone cord nervously in her fingers.

"Basically," Mac said, "the results were inconclusive as to the exact cause of death. The medical examiner says the calf's throat was torn open, but there was so much tissue mutilation that there's no way to pinpoint whether it was done by knife or teeth."

"Uh-huh," she said.

"Anyway, there were distinct tooth marks of canine origin on several of the bones and even some of the remaining tissue."

"Well, damn, Mac," she interrupted, "a dog could have

done that. There's not a rancher up here that doesn't travel around without at least one dog at his side." She had a sudden flash of Steve Slater in her mind, his lithe, well-muscled frame striding down the street to his pickup truck, the two large dogs in the back.

"Okay, okay," Mac said. "If a man did kill one of his head of cattle, or someone else's, he'd be wise to do just that, let his own dogs do some damage to the carcass. I talked to the powers-that-be in Washington this afternoon, and they concur—the teeth marks don't necessarily prove wolves were at fault here."

"So tell me some good news."

"Okay, well, the examiner said there were suspicious gashes on several of the bones."

"Knife marks," Brigitte said excitedly.

"Maybe. The trouble is, the marks could have been made by sharp teeth. Doubtful, but possible."

"Oh, baloney," she said. "We both know it was a knife."

"We don't know."

"Well, I do."

"I hope you're right, Brigitte. I honest to God do. Washington is forced to listen to these ranchers. They're a powerful lobby. What we need is concrete proof it's the ranchers hoodwinking everyone. The autopsy reports aren't really helping. If anything," he said grimly, "the canine tooth marks make it a lot worse for the pack."

"Damn."

"So how are you progressing?"

"Slowly." She sighed. "The funny thing is, even Bess Cantrell said today that the ranchers could be up to no good."

"So prove it. That's why you're there."

"I know that, Mac."

"And Washington's pressing. They want answers. Conclusive answers."

Again she sighed. "Okay. I'll go at it harder."

"I'd sure like to see this investigation wrapped up by Christmas," he said. "A real nice present."

"Me, too."

"Be careful, though. You know, Brigitte, when it comes down to it, you're a lot more valuable to us than the wolf pack."

"Well, thanks," she said, "but I disagree. It isn't this pack alone. It's the entire reintroduction program at stake. And that makes me feel awfully insignificant."

He said nothing.

"Well, I'm off to the shower. Gotta get glamorous tonight."

"A date?"

"Lord, no. I'm going to hit a country-western dance spot. Maybe a few beers will loosen some tongues. We'll see. It's time I start pushing a little."

"Well, take care and have fun."

"I'm sure it'll be a real blast."

She got herself decked out. She had to make a special effort, because most of the time she wore loose, comfortable clothes—baggy stuff, her mother called it. Tonight she changed her style, going totally Western.

She put on a crisp white shirt with blue-beaded fringe dangling from the yoke, and a midcalf-length denim skirt. Tall Western boots completed the outfit. She even put on makeup and blow-dried her hair till it stood out in casual wisps. It looked totally natural, despite thirty minutes of messing with hair spray and a blow dryer.

"Mmm, natural," she muttered as she gave herself a last look in the bathroom mirror.

Brigitte didn't necessarily feel ill at ease going into a singles' bar alone. In Denver she often met friends on a

Friday or Saturday night at hot new night spots. There were dozens and dozens of new bars and restaurants and loft apartments in old brick warehouses in LoDo. It was kind of neat—an old-fashioned city atmosphere, but everything inside was state-of-the-art.

She was comfortable meeting friends at the sports bars. She even went to baseball games alone. She was, after all, thirty-two and a nineties woman, and having a beer or soda or burger by herself was okay. You always found someone to talk to. The trouble was, every man she'd met since college was either already married or divorced and afraid of his own shadow when it came to relationships. Some had never been married and were scared to death of commitment. That's just the way it was nowadays.

Brigitte had blown her best shot at a good marriage in her senior year in college. John had desperately wanted to get married and raise a family. She'd chosen a career, instead. At the time, her heart had been breaking, but she'd convinced herself love would come again, that she could have both career and family. Well, so far she'd been wrong.

Brigitte strolled down Main Street toward the Yampa Tavern and sighed ruefully. There sure weren't many marrying types out there, not at her age. She had her career, true, but that wasn't doing much for her biological clock.

Brigitte took a breath before entering the tavern, and a notion stole unbidden into her mind. Maybe Steve Slater would be there. He was single, after all. But she dismissed the idea. Somehow she knew Slater wasn't the saloon type. He'd never look for company this way. And, Brigitte suspected, he'd have been married happily ever after if his wife hadn't died. There were his girls, too. Steve Slater wouldn't head off to a bar and leave them. Brigitte just knew that. Oh, well, she thought, she wasn't here to meet men, for Lord's sake. She was Mata Hari, and tonight she was in disguise—the country-girl-next-door.

Although the band wouldn't start playing for a half hour, the place was pretty crowded. Brigitte walked in, paid her five-dollar cover charge and looked around.

The place was larger than it appeared from the outside, apparently running the full width of the block from Main Street to Cottonwood Street. There was a huge U-shaped wooden bar, packed right now. There were fifteen or so tables, a row of booths along the east wall and toward Cottonwood Street was a dance floor and stage. The decor was Western.

Men and women milled everywhere, and Brigitte noticed immediately that she'd dressed right—all but the cowboy hat. She didn't own one.

She saw a seat open at the bar and slid onto it like a pro, smiling sweetly at the guy who'd almost gotten there ahead of her. She ordered a beer and poured it into a chilled mug. Lest her tongue get too loose, she thought, this beer better last awhile.

People around her chatted in a friendly manner, as if everyone knew everyone else, including her. Actually, a couple did recognize her and said hello.

The woman, who was sitting one stool away from Brigitte, leaned back and struck up a conversation. "You just started at Locals Corner, didn't you?"

"Yes," Brigitte said over the din.

"I used to work there for Bess. She's a neat lady. Real fair."

"Sure is," Brigitte concurred.

"I'm over at the insurance agency now. Used to be part-time, but it's getting better." Then the woman bit her lower lip. "Hey, sorry, I should introduce myself. I'm Margie, Margie Clark."

"Brigitte Hartman." They shook hands behind the man's back.

"You just move here?"

Brigitte nodded. "I'm looking to get out of the city."

"Well, Sweetwater's as good as they come. We don't even lock our doors."

"I've noticed."

"You from Denver?"

And so it went until the band began to play, and Margie and her man vacated their seats to dance.

Brigitte sipped on her beer—which was getting warm—and glanced around. It couldn't have been two minutes after Margie had left when a very handsome dark-haired man came in the front door. For an instant Brigitte's pulse quickened—was it Steve Slater?—but then she saw she was mistaken. She turned around in her seat, faced the bar and wondered about her reaction. Steve Slater was very good-looking. So what? Looks didn't mean a darn thing.

A few more minutes slipped by before someone finally approached and introduced himself as Cy Wendt. He asked her to dance.

"Sure," Brigitte said, sliding off her stool, "I'd love to."

Cy danced well, leading her in a counterclockwise direction around the floor. She didn't really know any fancy steps, but he was a good leader, careful not to let her trip up. The only trouble was, Cy was from neighboring Toponas. He sure wasn't a rancher. He worked for the county, in fact, as a building inspector. He knew Bess's husband, Stan Cantrell. What he didn't know was anything about the wolves. Brigitte gracefully bowed out of another dance and returned to her seat. She felt bad. Guilty. But, darn it, she couldn't afford to waste time. Mac had said he'd like this investigation wound up by Christmas. She had no time for the rudiments of social etiquette.

Over the next hour she danced twice more, both times casually bringing up the subject of the wolves by saying she'd first heard of Sweetwater when that wolf pack was introduced to the Flat Tops Wilderness. "I read about it in *Time,* and I always wanted to see this town. Gosh, I'm so sick of the city and all the crime." Then she'd get direct. "Is that wolf pack still around?"

But neither of her dance partners knew much about it, except for the cattle killings. Both were of the opinion that the reintroduction had been stupid. "The government didn't really think the ranchers would take this lying down, did they?" one partner said. "Yeah, I'm afraid man is here to stay on this land and the animals better watch out."

Back at her place at the bar, she was beginning to despair that the evening was a total waste when suddenly the seat next to her was vacated and a nice-looking blond man sat down. He didn't pay any attention to Brigitte at first, merely ordered a long-neck beer and swigged out of it with a sassy, cowboy flick of his wrist. Brigitte judged him to be about twenty-eight or so, a real Western stud, sure of himself. Not her type. Too young, too cocky. Nonetheless, she took an interest when she heard him talking to the bartender.

"Didn't see you at the meeting the other night," he said to the server.

"I don't go to Cattlemen's Association meetings, Chris, and you know it."

"Yeah, well," Chris replied, "people 'round here better quit paying lip service to getting rid of that wolf pack and do something concrete. It affects the whole town. If us ranchers get put out of business, then we don't have money to be spending in town. It's that simple."

"Hear, hear," came another man's voice from down the bar. "I say we got rid of fleas and bedbugs, and we sure as hell don't need 'em or want 'em back. Same goes for that damn wolf pack."

Brigitte cringed inwardly.

The same man said, "Hey, Garrett, buy you a drink?"

"Sure," Chris said with a nod, "thanks."

Holy cow, Brigitte thought, Garrett. This still wet-behind-the-ears brat was from one of the ranching families who'd had a calf slain. One of the really outspoken families. She'd even seen his father. Right.

She took a breath, and put a smile on her face. "Say," she said, getting Chris's attention, "I couldn't help overhearing that stuff about the wolves."

"So?" he said, turning to her, and she could see his demeanor change a hair. He was mildly interested. Not in what she'd said, but in her.

"Well," she said, "I'm new in town, and I keep hearing things about this wolf pack near here. I mean, is it true they've been killing cattle?"

"Damn tootin'," Chris said. "Just like we told the government they would. Hell, this wolf program was shoved right down our throats." He turned all the way around on his stool, knees splayed, and faced her. "How come I haven't seen you around?"

She shrugged. "I'm new here. I work at Locals Corner." She stuck her hand out. "Brigitte Hartman."

He took it and held it. "Chris, Chris Garrett. My dad owns a spread near town. Cattle ranching."

She laughed. "I gathered that."

He eyed her. "Hey, you want to dance?"

"Sure," she said, and she let herself be led off to the floor.

Chris wasn't a great dancer, but he had something, a way about him, that was both athletic and terribly masculine. He was overbearing, too, holding her so tightly to him during a slow number that she could feel him against her pelvis. He was a little hard, and that made her nervous. This wasn't what she'd intended.

She tipped her head back and smiled at him. "So," she said, "what would you do if you caught a wolf killing your cattle?'' She couldn't believe her audacity, pushing too hard, perhaps tipping her hand. Still, this wasn't an opportunity to be missed.

''Hell, lady,'' he said, ''not much chance of that. They're cowards, never show their faces. But, by God, if I do catch one, I'll shoot it sure as I'm standing here. Shoot it and the rest of the pack. Many as I can.''

''Wow,'' she said, the hair raising on her arms. ''Isn't that illegal?''

''Not if you catch 'em in the act.''

There were a hundred questions she was yearning to ask, but she didn't dare. He'd know for sure she was more than she appeared.

He was curious enough as it was. ''You know,'' he said, pressing himself against her, ''folks usually move away from small towns. It's kinda weird you moving to a place this little. A girl like you...''

''I'm a woman, Chris,'' she was quick to point out. ''And maybe I moved here to meet you.''

For a minute he looked bemused, and then he smiled. ''Very funny. You almost had me there.''

''I did have you,'' she said lightly.

They finally sat back down at the bar, Chris putting an arm around her shoulder possessively. In as friendly a manner as she could manage, Brigitte extricated herself.

''Chris,'' she said, teasing, ''I'm old enough to be your mother.''

He laughed. ''How old are you?''

''A lady never tells.''

''Come on.''

''Thirty-two.''

''Well, hell,'' he said, ''so am I.''

''Liar.''

He stuck a finger at his own chest and said, ''Me?''

"Uh-huh. You're not a day over twenty-seven, twenty-eight tops."

He made an annoyed sound and let it drop. "Say," he finally said. "Tomorrow's Saturday. I got it off. You wanna take a Jeep ride or something?"

Oh, no, she thought. "I, ah, can't."

"Gotta work?"

"Ah, no. But I'm way behind on errands, all that stuff."

"That doesn't take all day."

"I have to drive to Glenwood Springs," she said quickly.

Taking the hint finally, he shrugged. "Suit yourself. Maybe next weekend."

"Maybe," she allowed.

It wasn't long after Chris's invitation that she left the Yampa Tavern. The cold November air struck her face, stinging, and a million stars glowed overhead as she walked home. It had been an interesting evening. She'd learned, at least, that the men in this valley had no use for the wolf pack—though that wasn't really news. But she'd also learned that Chris Garrett would relish the chance to shoot a wolf. Or the entire pack. For a rancher that was hardly news, either, but his frankness, his overbearing attitude, seemed to go beyond the norm. Chris Garrett appeared to be a young man with the guts to live up to his words. And that told her plenty.

She let herself into her cabin and sank down into the single chair, prying off her boots, thinking. She probably should have accepted his invitation. She knew instinctively she could get a lot of information out of him, maybe even a bragging, knowledgable statement as to who, really, had killed those calves. Chris Garrett might go that far to impress her. But the idea of spending a day in the high country with him had been so repugnant that she simply couldn't do it. If by next weekend she needed the information he might provide, well, maybe she could force herself to spend a day with him. She'd cross that bridge when she came to it.

She changed into her warm flannel pajamas, brushed her teeth and turned out the lights. Tomorrow was going to be special. Tomorrow was her first opportunity to drive up into the wilderness, and if she was real lucky, she might find some sign of the pack. After all, she, better than anyone, knew their habits. And there was snow in the high country, she thought, drifting off into sleep. Snow. Maybe she'd find some tracks. Bess had said there might be pups. Pups, beautiful pups.

WHILE BRIGITTE DREAMED her pleasant dreams, a man quietly saddled his horse and whistled softly to his dogs. The fields were bathed in starlight, and the shadows of fences and trees stood out in sharp relief.

It was an easy ride, the two dogs loping along obediently beside him. He crossed Garrett ranchland, picking out familiar objects, a boulder by that fence, a stand of willowy cottonwoods in the field below.

It was a long ride, a mile or better. He kept his horse away from the occasional piles of snow that lay on the north faces of gullies and gently sloping hills. No point leaving telltale tracks.

And then, finally, he spotted the herd and stopped, eyeing the dark terrain, the dark humps of cattle near the fence line up ahead. The man's breath was heavy with excitement now, streaming out of his mouth in long white plumes in the bitter cold air.

He surveyed the area a moment longer, then gently spurred his mount, heading him toward a stand of aspens a hundred yards from the herd. A few steers rose to their feet, turned toward him, lowed nervously in the night. They were always nervous this time of year when they'd been driven out of the high country back onto home rangeland. But they'd present no problems.

He tied his horse to an aspen and whistled softly to the dogs. "Come on, boys, we've got work to do." And then he went on foot toward the herd, toward one particular heifer. At his side hung his big Buck knife, and stuck in his pocket was a garbage bag large enough to carry out the meat. In his right hand he held a lasso.

He approached the heifer and began to raise the lasso. Nearby, a large steer gave an alarmed, throaty warning, but the man ignored it. And then, suddenly, he stopped, aware of something. It was…

He heard it again. Clearly. A soulful, eerie howl echoing out of the mountains. His blood froze. A wolf. *My God,* he thought, *a damn wolf.*

He took a calming breath and lifted the lasso again. He wasn't really afraid of wolves, he told himself. In fact, it was ironic that he should hear one howling on this particular night.

He eyed the heifer again, began to swing the rope in slow, gentle circles over his head and then he let it go. The animal struggled. He neared, his dogs still at his side, their big paws tracking up the soft earth. He wasn't worried about his own tracks.

He went to work as the herd scattered, panicky. For a moment he felt that familiar surge of guilt, but it faded. Yes, the animal was valuable. But what he was doing was worth it.

CHAPTER FIVE

STEVE BUMPED ALONG in his truck and gritted his teeth, a feeling of déjà vu sweeping over him. This had happened before, over and over now—six times as of this morning.

Another dead animal.

He pulled up alongside Ben Garrett's truck and got out, signaling Shep and Boots to stay put. Ravens croaked and cawed from nearby treetops, flapping their coal black wings, angry at being disturbed at their feast.

"Goddamn," he muttered as he strode over to Ben's side and stared down at the mutilated remains of Garrett's heifer. "Damn, Ben."

"I'm so mad," Ben said, "I may lose it right here and now. And look at this." He pointed. "Wolf tracks all over the damn place."

Steve let out a low whistle and pushed his hat back on his head. "You call Fish and Wildlife yet?"

"Chris was supposed to call them right after he got hold of you. There better be someone up here in the next couple of hours or there'll be hell to pay. If they even think about dragging their feet this time, I'll have their heads. I swear, Steve, I'll call Senator Thurston myself and demand he take immediate action. And if I don't get action, me and my boys will track that damn pack of wolves down ourselves and shoot every last one of 'em."

"I understand, I really do, Ben." Steve hunkered down onto his haunches and eyed the remains, shook his head slowly. "It's Saturday," he said. "Might be hard to get

Hal up here from Denver. Tell you what. I've talked to Mac McCarthy down in Denver before. I don't know if you've spoken to him, but he's the head honcho. I'll go on back to the ranch and try to reach him. I'll tell him to find Hal and get his butt on up here. I don't care if it *is* Saturday, they owe us.''

Steve came to his feet, his gaze still on the torn carcass. "Chris called me and he may have called Brad Milligan and some of the other ranchers. If anyone else shows up, I suggest you keep their dogs away. We sure as hell don't want Hal saying our own dogs tracked up the area. This time we've got proof, I'd say. You be all right up here while I go on back and make that call?''

"Yeah, sure,'' Ben said, his rage barely in check, "I'll wait. Besides, my boys will be here soon. We'll all wait. Just tell that McCarthy to make it quick.''

Steve put his hand on Ben's shoulder. "I'm sorry about this. I'm sorry those SOBs at Fish and Wildlife ever got involved in this valley.''

"Yeah, me, too,'' Ben said, staring fixedly at his dead heifer.

Steve was back home and on the phone to Mac McCarthy before eleven that morning. "Hal's on his way,'' Mac told him. "Left Denver about an hour ago. He'll get directions to the Garrett ranch once he gets to Sweetwater.''

"Look, McCarthy,'' Steve said, "no runaround this time. No inconclusive autopsies and all that bull you guys dish out so good down there. The ground near the dead heifer's littered with tracks. Wolf tracks.''

"No one's had his dogs…?''

"Damn it, no.''

"All right, all right,'' Mac said. "Hal can take a few casts of the prints. But, Slater, it's still going to be inconclusive. Unless we get one of the big male tracks, there's no way of telling if domestic dogs…''

"I told you, there were no, and I repeat, no dogs up there. Ben Garrett's keeping an eye on the site himself right now. We're not going to blow this, McCarthy. This is it for the damn wolf pack."

"Now don't go off half-cocked there, Steve...."

"My name's Slater. Only my friends call me Steve," he said, and he hung up.

It must have been a full minute before Steve had calmed himself enough to realize that both his girls were standing in the doorway, still clad in their pajamas. He could see Jeannie's lower lip trembling and the fire in Heather's eyes.

It was Heather who spoke. "All you do is yell these days, Dad. That's all you do."

"Now, look," he began.

"You know what?" she went on. "Some of the kids at school are saying you ranchers are killing your own cattle and blaming the wolves."

Steve felt his jaw drop. "What?"

"You heard me."

A hiccuping sob escaped Jeannie, but Steve was too irate to notice. With all the control he could muster, he said, "Are you crazy, Heather, or just plain stupid?"

"I hate you," she whispered, tears in her eyes now, and she took Jeannie's hand and led her back upstairs.

Steve sank into a living room chair and hung his head, letting out a low whistle. This couldn't go on. He knew that he had to communicate with Heather again. And he couldn't forget Jeannie, either. Every time her older sister got away with that trashy mouth of hers, Jeannie was learning that it was okay to back-talk and insult, to wound people. Heather's words were a knife in his gut. He couldn't imagine the effect they had on her younger, more sensitive sister.

But what was he going to do? Get counseling? He couldn't imagine that, baring his soul to some uppity stranger. It was pathetically obvious the trouble they were having: Heather had lost her mom just when she most desperately needed her. Hell, Steve thought, they'd all needed Leslie.

He remembered Ben's dead animal abruptly and realized he ought to be driving back out there to tell Garrett Hal would be here in an hour and a half or so. But he needed to deal with the girls first. This had gone on long enough. And, he realized, he still hadn't talked to Heather about that shoplifting. But if he brought it up, they'd only start to yell at each other. Unless...

It struck Steve that he needed a new approach. That woman at breakfast had made some reasonable suggestions. Maybe, well, maybe he'd go up to Heather's room and try a new tack. After all, he had nothing to lose. "I hate you," his daughter had said. Yeah, he guessed they'd about hit bottom.

It took a lot of courage for Steve to climb the stairs and face his girls. He steeled himself, however, and first tapped on Jeannie's door. "Hey, honey," he said, going in, "you okay?"

She was sitting on her bed and only sniffed silently at him.

"Ah, sweetie," he said, "it'll be okay. Are you upset about the wolves or Heather or all of the above?"

"Everything," she said hoarsely.

"It's going to all work out, you'll see. I'm going to talk to your sister right now and we'll get back on track."

"Heather said she hated you, Dad."

"That's just talk, sweetie. Heather's hurting inside and it's just talk. We love each other."

"Dad?" Jeannie asked in a trembling voice, "is Heather going through puberty?"

Oh, God, he thought. "I guess so. Sure, I know she is. It can be tough."

"Will I get mean like that?"

Steve went over and sat next to her and hugged her. "No. We won't let that happen. We're going to start being a family again. Okay?"

"Okay, Dad. I love you," she said.

He was as nervous as a kid on the first day of school when he knocked on Heather's door.

"I want to be alone," she called out.

He ignored her remark and went in.

"Dad."

"This'll only take a minute," Steve said in a neutral tone. "I've got two things on my mind, and I'm asking you to hear me out. Okay? No argument?"

She glared at him through dark eyes so much like his own. Then she shrugged, her lips compressed.

"You aren't going to like the first thing I've got to say, but it's time. You're almost an adult, honey—a few years to go. I want to start right here and now treating you like the young lady you're becoming. No more kid games."

She just sat there staring at him.

"Today you're going to walk into town and talk to Mrs. Cantrell at Locals Corner."

"No way!"

"Yes way, kiddo. You owe her an apology for stealing."

"I...can't! I won't! And it's miles!"

"You will do it." He put up a hand to ward off the fit she was about to throw. "That's the bad news," he said quickly. "The good news is that tomorrow I'm going to teach you to drive the truck."

"What?"

"You heard me. I need some help around here from time to time, and you're old enough to be driving around the ranch."

"You mean... Like by myself?"

"Soon as you can handle the truck, sure, by yourself."

"Oh," she said.

"But, honey, first that walk to town."

"Do I have to?"

He nodded soberly. And then he figured, what the hell, and he told her about the time he'd taken the penknife.

"You did?"

"Yep. And I took the same long walk you're going to take."

She looked at the floor and finally, miraculously, nodded slowly.

"Okay," Steve said, relief washing over him. "Tomorrow I don't care if the wolves slaughter my whole herd, we're teaching you to drive. You're going to be a woman before you know it, and you'd best learn these things. Is it a date?"

"Sure," she said, looking up. "Sure."

"Okay. I've got to go on back to Garrett's ranch, but I'll be home before dinner. You better get going into town."

"Can Jeannie come?"

"If she wants to."

"I'm going to hate this," Heather muttered.

"Well," Steve said at the door, "so did I. But once it was over, that was it. Your grandfather never said another word to me about it. And I won't say another word to you. Deal?"

"I guess," she said sullenly.

Steve got back to Ben Garrett's ranch later than he'd anticipated. And when he finally did arrive, it looked like a darned town meeting. Ben, of course, was there, and so was Chris, his eldest, along with the middle boy, Jim Garrett. As well, Brad Milligan had stopped by to survey the site as head of the local chapter of the Cattlemen's Association. And Hal Franklin had arrived. Just. He was standing next to Ben, staring down at the dead animal, one hand thoughtfully rubbing his beard. He was muttering about the ground being messed up by footprints.

But there was someone else there, too, surprising Steve totally. Brigitte Hartman was standing with Chris Garrett, talking.

Steve got out of his truck and strode over. He nodded to Chris and then automatically tipped his Stetson to Brigitte. "Didn't expect to see you here," he said.

She smiled warmly and looked embarrassed. "It's a long story. I parked my Jeep at the Hanging Lake Trailhead, and I had this Forest Service hiking map... Anyway, I was just going for a short hike and, well, I must have made a wrong turn." She shrugged. "I never meant to trespass or anything. Mr. Garrett over there, well, Ben, that is, waved at me and here I am. Good thing, too, because Lord only knows where I would have ended up."

"Uh-huh," Steve said.

"I imagine a person could get pretty lost up here."

"Uh-huh," he said again, staring at her. He spoke to Chris then, mostly about the killing. But even as he and Chris talked, he was acutely aware of Brigitte, and he wondered how he could have missed noticing what a nice-looking woman she was. Must have had other stuff on his mind yesterday morning.

She looked so pretty standing there with her short blond hair tousled by the breeze and her cheeks all rosy from her walk. She had the biggest blue eyes and a nice nose, turned up just a tad. Her teeth were white, and she smiled readily, friendlylike, a smile that would tug at any man's heart. And when she wasn't smiling, her mouth was adorable, turned up at the corners, her lower lip full, almost pouty. He couldn't take his eyes off her mouth.

Steve couldn't have told anyone what a woman had worn on the most memorable occasion, but for some reason he took in Brigitte's outfit and thought somehow that it suited her. She wore loose clothes—casual, outdoorsy things. They hid her figure, although he could imagine what was underneath the faded jeans and loose green turtleneck and old blue down vest. The faded colors seemed to make her own high coloring that much more pronounced. He wondered then if he'd ever before seen eyes the true color of the Colorado sky.

He spoke to Chris a few more moments, then strode over to Ben and Brad and Hal, nodding at Jim Garrett, whom he didn't know all that well. But even as the men conversed, their voices often raised, he found himself searching out Brigitte, finding her long-limbed figure over by the fence. A coltish figure, he thought once before catching himself and rejoining the conversation.

"Don't know how much longer I can keep the ranchers in check," Brad was saying to Hal.

"Either you trap and destroy that wolf pack before winter sets in or I'll damn well do it myself," Ben was threatening the USFWS agent.

"My dad means it, mister," Jim put in. "We've had it."

Steve himself didn't say much. He didn't have to. Hal was getting the message loud and clear. And then, when Hal finally went back to his truck and got his equipment, Chris and Brigitte walked over.

"What's he doing?" Brigitte asked as Hal poured a ready-made mixture into several of the wolf tracks.

"He's taking a cast of the paw prints," Ben replied. "As if we need them."

"Oh," Brigitte said, apparently interested. And then she squatted down alongside the mutilated carcass and studied it. Steve was surprised. This wasn't women's stuff. Not at all. Yet she didn't seem upset or the least bit squeamish. Rather, Brigitte Hartman somehow fit into the scene, as if she were in her element, comfortable up here in the high country.

"A real shame," she said, coming to her feet, meeting Steve's gaze. "A real waste."

"Tell that to Hal over there," Steve said darkly.

But she only smiled and bit her lower lip. "I don't think I need to. I think he's hearing enough already."

"Let's goddamn hope so," Ben ground out.

Hal worked the area for some time, collecting the paw casts when they'd hardened, bagging the carcass. Jim helped him load it into his truck for transport to Denver.

"The autopsy results will take a couple weeks," Hal told the group.

"Like we don't know that," Brad Milligan said dryly.

"I don't give a tinker's damn about the autopsy," Ben said, his face flushed. "We want action, and we want it now."

"He's right," Steve said to Hal in a calmer tone. "We've had a bellyful of your wolves. Get rid of them."

Hal climbed into his truck and rolled down the window. "I'll be talking to Mac McCarthy soon as I get back to Denver. I'll let him know how you feel."

"Passing the buck," Chris muttered.

"Yeah," echoed his brother Jim. "Then this McCarthy can pass it along to *his* boss. Nothing ever gets done."

"Goddamn bureaucrats," Ben said.

"I think I'll resign my spot with the association," Brad muttered. "This is driving me nuts."

They were all heading to their vehicles when Steve turned to Brigitte, who was standing there, the sun dancing in her hair.

"Your car's at the Hanging Lake Trailhead?" he asked.

"Yes," she said. "If you'll just point me…"

"Well, it's over that ridge." He nodded. "About three miles or better. No way are you going to walk that before dark. I'll drive you."

"Oh, I couldn't…"

"It's not open for debate," he said. "Now hop in the truck."

"I really…"

Steve stopped in his tracks. "I spent half the morning arguing with a female already, so don't you start in. Okay?"

She laughed. "Okay, boss, lead the way." And then she saluted him and he found himself smiling.

It was an odd thing, Steve realized as he drove along the rutted ranch roads, but everything seemed new, different. They talked about Heather as he drove, but he hardly knew what was said. He was aware only of the oddest things: the clarity of the late-afternoon light, the scent of pine and dust, and a woman, the sound of her voice over the groan of the engine, the smooth feel of the steering wheel slipping easily through his hands. His senses were alive, he realized, and that notion stirred a long-forgotten part deep inside him.

The road leading off Garrett's land eventually met up with the one that ran past Steve's own ranch. He meant to take it a mile and a half to the turnoff that would lead to the Hanging Lake Trailhead. But when he stopped at the turnoff and saw his house in the distance, he couldn't help glancing over at Brigitte and voicing his thoughts.

"Come to dinner tonight. That's my spread down there—" he pointed "—and afterward I can drive you back to your car."

She looked at him and smiled, and he saw the last golden light dance in those blue eyes. "I couldn't do that," she said.

"Why not?"

"Well, I just couldn't impose."

Steve cocked his head. "That's not a reason."

"Yes, it is. I don't do this sort of thing."

"That's still a lousy reason."

She sighed heavily. "Steve, I don't think Heather and..."

"Jeannie," he filled in.

"Yes, Jeannie, well, I don't think they'd appreciate my company."

"You're dead wrong," he said. "The girls would be delighted to see a new face in the house."

She considered that, then shook her head. "Heather will be embarrassed."

"I don't give a rat's... Well, never mind that," he said. "I'm asking you to dinner for me."

"Oh," she said.

"What I mean is, it would be nice to have someone else at the table to talk to. I'd like it. And believe me, so would the girls."

"Well..."

He turned toward his house. "It's settled, then."

"I guess it is," Brigitte said, and he gave her another quick sidelong glance. He felt very much alive.

ACROSS THE MOUNTAINSIDE and down in the next valley, Ben and his two oldest boys arrived at their ranch house in separate trucks.

Audrey, his wife, was there at the door to greet them. She waved and called, "Hi, honey!"

Ben got out of the truck and waved back. Despite his anger over the dead heifer, he still felt a stirring in his loins whenever he looked at his new wife. She was twenty-seven years younger than he was. Hell, she was only two years older than Chris. Ben knew folks talked about that, but he couldn't have cared less. He and his three sons' mother had been married for thirty years before their divorce. He'd been faithful for the most part but, damn, that woman had borne his sons and then turned off sexually as if she'd thrown a switch. She lived in Glenwood Springs now, and the boys saw her frequently, but Ben had no feelings left for her whatsoever. For most of their married life she'd been as cold as a dead fish.

Now Audrey... That was a different story. Ben had met her at the annual Stockman's Show in Denver two years ago. She was from Cheyenne, Wyoming. She'd been married before, to a rodeo star, but it hadn't worked. Luckily for Ben. This lady was on fire, and there didn't appear to be an end in sight.

Audrey put her arms around him and kissed his cheek. "You poor thing, up there all day long," she said, leading him inside. "You must be famished. I've got an early dinner all ready."

"You cooked?" Ben tossed his jacket and hat onto a living room chair.

"Sure did," she said. "I let Maria go early. I was so bored without you, honey."

Ben's sons had gone to their respective rooms to clean up, so he pulled his wife against his chest and kissed her thoroughly.

"Mmm." He sighed, coming up for air. "If I wasn't so hungry, I'd take you on back to our room." And he meant it. He could be with her that way morning and night, and sometimes, when the boys were out on the range, in the afternoon, too.

Darn tootin', he thought. His wife had a way about her that stirred his blood. She was so pretty with her dark hair and bright green eyes. A knockout, really, and Ben was terribly proud that she was his. He recognized, too, that his oldest boys, Chris and Jim, appreciated her sensuality. But that didn't bother Ben one bit. She was his. Let them find their own women. He was pleased, in fact, that they were both virile young men. Jim was quieter, true, but Ben knew that still waters ran deep. And Jim was all man. Ben's youngest, Dave, who was still in high school, already promised to be the biggest ladies' man of the three.

You bet, Ben thought, he had three fine sons. Real men.

He kissed the top of Audrey's shining dark head and patted her bottom. "So where's that meal you promised?" he said.

Almost every evening they ate together family-style in the dining room. Ben liked it that way, his young wife and handsome blond sons surrounding him. It was already understood that when they married they'd build right there on the ranch, too, and always be a family. He looked forward to those days, his sons and their wives and lots of grandchildren.

Audrey had prepared a roast—beef, naturally—and browned potatoes and onions and carrots around it in the oven. They had beer with dinner. While Ben stood at the head of the table and carved the meat, he thought about the day and realized what it was that infuriated him so damn much.

"You know," he said, laying a slab of beef on Dave's plate, "if those goddamned wolves had gotten that heifer up on federal lands, I might have been able to stomach it better. But on my land... Right on my property. Somehow that was the last straw."

"Next thing you know," Chris said, "they'll be right at our door."

Audrey's eyes widened.

"It won't come to that," Jim said quietly.

"Oh, yeah?" Ben said. "If no one stops them, that's exactly what will happen."

"So we go out and shoot them," Chris said matter-of-factly.

"There's big fines for that, and jail time," Dave said. "We learned that in school."

"That's that tree-hugging biologist you got for a teacher this year," Chris said. "Damn bleeding-heart liberal."

Ben put up a hand, and they all obediently fell silent. "The way to handle this," he said, "is to force the government to get them off the land. The state Cattlemen's Association meeting's coming up in January, and our local chapter will be ready."

"What if the state doesn't listen?" Jim asked. "I mean, we're the only area with the wolf problem."

"Then we act on our own," Ben said.

"I wonder if anyone would really blame us if we acted on our own right now, before the snow sets in too deep to track the pack," Jim put in.

"Oh, gosh," Audrey said, "all this talk about tracking and shooting... I mean, Ben, the government pays you for a lost animal, doesn't it?"

It was Jim who snorted in derision.

Audrey said, "What?"

"Go ahead, tell her." Ben nodded at his middle son.

"It's like this," Jim said. "You remember the calf we had killed last spring?"

"Well, sure."

"Fish and Wildlife said there was no proof a wolf did it. It took four letters and God knows how many phone calls to get them to pay up. Why should we have to suffer like that?" He was speaking to Audrey but looking at his father for confirmation.

"Jim's right," Ben said. "It's the ranchers who're being penalized. You're a woman, Audrey. You don't understand. To a man, his land and his herd are as important as his family. It's all the same thing. When a wolf attacks my herd, it might as well be attacking young Dave here."

"Dad's right," Chris said. "Washington stuffed this down our throats and we're choking."

Ben nodded. Then he rose to his feet, beer glass in hand.

"I propose a toast," he said. "Here's to the wolves. The only good one's a dead one."

The boys all rose, too. They chorused, "To dead wolves!" and clinked their glasses, laughing.

"It's okay," Ben said to Audrey later that night as he reached for her in the living room. "I don't expect you to understand. You just keep cooking up a storm like today and that's all I'll ever ask of you. Well," he said, smiling, "and maybe one or two other little things."

CHAPTER SIX

BRIGITTE FOLLOWED STEVE across the drive to his house and felt her stomach knot with tension. It had been a rough day already, and she wasn't at all certain she could handle this dinner thing properly. She needed time to think, to sort everything out in her mind; what she didn't need was a confrontation with his daughter.

On the other hand, that closed door had suddenly sprung wide open. She'd been waiting on pins and needles for something like this to happen. She'd wondered if it ever would, and then he'd just up and asked her: Come to dinner.

She couldn't refuse him. Especially after today. Another dead animal. When Mac had called her early this morning, the wind had gone right out of her sails. And then she'd had to figure out how to get up to Garrett land and study the scene without arousing suspicion. Of course, Hal had been there, too, and she'd felt as if everyone knew, as if everyone could tell they were avoiding eye contact.

She'd stood in that field and waited for Steve or Chris or Ben or even the easily rattled Brad Milligan to say, "What's going on here? You two know each other?" But no one had noticed. Thank God.

Steve whistled at his dogs, and they raced ahead toward the door. Brigitte watched them and had to wonder if those tracks near the carcass had been made by these same dogs. It was a possibility. It could be Steve behind the cattle killings.

That thought hurt. She liked him. He had an appealing, quiet strength that drew her despite the alarms blaring in her head.

"This is it," Steve was saying, "the old homestead. Watch that step there."

His home. Guilt swept over her. She was lying to him, lying to everyone. The reason for her was just and fair. But certainly, right now, she was questioning her methods.

"Oh, boy," she said.

He stopped and turned to her. "What?"

"Well, you know," she said, collecting herself, "Heather. I'm still not sure this is a real good idea."

"Look, this is my house. I'm an adult, and I don't need permission from my fourteen-year-old daughter to bring a friend home for dinner."

"Okay, sure. I just don't want to cause any more trouble between you. I figure I've caused enough."

"You didn't cause it. Heather did."

"Mmm. Well, Steve, she may not look at it quite like that."

"Come on in, Brigitte, and don't worry about Heather."

She managed a smile, shrugged and followed him inside. "Once more into the breach," she said lightly.

The mudroom was cluttered with shoes and boots, a big bag of dry dog food in the corner. Beyond that was the kitchen, a cheery place, all white cupboards with glass fronts, a counter around the perimeter, an island in the center. Lots of notes were stuck onto the refrigerator door with magnets.

"Heather! Jeannie!" Steve called. "I'm home. We've got a guest for dinner."

A young girl raced in from another room. "Daddy!" She stopped short upon seeing Brigitte. "Hi," she said shyly.

"Jeannie, this is Brigitte Hartman. She's new to Sweetwater, and I've asked her to dinner."

Brigitte went to the girl and held out her hand. "I'm glad to meet you, Jeannie."

The girl put her own hand out and stared at Brigitte. She looked quite different from Heather, with blue eyes. She appeared to be very young, but she could have been about twelve.

Then Jeannie looked at her father and said, "But there isn't any dinner."

"What you mean, kiddo, is that it isn't made yet."

"That's what I mean, I guess," Jeannie said doubtfully. "Dad."

They all turned toward the voice. Heather stood in the doorway, her expression stormy.

"Hi, Heather," Brigitte said, trying to break the strained silence.

"I don't believe this," Heather said.

"Heather," her father warned.

"Dad, I really don't believe this." Her voice dripped with disdain.

Steve turned to Brigitte. "Give me a minute," he said. Then he went to Heather, took her arm and led her into the living room.

"Well," Brigitte breathed, "I warned him."

"What?" Jeannie asked.

"Your sister and I know each other. We met the other day. I'm afraid I had to... Do you know what happened?"

Jeannie nodded soberly.

"Well, I'm the one who did it. Heather is probably not too thrilled to see me here."

"How come Dad brought you home, then?"

"Here, sit down with me. I walked miles today."

Brigitte took off her vest and hung it over the back of a chair. She ran a hand through her hair, making it look more windblown than it already was.

Jeannie sat, back straight, hands folded in her lap.

"Your dad and I met the other day, and then again today, up where the animal was killed. I guess he's just being friendly, neighborly, you know, because I don't know many people in town yet."

"Where did you come from?"

"Denver."

"Oh."

"So that's the story."

Jeannie smiled. "My dad's real nice, isn't he?"

"He sure is."

"But I can't figure out why he brought you here for dinner. He's not a very good cook. He can only do eggs and stuff."

"Say, I've got an idea. How about you show me what you've got in this nice big kitchen and I'll help cook dinner?"

Jeannie was pointing to packages in the freezer when Steve came up behind Brigitte. She turned and met his gaze questioningly.

"It'll be fine," he said quietly.

"And did she…?"

He nodded. "Bess gave her a big hug, and I guess they both sort of cried a little, and…"

"That's wonderful," Brigitte said fervently. "That's great!" She put her hand on his arm and squeezed it in a friendly gesture, but when she saw his face go still, she snatched her hand away. *Careful,* she told herself.

"Yeah, that's good," he said.

"Is she still mad at me?" Brigitte asked.

"She'll be polite," Steve said evenly. "She promised."

Brigitte rolled her eyes. "Oh, good. Death by politeness."

"Dad, what were you going to make for dinner?"

Steve looked at his youngest daughter. "Gosh, I haven't thought about it. What do we have in there?"

"Aunt Naomi's squash casserole and Grandma's pea soup and, hmm, I guess that's some leftover spaghetti."

Brigitte held up her hand. "Save that stuff. I'm cooking, okay?"

"I didn't ask you here so you could cook."

"Jeannie told me you're not much of a chef, so the cat's out of the bag. Besides, I'd rather cook than do the dishes afterward. Deal?"

"Let her, Dad."

"I'm outnumbered, I guess."

"Okay, Jeannie, you show me where everything is. Steve, you clear out, okay?"

"Brigitte, I didn't really…"

"Go on, honestly."

He held her gaze for a moment, as if trying to gauge whether she really meant it. She cocked her head and smiled. She would have patted his hand, but she was cautious about touching him now. She was beginning to believe this could be the first time he'd had a strange female in the kitchen since his wife died.

"Go on, Dad," Jeannie put in.

"I wouldn't mind a shower," he admitted, and he headed toward the staircase. It was then that Brigitte noticed he wore a big Buck knife in a leather sheath on the back of his belt. It ran through her mind that such a weapon could do a lot of damage to a carcass. Of course, all ranchers carried knives, she told herself. Still, she filed the knowledge away. Just in case.

Brigitte found that her dinner choices were limited. There was lots of food, but it was a pretty unimaginative collection. Easy stuff that a man and two kids could whip up on short notice.

"Well," she said, hands on hips, looking into the refrigerator. She turned to Jeannie. "Do you guys like chicken?"

"I guess so."

"Mexican chicken casserole?"

Jeannie shrugged. "It's better than spaghetti or meat loaf or frozen pizza."

"It sure is."

So Brigitte started in, cooking the chicken, making the sauce: green chilies and onions, then some tortillas cut in strips. She directed Jeannie to strip the meat off the chicken while she grated cheese.

"So," she asked, "what grade are you in, Jeannie?"

"Seventh."

"Do you like it?"

"Uh-huh. I have a nice teacher this year. And we've started Spanish. I like that."

"It's always good to have a second language."

Together they layered the casserole, and Brigitte put it in the oven.

"You doing all right?" Steve asked from the doorway.

"Just great," Brigitte said. "It'll be about an hour."

"Dad, she made Mexican chicken casserole."

"Sounds good." He looked at Brigitte. "I really appreciate this."

His hair was damp, slicked back close to his head. He wore faded jeans and a red wool shirt and moccasins. He'd been upstairs taking a shower, she remembered, while she'd been cooking, and a brief flashing image of Steve in the shower passed in front of her eyes.

"Brigitte? Do you want me to set the table?"

She jerked herself back from the errant thought. "Oh, sure," she said. "The table. That'd be fine."

"Make Heather do it," Jeannie said. "She hasn't helped at all."

"That's okay," Steve said. "I'll do it."

The three of them sat at the kitchen table and talked while dinner cooked.

"Where's Heather?" Jeannie asked.

"In her room. She's listening to her music," Steve said. "She's acting dumb."

Brigitte gave a little laugh. "We all act dumb sometimes. The important thing is to realize that it's dumb, and the other important thing is to be able to laugh at yourself."

"I don't think Heather's laughing right now," Jeannie said.

"Maybe not, but someday she will. She'll tell her kids all the dumb things she did, and they'll all laugh."

"Tell me something you did," Jeannie said.

"Oh, gosh, let's see. There are so many. Oh, there's the time when I was little, younger than you, and I was playing beauty parlor with a friend and we cut each other's hair. I mean short. And my mom had hysterics when she saw us. Ooh, was she mad. I was so scared I cried, but it grew out, and now I can laugh at what I must have looked like."

"Dad, what did you do that was dumb?"

"I never did anything dumb," he said drolly.

"You did, I know you did," Jeannie said. "Tell us."

"Well, I might have done one little thing once."

"Tell us."

He shook his head. "I had a calf I was raising for a 4-H project. Pretty little thing. He was like a pet. So one day I decided to ride him. Heck, I was only ten or eleven. I was going to be a bull rider, see. I got on him, and he bucked me off into a mud puddle."

Jeannie laughed. Over her head Brigitte's eyes met Steve's. He smiled at her, the first time she'd seen him really open up, and it was a boyish grin, changing his whole face so that he looked younger and carefree and achingly handsome.

"Good one, Dad," Jeannie said.

Brigitte tore her gaze from his and stood. "Jeannie," she said, "show me where your salad bowl is. I'm going to make a nice, big salad. Oil and vinegar dressing all right?"

When the casserole was ready, Steve sent Jeannie to fetch her sister.

"I hope she's not too upset," Brigitte said to Steve.

"Don't worry about it. She'll be fine."

"I don't want to cause trouble between you."

"Look, Heather's got to take responsibility for her behavior. This is a good thing, believe me."

Heather came to the table quietly, chastised. Half sulking, half defiant, but polite. Brigitte heaved an inward sigh of relief.

"This is good," Jeannie said about the meal.

"It's great," Steve agreed.

Silence from Heather, but she was eating, all right.

"This is a lovely room," Brigitte said. The dining room had old-fashioned narrow paneling halfway up the wall, then a border of flowered wallpaper around the walls right under the ceiling. Very Victorian but not busy. Very attractive.

"We never eat in here," Jeannie said. "Not anymore."

"We have a guest tonight," Steve said.

"Only when it's a holiday or something, and Grandma comes, or Aunt Naomi. Like Thanksgiving. We'll eat in here. We'll have a big turkey and stuffing. Grandma always makes the sweet potatoes."

"Sounds delicious," Brigitte said.

"We used to eat in here more," Jeannie went on blithely. "Lots of times. When Mommy was alive. She liked to eat here. She fixed this room up herself, you know, and…"

"Jeannie." Heather finally spoke. When Brigitte looked at her, she saw the girl's face was white and strained, and Steve's face… She couldn't tell, because he was pointedly staring down at this plate.

"But I…"

"Jeannie, will you just be quiet about all that," Heather said fiercely.

Wow, Brigitte thought. These kids were not dealing with their mother's death very well; at least Heather wasn't. And neither was Steve, it seemed. You'd think by now they could talk about her. It was healthy, wasn't it? She glanced at Steve again. His head was bowed, his hands resting on either side of his plate. Jeannie's face was stricken, and Heather—her expression was cold and distant, as if she'd withdrawn to somewhere else. Brigitte's heart went out to them.

She reached over silently and patted Jeannie's hand. "It's a very pretty room," she said, trying desperately to dispel the pain-filled hush. "Your mom had terrific taste. Did she fix up the kitchen, too?"

"Uh-huh," Jeannie whispered.

"What a treat it is cooking in it. It's way better than the one in my apartment in Denver." She turned to Steve. "It must have been quite a job remodeling the kitchen. Did you do it yourself?"

He raised his head, his expression grateful. "I did some. Hired a crew for the rest. It sure was a mess in there for a while."

"I remember when my mom fixed up our house. Lord, what an awful thing to go through. You wish you could just move out, don't you?"

"Where are your parents?" Jeannie asked.

"Bozeman, Montana."

"You're from Montana," Steve said.

"Yes, but that was a long time ago. I went to college there, then I left and got a job in Denver and…" Oops, careful.

"What kind of job?" Jeannie asked.

"Oh, you know, secretarial. Despite some drawbacks, I like the city. It's a lot of fun."

"I'd like to live in the city," Heather said. "New York or San Francisco or someplace like that."

"Not Denver?"

"Denver's okay,"

"Only okay?"

Heather shrugged. Well, at least she was willing to talk now.

"Have you ever been to any of those cities, the big ones, like New York?" Brigitte asked.

They shook their heads.

"Steve, you should take these girls to a big city. They'd love it."

"Me?" He gave a short laugh. "I'd be scared of getting mugged."

"You go to Denver, don't you?"

"Oh, sure, we go shopping, although usually I get their aunt to take them to the malls. And we do the National Stock Show in January. Some movies, maybe. But I don't have a lot of time to get away. I can't leave my hired hand alone for more than a couple of days."

"I guess not."

"That's the trouble with being a rancher," Heather said. "You don't get vacations. Last year Tory Hanson's parents took her to Washington."

"But just think of the advantages you have," Brigitte said quickly. "All this freedom. All the cattle around you. And your dogs. Did you know in cities a lot of places don't allow pets? Some don't even allow children."

"Really?" Jeannie said.

"You've got a special kind of life here. You don't realize it yet maybe, but you will." Brigitte paused. "And I hear ranchers' kids get to drive when they're real young. Big trucks and tractors. I would have loved that."

Heather gave her a swift sidelong glance.

"Yeah, I'm going to start Heather driving tomorrow," Steve said casually.

"I bet you're excited," Brigitte said. "Do you have drivers' ed at school?"

"Yes, but I won't be old enough till next year."

"What grade are you in now?"

"Ninth."

"She's a freshman," Jeannie interjected.

"Do you like school, Heather?" Brigitte asked. Keep the girl talking. Maybe she could be a back door to Steve and any knowledge he might have about the cattle killings. That was what she was here for, after all, though the thought gave her a twinge.

"It's okay. It's too small. I want to go away to college, someplace big, in a city."

"Don't you think it's too soon to be thinking about that?" Steve asked.

"No," Heather said. "Dave's already decided where he's going to apply next year. And he's only two years ahead of me."

"Dave?" Brigitte asked politely.

"Dave Garrett, Ben's youngest son," Steve said.

"That's her boyfriend," Jeannie put in.

"Shut up," Heather said, embarrassed. "He's just a friend. He's got his license and he gives me rides to school sometimes, that's all."

"Well, you told me…" Jeannie began.

"Jeannie."

Oops, steer clear from that subject, Brigitte thought. "Where does he want to go to school?" she asked.

"He'd like to go to Cornell, to the veterinary school there, but it's too expensive. So Colorado State is the next best."

"Well, he sounds like a sensible young man."

"He is," Heather said. "Not like his crazy brothers."

Steve laughed. "Heather, that's not nice."

"But it's true, Dad. You even said so yourself."

Steve blew out a low breath. "Maybe I did, but it's not for public consumption, kiddo."

Heather seemed to hesitate, as if deciding something, then she blurted out, "Dave asked me to the Christmas dance."

Steve stopped his fork halfway to his mouth. "What?"

"Dave asked me to the Christmas school dance," she repeated.

"You can't go. You're too young."

Heather's dark eyes glowed with sudden anger. "I knew you'd say that. So what if everybody else in the school's going? I can't go!"

"Heather, please, let's discuss this later," he said quietly.

Surprisingly, Heather turned to Brigitte. "Tell him how old-fashioned he is!"

Brigitte was taken aback. Good Lord, to be in the middle of a family quarrel... "Heather, I can't really get involved. It's your father's decision."

The teenager narrowed her eyes. "But you were my age once. You must have an opinion."

Brigitte turned to Steve. "Oh, honestly, I can't interfere in this."

"Go ahead," Steve said. "I'd like your opinion. A fourteen-year-old going out with a kid two, three years older, driving those dark roads."

Brigitte drew in a deep breath. "This is really none of my business."

"Go on, tell him," Heather insisted.

Brigitte rolled her eyes and ran a hand through her hair. "I'll tell you what I think, but it's only one side, you know." She paused to consider how to phrase her thoughts. "Okay. First, Heather, will there be any drinking before or after the dance?"

"No."

"Will there be chaperons at the dance?"

"Of course."

"Well, then, I'd say it's okay as long as you're home by whatever time your dad decides."

"See?" Heather said.

"I heard her," Steve muttered.

"I hope I haven't put my foot in it," Brigitte said. "Steve?"

"Maybe I am old-fashioned," he growled.

Heather smiled broadly.

Brigitte had only one more thought. "Do you have a dress to wear?"

"I was going to wait to bring that up," Heather said, so serious and mature, Brigitte had to keep her smile hidden.

"Oh, God," Steve groaned.

"I'll get Grandma to take me shopping," Heather said quickly.

"Hey, I can take you. Grandma's too far away," Steve said.

"I want to go, too," Jeannie added.

"Well, kids, you know, I was thinking we should take a trip to Glenwood Springs. Christmas shopping. If you can't find anything then, you can order a dress."

"Yes!" Jeannie shouted.

"We could spend the whole day."

"I think that's a very good idea," Heather said with great dignity.

"Okay, then, it's decided. After Thanksgiving," Steve said.

"So I can go to the dance?" Heather pressed.

Steve grumbled something under his breath. "Yeah, I guess so."

When they'd finished the ice cream Jeannie had dug out of the back of the freezer, Jeannie and Brigitte sat at the kitchen table while Heather and Steve did the dishes.

Brigitte put out of her mind the reason she was there in that warm, comfortable kitchen. Now that Heather had thawed out some, it was very pleasant. She wondered what Steve's wife had been like, how their marriage had been. She'd learned a little from Bess—that her name had been Leslie, and she'd died three years ago in a freak fall from a horse—but she'd been careful not to appear too curious. As it was, Bess had given her a knowing wink and said, "He's some hunk, isn't he?"

After the dishes the girls went upstairs to watch TV, and Steve and Brigitte moved to the living room with fresh cups of coffee.

"They're great kids," Brigitte said.

"Thanks."

"You're a good father."

"I try my best. It's hard...."

"I can imagine. No, I can't—I can't even get close," Brigitte said with feeling. "I've never been married, much less had kids."

"Why not?" he asked.

She looked down. "Oh, I don't know. I wanted to get away, live in a city, be independent. My job..."

"Hell, a secretarial job doesn't sound like enough reason not to get married. You could still work, anyway."

"Uh, sure, I know. It... Well, it just hasn't happened. Men nowadays, the ones I meet, are either already married or scared of commitment."

"Are you afraid of commitment?"

"I don't think so. I don't know. No one's given me the choice yet."

He looked at her, his gaze dark and unreadable. "Sorry for the personal questions. It just seems you're real good with kids, and I wondered..."

"No problem. I haven't got anything to hide." *Liar,* she thought.

"The business with Heather, the dance. You were right, but I worry about her so much. And the Garretts…"

"You said something about Dave's brothers."

"Yeah, and Ben, too. He's pretty intense. I guess Dave's the most sensible of them, but he can be kind of wild, too."

"Heather will be perfectly fine."

He rubbed his eyes with his hand. "Yeah, sure, I know."

"The Garretts," she ventured. "You know, I met Chris last night."

Steve looked at her intently. "Last night?"

"At the Yampa Tavern."

"You were at the tavern?"

"Sure, why not?"

"Well… No reason, I guess."

Brigitte shook her head at him. "Anyhow," she said, "Chris seemed nice enough. Maybe a little outspoken."

"*Nice* is not a word I'd use to describe Chris."

"Really."

"I suppose it's Ben's influence. He's raised his boys to be tough and somewhat wild. Kind of like him. You know, men's men, that sort of thing. Ben's a stubborn one, too, stubborn and proud." Steve shook his head. "You should have heard Ben at the cattlemen's meeting the other night. Ranting and raving about shooting the wolf pack…"

"Wolf pack?" Brigitte's heart was thudding. Here it was, falling right into her lap. "You mean the same wolves you were all arguing about up on Ben's land today?"

"They're the ones, all right. They were set loose last year up in the Flat Tops Wilderness. They've killed six head of cattle so far."

"Oh, wow," she said carefully. "I didn't realize today it was the same wolf pack. You're talking about the ones that were on the cover of *Time?*"

"Yeah, those are the ones. Jeannie has that picture, the one of the pair of wolves. She's crazy about animals. You put a picture of some dumb cow on the cover of *Time* and no one would pay attention. But a wolf…''

''They're beautiful.''

''They're evil. They have pups and pretty soon they'll overrun the valley, and no one's stock'll be safe. Wolves are vicious predators. They're man's direct competition.''

''You don't think there's room for both?''

''You want my personal opinion? No, I don't.''

''But I thought there was some kind of fund to pay ranchers back if they lost stock. There is up in Yellowstone, isn't there?'' Brigitte said cautiously.

''Yes, there is, but our claims are on hold right now until Fish and Wildlife proves to their own satisfaction that our stock was killed by wolves.''

''They aren't sure? Well, what else could it be?''

He shrugged, his dark brows drawing together. ''Martians? Ghosts? Who knows?'' He leaned forward in his chair, elbows on his knees. ''I know you're from the city, and maybe you aren't aware of this, but we ranchers walk a thin edge all the time. We're at the mercy of the weather and all kinds of natural phenomena, but now we're also at the mercy of bureaucrats two thousand miles away who don't know a damn thing about how we live and who seem to care a hell of a lot more about a pack of mangy wolves than they do about us.''

''You feel strongly about this,'' Brigitte said softly.

''Yeah, I do. And that's probably the longest speech you'll ever hear me make.'' He smiled. ''I don't usually mouth off like that, but this wolf thing has been a real problem lately. Well, hey, you saw that heifer.''

''Hmm.'' *And the paw prints there were not made by wolves,* Brigitte wanted to say.

''I'm boring you.''

''Oh, God, no. Not at all.''

"That was a good dinner you cooked. I'm afraid we, uh, don't exactly come up with gourmet menus around here."

"That wasn't gourmet," she said.

"And Heather... She came around some, didn't she?"

"Yes, she did."

Steve raised his coffee cup to take a last sip, then set it down. "I guess I'd better take you back to your car."

She looked at her watch, surprised to see how late it was. "I'm keeping you up," she said.

"Not really. Let me tell the girls where I'm going."

When he was gone, Brigitte sank back against the chair, closed her eyes and blew out a long breath. Wow, he'd really opened up to her. He'd sounded totally sincere, and she simply couldn't believe that Steve was a man who was killing cattle just to blame it on the wolf pack. No way. Not Steve Slater, with those dangerously long eyelashes and all that anxiety over his daughter's date for a Christmas dance. It couldn't be him. On the other hand, Ben Garrett and his sons might be worthy of some more investigation.

"Ready?" Steve asked, standing in the doorway.

She sprang up, a little too fast, feeling guilty and flustered. My God, what if he knew what she'd been thinking?

"Sure, I'm all set," she said.

He drove her back to her car in his muddy truck. All ranchers had muddy trucks. And he had a gun rack on the rear window of the cab, too, although there was no shotgun in it. But then, the cattle hadn't been shot, had they?

"It was a nice evening," she began. "I really enjoyed it."

"So did I."

She was terribly aware of his closeness in the cab of the pickup. Her skin prickled with his proximity, as if there were static electricity in the air. She could smell the masculine scent of him, and her fingers itched to reach out and touch the hardness of his thigh through the tight denim of his jeans. She hadn't felt like this around a man in a long, long time.

"It's good to meet local people," she said, searching for neutral topics. "In Denver, everyone's getting so suspicious of strangers, it's hard to meet people. 'Course, I've been there long enough now..."

"How long have you lived there?"

Careful. "Six years."

"All at the same job?"

"Uh-huh."

He took his eyes off the road for a second and gave her a quick look. "Somehow I can't picture you at a desk job."

"Why not?"

"Oh, I don't know, just something about you."

"I happen to be very good at my work," she said in an injured tone.

"I'm sure you'd be good at anything you did. You seem to be, oh, I don't know, more into action, more... But what do I know?"

She sneaked a peek at his profile. Was he suspicious of her?

"And why Sweetwater? Why here? There's nothing much here for someone like you."

"Someone like me. What does that mean, Steve?"

"Someone single, young, female, smart." He hesitated. "And pretty."

She felt a jolt of heat inside, a fluid warmth that surprised her. "So all the women in Sweetwater are ugly?" she asked flippantly.

"You know what I mean."

She said nothing, only shifted on the seat, horribly uncomfortable, yet gratified in some indefinable way.

A moment later he continued. "Did you come here after some particular guy?"

She gave a surprised laugh. So that's what he'd been

after. "No," she replied, "no guy. I just wanted out of the city. I got mugged, and it scared the heck out of me. I took a leave from work, got in the car and drove. I liked the name of this place—Sweetwater. That's all there is to my story." *Liar,* she thought again.

"I'm glad you stopped here," he said gently.

She turned her head toward the side window, looking at the dark scenery flowing by. My God, what was happening here? And she felt ugliness coiling deep inside; she was deceiving this man, lying to him, and he was so nice and obviously interested in her. A strong urge built in her to blurt out the truth, unburden herself to him. She couldn't, though. Not until she learned what she'd come here for. Her first responsibility was to her boss, her job, the wolves.

But, dear Lord, she hadn't expected anything like this to happen. She'd thought it was going to be easy. She hadn't expected to like one of the suspects.

"Maybe you'll stay," he said.

"Maybe," she allowed.

They were almost at the place she'd left her car. She was glad; this was too difficult. Had Mata Hari felt this way?

There it was, the moonlight glinting off the bumper of her Cherokee. She started unzipping her vest pocket to get at the keys as Steve rolled to a stop beside the Jeep.

"Thanks," she said a little breathlessly.

His arm lay along the back of the seat, and she was achingly aware of its nearness. Then she felt his fingers brush her hair, lightly, and her stomach curled with fear and pleasure.

"Steve…" she managed. She reached for the door handle, but he stopped her.

"It's been a real long time for me since I've even looked at a woman, Brigitte," came his voice in the darkness. "But you…you're so…"

"Maybe we better not…" she started, but her voice

faded into nothingness as his fingers touched her neck. She shivered.

"Would you mind if I kissed you?" His voice was low, a little rough, and she couldn't see his face, his eyes. Everything was in shadow.

"Do you…ah, always ask permission when you want to kiss a woman?" she whispered.

"I haven't kissed anyone since my wife died," he said flatly. "I don't know what the rules are anymore."

"Oh, God."

"I'm not trying for pity, Brigitte."

"No, no, I'm only…"

"Should I say please?"

His fingers played on her neck, around to her throat, raising goose bumps.

"Yes," she breathed, leaning against him, knowing this was a mistake, a terrible mistake, but unable to stop.

"Please," he said in that gravelly voice.

His lips came down on hers, and she turned her face up, up to the warm shadow of him over her, to the feel of his mouth and his scent, the scratch of his whiskers. She felt weak, as if he were drawing out her strength, yet burning inside at the same time. She opened to the sweet nectar of his mouth and heard the swift intake of his breath. His hand came up to trace circles on her cheek, trailing fire from his fingertips.

He broke away finally, and they stared at each other in the night shadows.

"My God," she whispered.

"Yeah."

"I…I'd better go. It's late."

He brushed her lips lightly. "Will I see you again?"

She felt shaky. "Sure. I'm at Locals Corner. Five days a week. I…"

"What're you so scared of?"

"Nothing. I'm not scared." She stopped abruptly, then she said, "You. I'm scared of you."

"Why? Brigitte…"

"Men weren't in my plans. Relationships…" She shook her head.

"I'm harmless," he said.

"The hell you are."

He stroked her cheek. "I like you. It's a real strange feeling. It's been so long."

"Steve, please don't."

He drew back. "Okay, Brigitte Hartman, go on home. I'll be seeing you."

"Thanks for the ride."

"Thanks for dinner."

"Good night." She opened the truck door and climbed down.

"You drive carefully now," he said.

Then she was in her Jeep, fumbling with the key in the ignition, the engine catching, turning the lights on, and she saw Steve's truck pulling away, back down the road, rear lights fading into two red eyes.

She sat there for a moment, slumped over the steering wheel, her heart racing, her eyes squeezed shut. Then she straightened and pulled the Jeep onto the road, holding the wheel too tightly, her knuckles white.

She glanced up into the rearview mirror and met her own eyes. "You stupid idiot," she finally said, "what are you going to do now?"

CHAPTER SEVEN

THE SUN RODE low on the horizon these days. The wolf pack knew it was close to the darkest day of the year. It was cold; moisture froze into rime on the guard hairs of their remarkable two-layered coats, which kept them warm even in the Arctic. The members of the pack ranged the gamut of color from white to black, although most had fur that was grayish dun with paler tips at the ruff and a dark stripe along the back.

Game was plentiful in this new land they had made their own, huge herds of elk and deer wallowing heavily in the deep mountain snow while the wolves raced across its frozen surface on long, spindly legs.

Star's three half-grown pups hunted with the pack now, learning their jobs. But they still loved to play, dancing and twisting, tunneling their noses in the snow. One stopped, ears cocked, then ran to his mother, licked her muzzle, paraded around in the trampled snow. Another pup pounced on a dead branch, brought it to Auntie Mame proudly, laid it down in front of her.

The third pup taunted Uncle Joe, making mock rushes and attacks until the older wolf grew irritated and, with a growl and a snap of his jaws, straddled the youngster into submission.

It was a chill dawn, gray and grainy as a photograph, the time known in old European legends as the Hour of the Wolf. Silverfoot had led the pack down into a valley, following the scent of a fresh kill. Warily the pack approached the dead animal, listening, testing the air with small nudging motions of their noses. The scent of man and machine and dog and cow mingled, and normally the pack would not have been in this area, as their territory lay higher in the mountains. But today, chance brought them to this place, to a dead deer, conveniently cut open, its blood spilled and scenting the air for miles.

Star stepped closer, smelled the air, her golden eyes searching the area. When she approached the carcass and bent her head, the rest of the pack followed. A meal that didn't require a long, energy-depleting chase was not to be squandered.

Auntie Mame felt the blow before she heard the gun's report. All the wolves stopped as if they'd walked into a wall, hackles raised, three-centimeter-long eyeteeth showing. Their furry sides sucked in and out with their breathing as they tested the air for danger.

Then Auntie Mame took a few uncertain steps and, as if very tired, she sank down, panting, whimpering, and turned to sniff at the blood on her side.

Her head too heavy to hold up, she let it fall. The pack came close to sniff, to lick her muzzle, to nudge her with cold, damp noses. But her golden eyes had lost their fire, reflecting only the pale morning sky. She was dead.

Star sat on her haunches and howled, a wail that quickly reached its pitch, then tapered, with several long harmonics, to a tremolo. The other members added their own voices to the funeral dirge, then they disappeared into the brush, elusive wraiths in the dawn, leaving only the bloody trampled snow and the two dead animals behind.

BRIGITTE SAW STEVE through the window of Locals Corner—he was filling his truck with gas. He stood there waiting, hands in his pants pockets, dressed in his denim jacket and scuffed cowboy boots, and he looked so good to Brigitte, so absolutely right, his gaze unfocused, his black brows drawn together as he squinted off into the distance. A storybook hero, she thought, like John Wayne in those Westerns where the good guy always wins. Only, Steve's hat wasn't white; it was a battered and dusty brown.

He'd be inside in a second to pay for the gas. She flushed and turned away from the window, busying herself restocking the candy bars. Lord, she was acting like a schoolgirl.

She could feel the touch of his lips on hers still; she'd felt them all day yesterday and woken up this morning savoring their remembered pressure. And he'd asked, he'd actually asked, if he could kiss her. He'd said he hadn't kissed a woman since his wife had died—three years ago. Why now? Why her?

Maybe she should leave Sweetwater, simply call Mac and tell him she'd done the job so damn well that now she had a crush on one of the suspects, and there was no way she could judge his guilt or innocence anymore. Pack up and leave.

Steve came in then, ringing the bell over the door, and she couldn't help smiling at him.

"Morning, Brigitte," he said, and his face lit up with an answering smile.

"Hi, there," she said. She was aware of Bess behind the cash register, grinning like an idiot.

"Nice day," he said. It wasn't a nice day; it was gray and damp and cold. Downright miserable.

"Uh-huh," Brigitte answered.

"Hey, Bess," he said, stepping up to the register. "How you doing?"

She took his credit card and ran it through the machine. "Didn't realize you knew Brigitte so well," she said off-handedly.

"Uh, yeah, we met a couple times."

"Cute, isn't she?" Bess asked wickedly.

Steve gave Brigitte a level look, then took his time turning back to Bess. "Yeah, she's cute," he said dryly.

Steve got his card back, slid it into his worn wallet, signed the receipt. Then he seemed to hesitate.

"Need anything else?" Bess asked.

"Uh, no." He turned to leave, reached the door, then spun on his heel to face Brigitte, who stood there with candy bars in both hands.

"Brigitte," he said. "I thought..."

She cocked her head and waited.

"Uh, I wondered..." He pushed his hat back with a thumb.

"Is something...?"

"I'd like you to..."

They both spoke at once then stopped, embarrassed.

He took her arm and led her a few steps away so that the candy bar stand hid them from Bess. "I'd like you to come to Thanksgiving dinner," he said.

"Oh."

"My mom will be there, and my sister Naomi, her husband and their kids. It's a family thing, you know, every year. Maybe you don't want to, though."

Pack up and leave, Brigitte thought. *Sure.* But Steve was waiting, his dark eyes serious.

"I'd love to," she said, and he looked so relieved, she almost laughed and said something light and amusing.

The rest of the day went straight to hell.

The llama rancher stopped by Locals Corner about ten that morning, a man by the name of Hank Ritchie, and he told Bess and Brigitte the news.

"Did you hear the latest?" he asked while laying out dollar bills for his gasoline.

"What's that?" Bess asked.

"Andy Hecht found a dead wolf on the highway this morning."

"What?" Bess said.

Shock hit Brigitte like a bludgeon, taking away her breath.

"Yeah, he was just driving into town, and there it was. Cut up some, I heard, and with a note."

Oh, God, no! Brigitte cried silently.

"A note?" Bess said.

"Something like, 'One less wolf to kill our cattle.'" Hank shook his head. "I'm not in favor of that kind of stuff. I have six-foot fences around my llamas, and a big dog. Never had any trouble, not even with coyotes or mountain lions."

"Good Lord," Bess said.

"Andy went to the sheriff about it, I guess. I heard it from Lou Dobson, who was in paying a fine at city hall. Hell of a thing."

Brigitte made her feet take her closer to Ritchie. Her stomach was lurching and she could hardly breathe, but she tried to sound normal, tried to calm herself.

"How did the wolf die?" she heard herself ask.

"Shot, I believe."

She closed her eyes, forced herself to say, "How awful," when all she wanted to do was scream and sob and race to a phone to call Mac.

"Do they know who did it?" Bess asked.

"Nope, not a clue."

"Oh, boy, is this going to cause a stink," Bess said. "Wait till the media gets hold of this!"

"Excuse me a sec," Brigitte said. "I've got to go to the rest room."

She sat on the closed seat of the toilet and gulped huge lungfuls of air. She put her face in her hands and rocked back and forth. This is what she'd been sent here to prevent! Exactly this! And she hadn't heard a thing, not a word. Who'd done it? How had they found the pack? How had they gotten close enough to shoot one of the wolves? Who? *My God,* she prayed, *please don't let it be Steve.*

It couldn't be Steve. He couldn't have driven up this morning and asked her to Thanksgiving dinner right after he'd shot a wolf and thrown it on the highway. It wasn't possible.

Brigitte took a deep breath and stood. She checked her face in the mirror; she looked okay, a little pale, but okay. She had to go out there now, go to work—and listen to people, ask questions and try to glean a hint of who had done this.

`And she certainly had to go to Thanksgiving dinner at the Slaters'.

"You all right?" Bess asked when she reappeared.

"Uh, fine. You know, cramps."

Nobody talked about anything else except the dead wolf that day. Everyone who came in had an opinion. Maddy Linder bought cigarettes and stated that she'd seen the UFO land that morning, and she knew the aliens had done it.

Brigitte learned that the wolf who'd been killed was the one named Auntie Mame, the beta female. She felt grief wash over her, grief and a terrible frustration that she'd been so powerless to stop this thing from happening. Auntie Mame—a sweet-tempered female, shy, but the best, most patient hunter.

She also learned that Brad Milligan had called a Cattlemen's Association meeting for that evening at city hall and that all kinds of threats had been heard from various people, that the sheriff was real upset and had been on the phone to Denver to Fish and Wildlife and to the state attorney general.

"Wow," Bess said. "Anyone taking bets on who did it?"

"Not yet," said one resident, "but I'll put my money down the minute someone organizes a pool."

On whom? Brigitte wondered. She had to call Mac—and soon.

Right after lunch the first television van rolled down the street past Locals Corner. Cars started arriving, too, with logos on the doors: Channel 4, the *Denver Post.* "Look at that," Bess said, "a media blitz in Sweetwater. You'd think Princess Di was here."

Brigitte gazed out the window, wondering what all the newspeople were going to say. They'd probably whip up such a frenzy that it'd be harder than ever to reconcile the ranchers with the pro-wolf factions. They'd done it in Montana and Idaho and Wyoming, covered the reintroduction there with such intensity that sometimes they'd thrown fat on the fire. It was bad enough a wolf was dead; now the press was arriving to pick over the bones.

She couldn't keep her mind on work. She tried, but she made mistakes, forgetting things, ringing up the wrong prices, erasing the total on the gas pumps before the customer had even paid. She was so bad that Bess told her to go home and take some aspirin.

"Sorry," Brigitte said.

"You look like hell. I think I'll be better off without you. Do you always get like this?"

Brigitte gave her a sickly smile. "Not always. I promise I'll be better tomorrow."

"Go on, scoot. You'll be sorry when Dan Rather comes in to interview me."

Brigitte was close to tears on her way home. She knew she had to keep it together, because she had to call Mac instantly, but she hurt almost as much as if a member of her family had died. And to make it worse, she felt guilty— she should have found out that this was going to happen. She should have known!

She called Mac the minute she got in her cabin.

"I'm just about out the door," Mac said. "I have to be

there for some damn meeting at seven. Brigitte, what in hell went down?''

"I don't know! I had no clue it was going to happen, honestly, Mac. And I have no idea who did it. Nobody seems to know. Oh, God, Mac, I feel so bad.''

"This is some fine state of affairs. I have to play politician now, and I'm getting it from both sides. Goddammit, Brigitte...''

"I was getting so close, really I was. Steve Slater's been real friendly, and I...I figured I'd get a good feel soon. And then this happened. Out of the blue. I swear, there was no warning, nothing.''

"Well, hang in there. Keep your eyes and ears open. Hal and I will be there this afternoon.''

"Don't even look at me, Mac. Don't blow my cover.''

"I don't know you.''

"That's right. I'll try to make the meeting. I guess I'd better be there, hadn't I?''

"I'd say so,'' Mac went on. "I won't be able to talk to you until I'm back here in the office, Brigitte, but you can leave me messages anytime. Even at home. This has turned ugly, and more than ever I need you to figure out who did it. We'll nail this person. We can't let this happen again. You hear me, Brigitte?''

"Yes.'' She cleared her throat and said it loud enough for him to hear. "Yes, I hear you.''

By the time the Cattlemen's Association was due to meet that evening, the town of Sweetwater was in an uproar. Brigitte forced herself to go out for an early meal at Rosie's Café, just so she could listen to the talk. What she really wanted to do was curl up in her bed and suffer quietly. But she still had a job to do, so she dragged herself up and went out to pick at the Monday-night special.

Everyone at Rosie's was discussing the big event. A news crew sat at a table eating dinner, looking very big-city, very out of place. Some of the diners stared at them curiously. Brigitte kept her head down.

Her waitress asked her if she was going to the meeting tonight. Everyone was going to be there. Brad Milligan had declared it an open meeting because the USFWS wanted it on record, a public affair.

"Pretty exciting, isn't it?"

"Mmm," Brigitte replied.

She tried to eat the mashed potatoes and chicken-fried steak. She really tried. But all she could think of was going to that meeting and seeing Steve there. What if he stood up in front of all the cameras and microphones and incriminated himself? What if he hadn't actually done it himself but knew about the plan to shoot the wolf and agreed with it?

Misery swept over her in waves. Auntie Mame was dead, the whole reintroduction program she'd worked so hard for was in jeopardy, some angry man was out there with a gun and more bullets.

And Steve Slater. Widower, nice guy, a struggling single parent. And maybe a wolf killer.

City hall was lit up like day. Satellite vans were parked side by side, obstructing the front door. Men and women roamed restlessly, holding microphones, talking, yelling at cameramen who trailed behind, video cameras on their shoulders like second, high-tech heads.

Some of the newspeople were standing still, talking into the cameras. "It's a cold November evening in Sweetwater, Colorado, where this morning a wolf from the Flat Tops pack was shot and killed, then mutilated. Agents from the U.S. Fish and Wildlife Service are on the scene..."

Brigitte made her way through the crowd, numb, her eyes searching for only one person, but she didn't see him until she was inside the packed meeting room. He was there, sitting up front with the other ranchers. She recognized them all now: Ben Garrett, two of his sons, Andy Hecht, Tom Morehead, Bill Ramsey, Brad Milligan, the Robertsons.

She had to stand on tiptoe to see over the crowd, but she finally located Steve. He looked very serious, worried, his brows drawn together. She asked herself if he appeared guilty, but she couldn't answer the question, and her heart hurt to think that he might have done something so awful as killing Auntie Mame.

Ben Garrett bent his head to say something to Steve, who nodded soberly and looked over his shoulder at the crowded room.

Brad Milligan finally called the meeting to order, and the din died down. "I want to start by advising everyone to stay calm and speak in turn. I also want to thank Mac McCarthy and Hal Franklin from the USFWS Denver office for being here. Now, you all know what this is about, what happened this morning. Fish and Wildlife will examine the carcass and we'll get the report when it's done. It's clear that the wolf was shot with a high-powered rifle. She was mutilated, and there was a note on her saying, 'One less wolf to kill our cattle.' That's all we know, folks. The sheriff asks everyone with knowledge of this crime—" At this, the crowd buzzed angrily. "Of this incident, to please talk to him. Any information will be treated confidentially. I now turn the meeting over to Mac McCarthy."

Brigitte saw Mac rise. He was a small man with a big man's ego. He looked out over the crowd for a long, pregnant moment and then launched into his speech. "This is serious business, people. It's a felony to kill an animal tagged as an endangered species by your federal government. It can bring you a year in jail and a $100,000 fine. We have tried our best to listen to your concerns as this reintroduction plan was set up, and we've been fair to you. It's our honest belief that you should be fair to us." And on he went. Brigitte had heard it all before—all the reasons for reintroducing wolves, all the planning, the knowledge of wolf habitat and behavior, the way it had worked in Yellowstone and Idaho.

"Ignorance and murder, that's what I call this," Mac said angrily, "like burning witches in the Middle Ages. People, we've got to find out who did this and stop them."

Someone in the packed room yelled out, "Your damn wolves are the murderers!" There were cries of agreement, an answering buzz. Video cameras whirred, taking it all in hungrily.

"Whoever shot that wolf's a hero!" another man shouted, and the men with cameras pivoted toward him.

Next to Brigitte in the back of the room, a well-dressed lady stood in front of her cameraman, looking at papers in her hand. Then she straightened up, stared into the camera, and intoned, "I'm in the meeting room of city hall in Sweetwater. You can hear the agitated crowd behind me, angry because of the cattle that have been killed, divided over the reintroduction plan. What's at stake here in Sweetwater is nothing less than an entire system of values and a way of life. The small rancher in Colorado is an endangered species just like the wolf, and they are in direct competition according to the ranchers. There's trouble brewing in Sweetwater, and the wolves are only the catalyst."

Hal Franklin was standing. He held a hand up to quiet the crowd, but it took some time. "I've been up here a lot of times in the past year. I know you people and I respect you. Most of you are as honest as they come, but we have evidence, scientific evidence, that leads us to believe that the six head supposedly killed by wolves have actually been killed by a man or men and made to look like..."

He was cut off by howls of derision. Fists waved in the air. Next to Brigitte a woman yelled, "Stupid city slickers!"

Brigitte closed her eyes and felt the anger of the crowd, like a great heartbeat, surging at her. She was nauseous— the air in the room was stale and hot. It occurred to her that this could be a scene from a Western, the scene in the saloon where the crowd turned into a lynch mob.

"Crazy sucker!" somebody called out. There was laughter, then more angry shouts. Brigitte's head started to pound. She was heartsick at the rage emanating from the crowd. Unreasonable rage, mob rage.

Gradually the noise died down. She couldn't see the front of the room, but someone—one of the ranchers—stood up and was quieting the throng, starting to speak. She craned her neck, but all she saw were the heads in front of her.

The voice, however, was familiar. Steve. Her heart clenched as she listened. "Everybody calm down," he was saying, his tone measured and firm. "These folks from Denver are getting a real bad impression of us. They're trying to solve this problem just like we are." He had everyone paying attention now, and he continued. "All right, we have these men here now and they're listening to us. So I'm going to give them my opinion. This business about some of us killing our own cattle is pretty farfetched. Until they have proof, I think it's not a real issue, but I'll tell you what is. Ranchers have a God-given right to kill predators that threaten their livelihood. Even the government allows us to do that. The trouble is, it's close to impossible to catch a wolf in the act, so that hasn't helped us at all. Wolves are predators and kill cattle, that's a fact. To call the shooting of this wolf murder is ridiculous. It's self-defense."

Cheers greeted this statement, wild clapping, shouting. But to Brigitte the noise meant nothing; she was going over and over Steve's words. He seemed to be defending whoever had shot Auntie Mame. Did he know who'd done it? Had *he* done it?

And yet he'd sounded so sensible, so calm and in control, unrattled. A man speaking his own well-considered opinion. Her mind jolted back and forth between the two possibilities, torn apart, unable to judge. Her headache got worse.

There was more—shouting and insults and rambling speeches that Brad tried to cut off when the crowd got restive, but Brad was pretty upset himself, so he wasn't particularly effective.

Hal and Mac spoke again, but someone in the audience challenged Mac to a fight—outside, no guns—and Mac retired in disgust.

Nothing was really accomplished at the meeting except to polarize both positions, Brigitte could see that. Brad lost control of the situation at the end, and everyone yelled and spoke at once, and some of the crowd swirled up onto the stage where the lectern was, and the sheriff had to escort Hal and Mac out the back way.

It was horrible.

Brigitte pushed her way through the crowd and finally got out into the fresh night air. She was standing there, trying to still her racing heart, when she saw Steve emerge from the front door. He stalked angrily through the people gathered there in buzzing knots, heading toward his truck.

Brigitte wanted so badly to go to him—for so many reasons—and find out what he thought of the meeting, how he'd reacted to the hate she'd felt, who he thought had killed Auntie Mame. She wanted to ask a million questions, and her mind did a strange balancing act. Part of her knew he'd give her calm, intelligent answers despite his own position. Yet another part told her he might be a liar and a criminal—and paradoxically, both sets of knowledge could exist inside her head and her heart at the same time.

She told herself she wanted to ask him these questions to assess his honesty, to get hints of what was motivating the ranchers, to gather information, but somewhere deep inside her she knew that was only a reason to get close to him. Sure, she wanted that information, but she also wanted—needed—to be with him, to know how he felt. As if that could somehow alleviate her pain and her guilt.

She didn't approach him. But the Western Slope reporter from Channel 9 stepped in front of him and thrust a microphone in his face. Steve frowned and said something, but the reporter didn't move, so Steve pushed him aside and strode past, getting into his truck, pulling out into the street and driving away.

Brigitte stood there for a time, not hearing the talk, the comments, the crude remarks around her as people began to drift away to their homes, their vehicles. She watched the taillights of Steve's truck until they disappeared into the night, and then turned and started walking back to her cabin.

By the time she got inside, she was crying. She never cried—this was nuts. She wiped her eyes and blew her nose and thought about it, but she couldn't figure out if her tears were for Auntie Mame or her future with Steve Slater.

BEN GARRETT GATHERED beer from the refrigerator and tossed one to each of his sons. They sat around the kitchen table, chairs pushed back, legs stretched out and crossed at booted ankles. Audrey sat with them, listening to their reports of the meeting in town.

"They got our point now, by God," Jim said. "They can't ignore us anymore."

"I'm sure glad someone did that wolf in. It was what we needed, all right," Chris said. "Dead cattle don't excite those tree-huggers, but kill a vicious predator and they go ballistic."

"Can't say I haven't thought about tracking down that pack and doing some killing myself," Ben said.

His sons exchanged glances.

"Don't look like that! Darn tootin', I've thought of it. Too bad one of us didn't do the job. But it doesn't matter now. Someone's got the ball rolling, and more power to him."

"Well," Audrey said, "I saw pictures of that poor wolf on TV. Whoever did it mutilated her. It's sick, and I'm glad you didn't do it."

Ben gave her an indulgent look and patted her leg. "Hell, Audrey, you're city folk. You don't know a damn thing," he said, and then he went back to man talk with his three strapping sons.

CHAPTER EIGHT

BRIGITTE SPENT a restless night. She felt as if she never really went to sleep, only teetered on that edge where sleep and wakefulness met.

She did dream once, though, of golden eyes staring at her through a dark tangle of forest. And when she finally got up at dawn, she was swept by that same, sick feeling of guilt that she should have been able to prevent the death of Auntie Mame.

She was in the shower when she realized how frustrated she was by these bullheaded, intractable ranchers. She'd been right all along; they were the same as the townsfolk where she'd been raised. Narrow-minded, all of them.

And that included Steve Slater.

It was never far from the surface of her consciousness that he could have killed Auntie Mame himself. Slaughtered her and then calmly driven up to the gas station yesterday morning, blood still fresh on his hands.

It could be Steve behind it all. Steve and his two big dogs. Steve who'd stood up last night at the meeting and openly declared his support for killing the wolf.

She was miserable all day at work, and Bess again took notice. "You still not feeling good, honey?"

"I'm okay. A little under the weather, I guess."

"You and everyone else in this crazy town. Seems like the whole town's out of sorts since that wolf thing yesterday morning. Sure has folks taking sides."

"I wonder..." Brigitte ventured. "I wonder who really did it."

"Coulda been any number of folks. Most everybody thinks it's one of the ranchers but, heck, there's no proof of that, is there?"

"But if it's a rancher," Brigitte pressed, "which one? I mean, who would you guess?"

Bess looked bemused. "Me? Who would I say? Well, I'd point a finger at Ben Garrett, or maybe even Brad Milligan."

"Why Brad?"

"'Cause he's the quiet type. Can't trust them. And he gets upset real quicklike, too. You never know what's going on with that man. Then, of course, there's Steve Slater. Now I know you're sort of fond of him, but beneath that quiet control, who knows what's brewing?"

Brigitte expelled a breath. "You said Ben Garrett."

"Oh, sure, Ben. He's the easy one for everybody to suspect. Heck, he blusters and rants and threatens to shoot the whole wolf pack."

"But just because he talks big doesn't mean a thing, does it? And there are other ranchers, too, others who've had cattle killed. There're the Moreheads."

Bess stopped what she was doing and eyed Brigitte curiously. "You sure do know a lot about these ranchers, honey."

Uh-oh. "Not really," Brigitte said matter-of-factly. "I just hear a lot of stuff, you know, like gossip at the tavern on Friday night." She shrugged.

"Oh, the tavern," Bess said. "How was that, anyway? You meet any nice fellas?"

Phew, Brigitte went on to tell Bess about her evening, thankful she'd slipped out of a potentially dangerous conversation. She shouldn't have said so darn much. *Stupid.*

By quitting time she was still riled up and frustrated,

feeling as if she were spinning her wheels. How could she like a man, have kissed him the way she had and not trust him?

She'd fretted all day long, wanting so desperately to see Steve and talk to him. She wondered at herself, questioned her motives. Was it to reassure herself or find out the truth? Suspicion and hope and longing fought and vied for ascendancy in her mind. She felt as if she were going crazy.

She couldn't fight her urges anymore when she got off work. She shut down the questions tumbling around in her head, went straight to her cabin, got into her Jeep and drove to the Slater ranch. There were things she absolutely had to know, and if she gave herself away, well, that was a bridge she'd cross when she came to it.

She pulled up in the Slaters' driveway, got out and took a deep breath, then went to the door, but only the girls were there. Steve, it seemed, wasn't in from the fields yet.

"Can you stay for dinner?" Jeannie asked.

"Oh, sweetie, I don't think so. I have things I have to do in town."

And Heather. "You can wait for Dad inside if you want." Polite but still guarded.

Brigitte waited in the kitchen. It was hard, her mind on what she needed to ask Steve, how she was going to ask him. She was anxious, her stomach churning. Where was he? How long before he got home? And Jeannie was talking to her all the time about this and that, needing adult female companionship, while clearly Heather still resented anyone other than her mother being in her home. And, really, Brigitte thought, what place did she have in this scenario?

She tried a neutral subject. "Any progress on your dress for the school dance?" she asked Heather, her stare going to the window, the driveway. Where was he?

But it was Jeannie who answered. "Heather ordered a dress out of a catalog, and Dad says it's too old for her."

"Shut up, Jeannie," Heather said, and she opened the refrigerator door and began to rummage inside.

"And Dave's too old for her, Dad says," Jeannie went right on heedlessly.

"Shut up."

Brigitte sighed. "Old is a funny thing, Jeannie," she said. "Two years when you're a teenager is a big difference in age. But when you're, say, thirty, it's really nothing at all."

"Dave's only seventeen," Heather put in defensively. "Lots of girls in my class date older guys. Older even than Dave. Jeannie's just an idiot. She doesn't know anything."

"I know lots," Jeannie said, and so it went until Steve finally drove up to the barn. They could see through the window that he was unloading rolls of wire fencing.

Jeannie opened the side door and called hello to him, and Brigitte collected her thoughts. She'd come here to get some answers. She'd been ready. But then she'd sat in his cozy kitchen, listening to his daughters, and now she had to get the wind back in her sails. What was she going to say to him? *"Steve, did you kill that animal?"*

She said goodbye to the girls and went outside, crossing the muddy yard, hands in her jeans pockets, jaw clenched.

"Hey," he said, smiling at her from the barn door. "I thought that was your car."

"Steve," she began, "can we talk?"

He looked at her questioningly. "Is everything okay?"

But she shook her head at his concern. "Everything's fine. I'm fine. It's just that there's something I've got to know."

"I see," he said, "and I take it I've got the answer?" He continued to unload the truck, and she followed him into the barn, steeling herself. *Come right out and ask him,* she thought. *Be straightforward. No games.*

She watched as he stacked the last roll of wire, took off his work gloves, slapped them against his thighs, dusting them off. "Okay," he said then, turning to her. "There's something you want to know. Ask away."

Brigitte took a breath and let it out, her gaze locked on his. "Did you have anything to do with killing that wolf yesterday morning?"

For a long, awful moment he merely stared at her, as if trying to digest her words. Finally he smiled slightly, humorlessly, and said, "You're asking if I was involved somehow?"

"Yes."

And then she saw his face cloud over. "You're asking me that?"

She nodded.

He leaned back against an empty stall and folded his arms across his chest, a muscle working in the flat plane of his cheek. "You have to ask that?" he said in a low voice.

"Yes."

"And what if I don't answer?"

"I don't know." She looked down at her feet and then back to his face. "If you don't deny it, then I'll have to think you were involved."

"Goddamn," he said under his breath. "You don't know me at all, lady."

"Maybe not. Right now I only know that you say you hate the wolf pack. You practically advocated hunting them down and killing them all."

"Since when is holding an opinion proof of a crime?" he asked.

"But..."

"Don't 'but' me. You've obviously got a burr under your saddle, and you think I'm involved."

"Look, Steve, I..."

"No, no backing off. Either you think I'm capable of breaking the law or you think I'm not. Which is it?"

She closed her eyes for a moment, then opened them, taking a breath. "I want to believe, I need to believe you're innocent."

He snorted. "You need to believe. What kind of talk is that? Why do you need to believe?"

She had to force herself to hold his stare, not to shake beneath the force of his anger. He suddenly seemed awfully big and tall and strong standing there, and she had to wonder: Did she really know the first thing about this man?

"I want to know," she said, "because I like you, Steve Slater, and I can't have those kinds of feelings for someone who'd go out and slaughter an innocent animal that way."

"Innocent," he said. "I guess that's the question here, isn't it? I don't happen to believe the wolves are innocent."

"That's not an answer."

He shook his head. "You'll have to figure it out on your own, Brigitte Hartman from Denver."

"I see."

"You know," he said, "this is a great country we live in, and there was a time that respect for minority rights meant something."

"What're you...?"

"What I'm saying is that I know most people support the damn reintroduction of wolves. But somehow ranchers like me got lost in this whole tree-hugging mania. I just want folks to remember that minorities' rights count, too."

For an uncomfortable time she held his gaze. She felt like crying. He was so down-to-earth, so centered, so...proud. It was impossible to fault him, impossible to get an answer from him, either. And yet she knew she had to decide who he was and what he was capable of. Nothing was going to work between them till she did.

Finally it was Steve who sighed deeply and seemed to relent. "You know," he said, facing her in the gathering darkness, "it's a female thing. I guess you sound like my daughters on the subject of those damn wolves."

"A female thing."

He shrugged. "Sure. Every woman in town's upset about that damn wolf. They get all squeamish."

"Oh, God," she whispered.

Then he unfolded his arms and put the back of his hand on her cheek gently. "I don't expect you to understand," he said quietly. "No more than I expect my daughters to understand."

Brigitte couldn't believe her ears. Where had this man been for the past thirty years? Hadn't he learned a thing about women? Squeamish.

With a telltale sigh, she turned from him, and his hand fell away.

"Hey," he said softly. "Hey, I'm sorry about that stupid wolf getting killed. It was the wrong way to handle things." And then he was behind her, his hands on her shoulders. He turned her around to face him, and every fiber of her tensed.

"Hey," he said again, so quietly she could barely hear him, and he lowered his head and brushed her lips with his.

The big, cold, dark barn suddenly seemed to close in around her. Steve moved his hands down her arms, bringing her against him, and the kiss deepened. She could feel the length of him pressed to her, the strength of him, and she could feel his desire. Everything in her quickened, and she returned his kiss, her arms going around his waist, her mouth opening to his.

But it didn't last. Despite her desire, despite wanting to

be in his arms more than anywhere else on earth, she drew back, wedging her hands against his chest.

Her head fell back and she drew in a long, quavering breath. "No," she said. "This is all wrong."

He tried to kiss her again, but she only laughed sadly and disengaged herself. "Steve," she said, "I'm not squeamish. I'm not the simpleminded female you seem to think I am."

"Brigitte, I didn't mean…"

"Oh, yes, you did." She backed toward the door of the barn. Then she laughed ruefully again. "I've never said this to a man before, Steve, but I can't help it. You're a Neanderthal."

"Hey, don't go like this. Brigitte…?"

But she turned and got out of there as fast as she could, the image of his wounded expression burned into her brain.

She drove back to Sweetwater too quickly. How could she have let him kiss her? And after the things he'd said. Oh, he was coy, all right, that business about how she had to decide who he was. It was merely a tactic to put off answering her about the wolves.

Squeamish, right. If only he knew!

And yet he'd said something… Something about killing the wolf having been a stupid way to handle the situation. Did that mean he was innocent? Or did it mean he'd been stupid to do it?

By the time she reached her cabin and dialed Mac's number in Denver, she was as confused as she'd ever been in her life. In spite of everything, she did like Steve. Too much. But he was so old-fashioned, so hopelessly stuck in that Western philosophy of "Don't fence me in, and get out of my face" that she simply couldn't deal with him.

Yet she'd practically melted in his arms. She'd wanted him to kiss her, to keep right on kissing her. She'd been dying for him to touch her. Damn. And double damn, Steve Slater knew it.

She talked to Mac about everything she'd learned since last night's cattlemen's meeting—which wasn't much. But Mac was barely listening. Instead, he was raving about the front page of today's *Denver Post.* "Did you see it? The front page?"

"Yes, Mac, I work at a minimart. Of course I saw it."

"Did you read the story? Did you?"

"I haven't had time, Mac. But I can imagine…"

"I swear to God, the *Post* is coming down on the side of the ranchers! The article gave a blow-by-blow description of every last cattle killing in the past year! They only mentioned once that there was a possibility the ranchers were behind the deaths! And that was on page three!"

"Mac, it's sensationalism. You know that."

"And this morning, I hadn't even sat down at my desk before I got a call from the governor of New Mexico! He wants to know what in hell went wrong with the wolf reintroduction in Colorado. He said he's rethinking the New Mexico reintroduction because his desk is littered with letters from ranchers and their lawyers, and he'll be damned, and I quote, if he's going to let the federal government screw up his reelection chances next year."

"Oh, Lord."

"Precisely. And what have you learned so far? Zip. Zilch. Nada."

"Calm down, Mac," she said.

"I will not calm down. I've given six TV and radio interviews today, and I've got six more tomorrow. Even CNN called. It's going national."

"Look," she said, "this has been coming to a head for a long time. That's why I'm here. And if you'd settle down and listen, I've got some news. Not much, but…"

"Go on."

"Everybody in town is talking about it now, Mac. Everybody. And they're taking sides. It's only a matter of time before something breaks."

"Time is just what we don't have. You heard that mob last night. They'd have us trap and remove the pack tomorrow if they could. And if that happens, it's all over for the wolves in the Lower Forty-eight. Every state in the West will refuse to consider reintroduction."

"That's not going to happen. We still have time. And maybe Auntie Mame's carcass will provide some clues. Can you hurry the autopsy? And the one on that last cow, the Garrett heifer?"

"I've already done that."

"Good," she said, and she sighed. "Give me till Christmas, Mac. You promised. Hold them off till Christmas and I'll have this thing solved."

"Uh-huh," he said. "Sure. Till Christmas. Tell me to be an optimist. Brigitte, remind me that sometimes things do work out."

"Okay, Mac, I will. And you'll see. I promise."

But as soon as she was off the phone, she felt the weight of her promise settle on her like a slab of concrete. There was no guarantee she'd learn a darn thing. And now she'd even blown the one real inside connection she had in this valley—Steve Slater. You didn't push a man like that away from you and expect him to come crawling back.

She awoke the following morning with a sense of dread that another wolf might turn up dead. It was only a matter of time. It might be Star or Silverfoot. It might happen today or tomorrow or next week. But it was going to happen if she didn't do something soon.

The sense of urgency was fierce when she got to work that morning. Christmas, she thought. A little more than four weeks off now. Mac had said he'd give her till then. Now it didn't seem like very much time at all.

Brigitte worked all morning; she knew she had to somehow get the afternoon off and do some real sleuthing around town. But she needed an excuse, something plausible to tell Bess.

As it turned out, however, the day was slow and all Brigitte had to say was, "It seems a shame your having to pay me to stand around. I could punch out and get caught up on my laundry or something."

"You wouldn't mind?" Bess looked relieved.

"Not at all."

"Well, hunting season's darn near over. It is going to get real slow."

"No problem," Brigitte said. "I appreciate whatever hours you can give me."

She started her Dick Tracy act at the same café where she and Steve had had breakfast. It was lunchtime, and the restaurant was pretty full. There was a joiners' area, ten chairs around a big table, and Brigitte suggested to the hostess that she sit there as a single and not take up a whole table to herself.

"Fine, honey," the hostess said. "If you can stand a bunch of the local boys, have at it."

Brigitte smiled apologetically at the six men already seated there. Two of them nodded at her. They were regulars at the minimart. She ordered a tuna sandwich and fries and casually listened in to the conversation. Not surprisingly, it centered around the dead wolf and all the media hullabaloo.

"You'd think it was the Oklahoma bombing or something," one of the guys said. "Hell, it's a dead animal, is all."

"Yeah, but a special one. The media loves all this wolf stuff."

Then someone else spoke up. "Too bad it isn't the whole pack. I say get rid of them all and be done with it."

"Now hold on, Ed," someone interrupted. "We all keep forgetting that the wolf was here long before man. Seems natural to have them back."

"Oh, come on," another man said. "How would you like it if you were a rancher and had the wolves feeding on your herd?"

"And they haven't even paid the ranchers yet for their dead livestock," the man called Ed reminded the group.

Brigitte saw an opening. She took a breath. "It's none of my business—I mean I just moved here and all—but I heard from someone that it could be the ranchers themselves killing the livestock and trying to pin it on the wolves."

The response she got was immediate and loud, everyone talking at once. "Not a chance!" "That's nuts!" "I wouldn't put it past a few of them." "I've heard the same thing, more than once." And even a name: "Ben Garrett. If anyone's doing it, my money's on Ben." "Yeah, maybe, but he sure has a sweet little wife, doesn't he?"

Everyone laughed. Even Brigitte forced a smile. She wasn't about to let the flow of the conversation ebb, though.

"I've met Ben," she said casually, "and he seemed nice enough."

"Nice?" someone said. "A loudmouth maybe, but not nice."

"That doesn't mean he'd kill his own cattle," she put in, "or that wolf the other morning."

"Oh," Ed said, "Ben's capable of it. Or any of his boys. Chips off the old block."

Then someone said, "Well, don't forget Slater. He can be hardcore, too. And didn't he have a calf killed?"

"Sure he did," was the reply.

"But so did Tom Morehead, I think."

"I know Tom Morehead did, you bet. But he's a calm one, wouldn't hurt a fly."

"That's right," someone else said. "It's not Tom."

Cross him off the list, Brigitte thought. Then she couldn't help asking about Brad Milligan.

"Brad?" Ed said. "Yeah, he's capable of that. Kind of a funny guy. Gets real quiet at times then real riled up. Short fuse."

The conversation ran on the same track all during the meal, but mostly the men talked about the media frenzy.

By the time Brigitte paid her check and left, she'd gotten about all she could from the boys. She walked down the street, heading to her cabin, and mentally went over her list of ranchers. The Hechts and Ramseys and Robertsons were all outspoken against the reintroduction, but none had reported slain cattle. And from what she'd heard and seen Monday night, none of them seemed the type to take matters into his own hands. But the names Garrett and Milligan, Morehead and Slater kept cropping up. She felt safe to eliminate Tom Morehead. Brad Milligan was a big question mark. That left Ben or his sons and, of course, Steve. She desperately wanted to cross Steve's name off, but she couldn't. And wasn't it Steve himself who'd told her she had to decide who he really was?

But she couldn't keep dwelling on Steve. Every time she pictured him, he consumed her thoughts. She wished Heather had never walked into Locals Corner that fateful day. She wished she'd never even heard the name Slater.

The idea of taking a drive up toward the Garrett ranch came to her during her walk. Why not? she thought. It occurred to her that she'd be driving right past Steve's place. She told herself that it didn't matter, that what had happened between them couldn't be allowed to matter.

It was a stroke of luck she'd driven by the Garrett spread when she had. A few minutes earlier or later, and she would have missed Chris entirely. As it was, it seemed the most natural thing in the world for her to stop and say hello when she saw him fixing a fence along County 123.

"Hi," she said, getting out of her vehicle.

He stopped what he was doing and thumbed his hat back on his forehead. She was painfully reminded of Steve. "Hi," he said. "What're you doing in this neck of the woods?"

"It's a nice autumn day. I'm just driving around."

"Don't have to work?"

"Oh, Bess let me go. It's real slow today."

He tossed a roll of wire into the bed of his pickup and leaned against the tailgate, eyeing her. "Saw you the other night at the meeting," he said.

"Everyone in town must have been there," Brigitte said matter-of-factly.

"Not really," he said. "Wouldn't have thought you'd be interested."

"It's hard not to be."

He grinned at her. "You're looking mighty pretty today."

"Mmm," she said, leaning against the truck, too. "Quite a media event, wasn't it?"

"I guess. Say, what are you doing later? I was going to stop in at the tavern for a beer..."

But she cut him off. "I couldn't believe all the news vans. I mean, you see them in Denver. But not a place like Sweetwater."

Chris shook his head. "It's about time they heard our side of the story, I'd say."

"Your side?"

"Sure. We want that wolf pack gone. I don't care if they put them all down, gas them, whatever. Just get rid of them."

Brigitte took a breath. "Wow, Chris, you sound as if you'd get rid of them yourself."

And then he laughed. "I would. Darn tootin' I would."

"I mean you sound as if you'd actually kill them."

And he laughed again. "You bet I would. Haven't you heard the ranchers' code? Shoot, shovel and shut up. Yeah," he said, growing suddenly very serious, "you bet I'd do it."

She stared at him. "Did you?"

"Did I what?"

"Did you shoot that wolf, Chris?"

For a long, strained moment he glared at her, and then his lips curved into a smile. "If I did, I wouldn't be telling you, lady, now would I? Besides, it's against the law. Now, how about that beer at the tavern?"

"Oh," she said, straightening, "I can't. I've got laundry to do."

"Laundry," he said.

"Uh-huh. Real exciting evening." She began to walk toward her car and then turned back to him. "Have a nice afternoon," she said.

"Yeah, sure," he replied, and he watched her go, studying her, frowning.

But Brigitte never saw that dark expression. In fact, she thought she'd pulled off the conversation quite well, and all the way back into Sweetwater she felt excited and alive. *It's the Garretts,* she thought over and over. *I know it's them.*

She was still thinking that, remembering the bragging tone of Chris's voice, when she opened the door to her cabin and a note fell to the floor. "Please come by the desk," it read.

She walked right over, expecting some new disaster. But when she entered the office, Edie Zimmer was smiling and pointing. "For you," she said.

Brigitte looked. Sitting on a coffee table by the front window was a big vase of flowers.

"Came about an hour ago," Edie said.

Brigitte savored the unopened card in her hand all the way back to her cabin. Her first thought was that it was from Steve. Who else would send her flowers? But then she decided they were from Mac, who'd been chewing out everyone in sight, who'd come down on her so hard on the phone. Sure.

Be from Steve, she thought as she sat on the side of her bed, the vase on the kitchenette counter. *Oh, please.*

She opened the little envelope, her heart thudding so strongly, she felt like a fool.

She took the card out and read, "'You're right. I'm from the Stone Age. Forgive me?'"

It wasn't signed. It didn't have to be. She read it again and laughed and then held it to her breast. Oh, Lord, she thought. Oh, Lord.

WHILE BRIGITTE HELD the note close to her heart and stared at the bouquet of flowers, Chris Garrett arrived at the ranch house and tossed his hat and jacket on a living room chair. "Hey, Dad," he called.

"In here" came Ben's reply from his den.

Chris entered and found his father and Jim watching the early-evening news.

"Look at this," Ben said. "It's the lead story on the five o'clock news."

Chris stared at the screen. Sure enough, there was a picture of the slaughtered wolf, Auntie Mame, and a reporter's voice overlaying it.

"Forget that," Chris said. "I think we may have a problem."

"Oh?" Ben turned down the volume.

"What's going on?" Jim asked, sitting forward in his chair.

"You know that girl who works at Locals Corner, Brigitte something?"

"She was up on the ranch when we found the steer," Jim put in.

"That's the girl," Chris said. "Well, anyway, she was out on a drive this afternoon, or so she said, and she stopped and talked with me for a few minutes."

"So?" Ben said.

"So she was asking all sorts of questions about the wolves. She even came right out and asked if I shot that bitch wolf the other morning."

Ben raised his gray brows.

"And I'll tell you what else. She was at the Yampa Tavern last Friday night, asking questions there, too. Plus I saw her Monday night at the meeting. And now that I think about it, it's awful coincidental she got lost hiking the other day and happened to end up right where our heifer was killed."

"What're you getting at?" Ben asked.

"I'm not buying the fact that some sassy, blue-eyed chick all of a sudden moves up here from Denver just to get away from the city. I smell a rat."

Jim frowned. "She's working for the feds. What else could she be?"

Ben was silent, thinking.

"I agree with Jim," Chris said. "And I think we should do something about it."

"Like what?" Ben asked. "We don't know anything for sure."

"I'll go to Denver." Jim looked from his older brother to his father. "I'll go tomorrow. I'll check up on her."

"Mmm," Ben said, and he rubbed his jaw. "And what if she is some sort of agent sent up here to spy on us?"

Jim grinned. "Why don't you just let me handle it," he said.

Again, Ben mulled that over. Finally he nodded. "Handle it, then. But don't screw up, son. We don't need any more problems."

"You can trust me, Dad," Jim said proudly.

Chris half listened to the exchange while he pictured Brigitte, the pretty, defiant tilt of her chin, the slimness of her back when she'd turned on her heel and left this afternoon. He hoped he was wrong about her. He hoped she didn't turn out to be some tree-hugging environmentalist. Yeah he thought, it would be a goddamned waste of one fine piece of woman.

CHAPTER NINE

STEVE TURNED OUT of his long driveway and drove toward Sweetwater, his daughters on the front seat beside him.

"I don't see why we have school today," Jeannie said, sulking.

"Grandma and Aunt Naomi are going to get here and we won't even be home," Heather put in.

"It's stupid to have school the day before Thanksgiving," Jeannie went on. "Can't we stay home?"

Steve sighed. "No. You've got the next four days off. Quit griping."

"But we could go shopping today," Heather said. "You're going all the way to Glenwood Springs, and we could stop at the mall."

"I'm not stopping at the mall," he said patiently. "I took the chain saw in to get repaired, and I'm picking it up and heading straight home."

"But when are we going Christmas shopping?" Heather asked.

"After Thanksgiving."

"Let's go Friday," Jeannie said.

"Maybe," Steve allowed, knowing full well he wasn't going to have time.

"Can we put the tree up early?" Jeannie asked.

"We have to cut it first," Heather pointed out. "Dad, can I drive when we go to cut it?"

"Sure," he said. "Sure."

"Dad?" Jeannie asked as he pulled up in front of the brick school. "Can you pick us up today?"

"Not today. Take the school bus. Someone's got to be home when your aunt and grandma arrive."

"Bummer," Heather said. Then she brightened. "Maybe Dave can give me a ride."

"Dave Garrett?" Steve frowned.

"He drives every day," Heather said.

"Can I have a ride, too?" Jeannie asked as she got out of the truck.

"No way," Heather replied, and the girls began arguing, forgetting to wave goodbye to their father.

An hour later he was in Glenwood Springs loading the chain saw into the bed of the truck with the dogs. Then he was on his way home again.

It began to snow lightly in Glenwood Canyon, the sky turning a dull, gunmetal gray. Wind whipped dust across the road and whirled it into spirals against the tall canyon walls, and the traffic on Interstate 70 slowed. Steve drove and thought about the upcoming winter, wondering if there'd be enough hay for the herd or if there'd be a heavy snow year and he'd have to buy hay at the midwinter premium. Of course, if there was a heavy snow cover, then there'd be plenty of irrigation water next summer. It was a trade-off. Everything about ranching was a trade-off.

He turned off the highway at the 133 exit and drove along the valley floor, the snow getting heavier. He switched on the headlights and wipers and decided it was time to put on the studded tires for the winter. He thought about Christmas and a shopping trip for the girls, about what he was going to get his mother this year. He thought about needing to replace a section of fencing on the east side of the ranch. Better do that soon, before there was three feet of snow in the gully.

He thought about the wolf pack, too, and wondered, as

did all the ranchers, if Fish and Wildlife was going to take action this winter. He doubted it. So did everyone else. The wheels of government ground mighty slowly. And the longer the government dragged its feet, the more likely it was that another wolf was going to show up on the road with a bullet in it.

His girls had gone nuts over the dead wolf last week. Jeannie had cried herself to sleep, and Heather had declared ranchers to be jerks—all but Dave Garrett. And Steve had pointed out, to no avail, of course, that when his daughters were grown and understood the economics of the situation, they'd think differently.

"Never," Heather had declared at supper one night. "I'll never, ever be a rancher."

And there was Brigitte. Brigitte, who was never far from his thoughts. What a mess he'd made of things when she'd found him in the barn and asked if he'd shot that wolf.

Why hadn't he given her a straight answer? He'd run the scene through his head a hundred times, and he could only surmise that she'd insulted his integrity. Hell, he despised the wolf reintroduction, but she should have known that he was law-abiding.

Then he'd kissed her. Called her squeamish and pulled her into his arms. Squeamish she was not. He remembered how she'd stood over Ben Garrett's mutilated heifer without flinching. And hadn't he thought at the time how easily she fit into the environment?

Leslie had fit into the rural life, too. But Leslie had been cut out to be a rancher's wife and a mother. She'd been happy being a homemaker, in her element. And, of course, she'd loved to ride alone in the high country....

He shook off the memory and thought instead of how very similar in some ways Brigitte was to his dead wife. But in other respects she was quite different, a thoroughly modern woman who could hold her own in any situation.

He couldn't imagine Leslie ever going by herself to a bar. And yet obviously Brigitte had, because she'd met Chris Garrett at the Yampa Tavern. She was a city girl, too, though Steve always had a hard time picturing her behind a desk.

He wondered then, as he'd wondered so often before, if she *was* going to put down roots in Sweetwater. Steve had a lot of questions about her, but mostly he put them aside and thought about the feel of her against him, the softness of her lips, the scent of her hair. He knew, he just knew they'd fit together like a pair of gloves.

He turned north on the county road that led to Sweetwater. In the back the chain saw shifted, and the dogs did, too. The snow was really coming down now in big wet flakes, starting to stick to the road in patches. Winter, he thought. Winter was always long. And lonely. It would be nice if Brigitte hung around.

Sweetwater lay a mile ahead, and Steve glanced at his watch. Eleven-thirty. His mom and sister and the two toddlers wouldn't get in till at least three or so. He had time. Maybe time to stop for lunch at the Elks Lodge in town. And then, of course, he needed to gas up the truck. He could have filled it in Glenwood, he supposed, but then he laughed out loud at himself. "Right," he said. All along he'd known he was going to stop at the minimart. He'd been subconsciously planning it for days, ever since he'd sent the flowers. The trouble was, how had she reacted to getting them? He didn't know. He thought all women liked getting flowers, but then again, maybe only Neanderthals sent flowers nowadays.

Ah, hell, he thought, driving down Main Street in the storm. He had to face her today. Tomorrow was Thanksgiving. He'd asked her to dinner, and he didn't have a clue whether or not she was still coming.

Steve pulled up to the pumps and got out, settling his

hat low on his forehead against the driving snow. He put the nozzle in the tank and then turned his back to the wind, hunching his shoulders. What, exactly, was he going to say to her?

His gaze shifted uneasily to the store. He could see through the big plate-glass window, but she wasn't at the register. Bess was. He looked back at the pump. Twelve gallons. Thirteen. What if she wasn't even here today? Should he call her? Just come right out and ask what time he should pick her up tomorrow? Or maybe that was assuming too much. God, he thought, he really did hate this. Dating, he guessed you'd call it. Dating was a real pain. It was so much easier to be settled, past all this uncomfortable stuff.

As it turned out, he almost bumped right into Brigitte as he was entering the store. "Oh," he said, not ready.

"Oh, yourself," she replied, and she gave him a heart-warming smile.

He was lost.

"I was wondering when you'd be by," she said, and he could see she was leaving, shrugging her arms into a navy blue anorak, pulling gloves out of the pockets. "I was on my way to lunch."

Steve untied his tongue. "I was going to get a bite, too. At the Elks."

"Oh," she said.

"Will someone please shut that door," came Bess's voice. "I ain't here to heat all of Sweetwater, you know."

"Ah, sorry," Steve said, and he reached into his back pocket for his wallet. He looked at Brigitte. "You want to have lunch with me?"

"Sure," she said. "I'd love to."

It was so easy, really, Steve thought as he parked in front of the Elks Lodge. He'd spent days trying to figure out how she'd reacted to the flowers, when all he'd had to do was ask her to lunch. And the first thing she'd said when they'd gotten into the truck was, "Thank you so much for the flowers. They're lovely."

Inside the lodge they shook off the snow and he hung up their coats, then signed her in as his guest. The place was pretty full, some of the guys were having lunch right at the bar. But a table opened up shortly, and Steve led her over and pulled out her chair.

"What a great old building," she said. "Has this always been a lodge?"

He gave her the history, what he knew of it. "The building was put up in '94—1894, that is. The Elks have always owned it. I guess Bill Ramsey's great-grandfather built the actual bar and did the wainscoting and window boxes."

"It sure is Victorian," she said, glancing around. "My dad was an Elk. I can remember going to picnics and family stuff when I was really little. But then, well, he was gone, and that was the end of it."

Steve nodded. "You said he left when you were what? Nine or something?"

"Something," she said, waving it off. "Not my favorite subject, you know?"

"I understand," Steve said, and he realized he wanted to know everything about her, every detail. It wasn't in him to pry, though.

Brigitte smiled. "You, however, are a good dad," she said.

"Well, the girls might disagree."

"I doubt that," she said. Then she smiled again. "Did you ever get that dress for Heather?"

"Oh, yeah," he said, "catalog order. She runs into the house every afternoon to see if the UPS truck's come."

"Her first real dance," she said, reflecting. "New dress… There's nothing quite like it. I think I broke out in hives."

"You did?"

"Uh-huh. I wasn't always so outgoing."

"And what made you outgoing?"

She shrugged. "A very long string of dating experiences, I suppose."

"But you've never been married." Steve stared at her, the way her dark gold lashes curled above her china blue eyes, the way her mouth tweaked up just a tiny bit at the corners. It was a delicious mouth, adorable, her lips pink, no lipstick on them. She had a long graceful neck and slim arms beneath her turtleneck sweater. Her hands were delicate and ladylike with short nails. She always wore clothes that disguised her figure, and he wondered what exactly she would look like, feel like, taste like. She was incredibly feminine, yet strong, as capable as any woman he'd ever known.

"No," she said. "Not yet. The poor saps don't know what they're missing, I guess."

"They sure don't," he said before catching himself, and they both laughed.

Lunch was the usual Wednesday fare—hamburger and fries or a chicken breast sandwich and fries. Plain and simple. They ate relatively quickly, because Brigitte had to be back to relieve Bess.

It was over a fast cup of coffee that Steve got up his nerve and asked, "Are you staying?"

"What?" she said.

"Are you staying in Sweetwater?"

She sort of pursed her lips and blew out a breath. Then she leaned an elbow on the table, put a fist under her chin and looked him in the eye. "I can't answer that," she said. "My leave lasts till Christmas. After that, well…"

Steve was puzzled. Why didn't she know? "I thought you were looking for a place to settle down. A safe place, away from the city."

"I am."

"Well, then, what about Sweetwater?"

"It's a nice town."

"I don't understand," he said.

She sighed and looked at her coffee cup. "Steve," she said, "things are kind of confusing. It's hard to explain."

"Then unconfuse me."

"That's not a word."

"Come on," he said. "At least try to explain. Why all the mystery?"

"It's not a mystery, really," she said, but he noticed that she wasn't meeting his eyes.

He tried again. "You tell me you work as a secretary and that your work's important, but you seem willing to consider staying indefinitely. I can't make sense of it."

"Why does it have to make sense?"

"Come on, Brigitte," he said. "You're being evasive and I can't figure it out."

"Then stop trying." She got to her feet, flashed him a quick smile and said, "I have to get back to work, really. Would you drive me?"

"Sure," he said, rising also and tossing some bills on the table for the waitress.

He followed Brigitte out to where they'd hung their coats in the lobby, helping her into hers. He was still confused, though, more than ever. And by the stiff set of her shoulders and the way she refused to meet his eyes, he had to figure she was hiding something. Something big. He'd always thought that, he realized. He just didn't know what it was.

He drove her back to Locals Corner and stopped in front of the door. The snow was still coming down wetly, coating the truck. The wipers swished, swished. He stared at the windshield and said, "There's someone in Denver, isn't there?"

She was silent for a long moment, and he could feel the tension mounting. "No," she finally said, "there's no one in Denver."

"But there was."

"No, Steve, it's nothing like that," she told him. "I promise."

"But there's something. I know it."

She refused to give him an answer. Instead she said, "What time tomorrow?"

"Oh," he said, "tomorrow. Right. I'll pick you up at three."

"Three. Okay. But I'll drive out."

"I'll come and get you," he said again.

"Steve." She opened the truck door and reached out and patted the snow off one of the dogs. "I'll drive. Really. I'll be there at three. And thanks."

"Okay," he said, and she was gone. He drove back to the ranch, the heavy chain saw and dogs in the rear, and he couldn't stop wondering what the devil it was about Brigitte Hartman that didn't quite mesh.

His mother, Ruth, and sister, Naomi, arrived about two minutes before the school bus dropped Jeannie at the bottom of the drive. Suddenly the house was filled with noise and bags of groceries, the toddlers, Johnny and Timmy, chasing the terrified dogs in and out of rooms.

"You two settle down!" Steve's sister yelled at her boys. "Sorry, Steve," she said. "They're getting to be real terrors."

Steve's mother gave him a big hug and then began putting the groceries away, ignoring the dogs and her grandsons as they raced around and around the kitchen. Steve finally put the dogs outside, and that was when Jeannie walked in, covered with snow.

"Where's Heather?" Steve asked.

"With Dave," Jeannie said, drawing out his name, Da-a-ave, and screwing up her face.

"Who's Dave?" Ruth asked.

"Oh, a neighbor's son. Hell, I think he's darn near eighteen."

"That's a little old for Heather, isn't it?" Naomi met Steve's eyes before she turned and scooped up her two-year-old, Timmy, into her arms and gave him a lecture.

"I don't know," Steve said. "Nowadays I don't know what the dating rules are."

"Is he a nice boy?" Ruth asked, looking in the fridge for room to put the turkey.

"I barely know him," Steve said.

"Ask him to dinner," Naomi suggested.

"Oh, yuck," Jeannie announced as she gave her grandmother a huge hug and kiss then went off to chase after four-year-old Johnny.

Heather arrived home not long after that, when Dave Garrett dropped her off.

"Oh, a boyfriend," Naomi teased, and, amazingly, Heather smiled shyly instead of flying off the handle.

Steve felt like a fifth wheel in the kitchen all afternoon. Still, he stayed, sitting at the old scarred table, reading the paper while his mother and sister not only fixed dinner, but began the preparations for Thanksgiving.

Wonderful, warm aromas filled the house. Naomi made homemade cranberry sauce and put two pies in the oven, Ruth cut green beans and packaged them. Sweet potatoes sat on the windowsill, a bag of gooey marshmallows beside them. All the fixings for the dressing were there, too. In the meantime, Ruth made the girls' favorite dinner, a big iron pot of stew and fresh rolls. Naomi fixed a green salad, and Heather set the dining room table.

Steve watched the women work and realized he hadn't yet mentioned there would be one more for Thanksgiving dinner. He wasn't sure how to tell them. He didn't want his mother and sister to take it all wrong.

They sat down to dinner at six-thirty, Johnny in a chair of his own, little Timmy in a booster seat next to his mother. Jason Tucker, Naomi's husband, wouldn't drive over till tomorrow.

"Let's see," Ruth said, counting heads, "there'll be eight of us, including the baby."

"Timmy's a baby, Timmy's a baby," Johnny chanted.

"Be quiet. Don't tease," Naomi said sternly.

"Jeannie's a baby," Heather couldn't help chanting then, and Jeannie stuck her tongue out at her sister.

Steve cleared his throat.

"Actually, Mom," he said, "there'll be nine."

"What?" Naomi said. "I count, let's see—" she paused, thinking "—eight."

"I know who's coming," Heather said. "Brigitte."

"Oh, wow," Jeannie said, brightening. "Is she, Dad? Is she?"

"Well," Steve said, looking at his bowl of stew, "I did ask her. Seemed the neighborly thing to do. She's new in town." He shrugged.

"Brigitte?" Ruth asked.

"Brigitte Hartman," Steve said, carefully buttering a roll. "She moved here from Denver. Or at least she's thinking about it."

"I hope she does," Jeannie said. "She's cool."

"She's a very nice lady," Steve remarked nonchalantly.

"And, Grandma," Jeannie went on, "she's really pretty. She cooked us dinner one night—a Mexican casserole."

"Hmm," Naomi said, grinning at her older brother.

"She's cool, isn't she?" Jeannie asked her sister.

"Oh, sure," Heather muttered.

Thankfully for Steve, the conversation turned to Christmas and what everyone wanted this year. No one knew except Johnny. "I want a truck!" he bellowed.

"Well, you'll have to ask Santa Claus," Naomi said as she started to clear the table.

"Santa Claus..." Jeannie smirked.

"Shut up," Heather said.

The sleeping arrangements were decided while Ruth, Naomi and Heather did the dishes. Jeannie watched the toddlers. "I'm putting you in my room, Mom," Steve said.

"Well, where will you sleep?"

"Down here on the pullout. It's no big deal. And Jeannie and Heather are bunking together, so Naomi and Jason can have the guest room, and the toddlers can sleep in Jeannie's room. It's all settled."

"Dad made us clean our rooms," Heather said.

"And the kitchen and living room, too," Jeannie announced.

"You did a great job," Ruth said, a dish towel in hand. "It hasn't been easy these past couple of years, and Grandma thinks you're doing wonderfully." She glanced at Steve, who only sighed and nodded.

Everyone but Steve and Naomi was in bed by ten. The snow was still coming down outside, and Steve and his sister sat in the warm living room near the fireplace, enjoying a brandy together. Shep and Boots were by Steve's feet.

"I don't know the last time I had a brandy before bed," Naomi said. "This is a real treat."

"I never have the time, either," Steve said. "Even when Leslie... Well, even then we both went to bed right after dinner. Exhausted."

"I know the feeling. Those two kids of mine are prematurely aging me. I should have had them when Jason and I were first married."

"Well, you got a business going instead."

"True. It's a balancing act."

"It's funny," Steve said, staring at the brandy he held in both hands, "but I could have a couple more."

"Kids? Good grief. You're over forty."

He stretched his long legs out in front of him and sighed. "I know. But look how many people we know who're having kids late. It's not a big deal anymore."

"True," Naomi said. "But you need a wife for that, big brother. Got someone in mind?"

"Hell, no," he said.

"Liar. Who is this Brigitte, anyway?"

"God, Naomi, a friend. Don't make more out of it than there is."

"Right. Your girls seem to think a lot of her."

"Jeannie does," he admitted.

"And Heather?"

Then Steve had to explain the whole story of how he and Brigitte had actually met in the first place.

"Oh, all kids snitch stuff," Naomi said. "Sounds like you handled it fine. And Heather's driving?"

Steve nodded. "But only on the ranch roads, you know. Not on the highway. She's learned pretty darn fast."

"My God, that makes me feel ancient. I remember when she was born. Seems like yesterday."

"Doesn't it?"

"So, go on about Brigitte. Have you dated?"

Steve shifted uncomfortably. "We haven't dated, not really. She cooked dinner here one night. It was after Ben Garrett had an animal killed, and we sort of ran into each other."

"You and Ben?"

"No," Steve began, but then he saw the teasing smile on his sister's face. "Very funny."

"So, tell me about Brigitte," Naomi prompted.

"Not much to tell. She's pretty, about thirty-two,

thirty-three. To tell the truth, I don't know all that much about her.''

''Why'd she move here, of all places?''

''Beats me. First off, she hasn't really moved yet. I think she's looking Sweetwater over. She says she wants to get away from all the crime in the city.''

''You don't sound very convinced.''

''Well, I'm not.'' He took a long sip of his drink, feeling its warmth all the way down to his belly. ''If I had to guess, I'd say she's trying to get over someone.''

''Hmm.''

''There's a lot about her that's a mystery,'' he said.

''Oh, a mysterious woman,'' Naomi said. ''Sounds exciting.''

''Maybe to you,'' Steve muttered.

''Well.'' Naomi rose and yawned. ''I hope something works out for you, big brother. I really do. We all have to get on with our lives.''

''Yeah, I suppose so,'' Steve allowed.

When Naomi had gone up to bed, Steve let the dogs out for the last time, then turned off lights and pulled out the living room Hide-A-Bed. Upstairs, everyone was sound asleep, and the house was suddenly quiet, the way it usually was.

He stripped down to his shorts and long underwear top and stretched out, hands behind his head. The last log in the fireplace hissed and crackled and shed a warm orange glow on the walls and ceiling.

He thought about lying there alone, and he knew he was ready to share his bed again. But with Brigitte? Someone he really didn't know at all?

He had a lot of questions. The funny thing was, they never seemed all that important when he was with her, staring into those blue eyes with those long, curved lashes, watching the way the wind caught in her short hair and tousled it, the sun playing on her face, her smile. When he was with her, something just clicked inside him. Like today, when she'd thanked him for the flowers. Hell, he'd felt as if he'd just won the lottery.

THE FIRST RAYS of sunlight found the Flat Tops and slid down the striated mountainsides, seeking the ravines and gullies, lighting the snow-touched land. In places, the fresh white powder was deep, three or four feet. In other spots there was only a light dusting, the land barren and windswept, forbidding. Cold. Yet home to Star and her pack.

The wolves still mourned Auntie Mame. Their high spirits had been dampened, and they often sat, raised their heads and howled, paying tribute to her memory. It was as if there were a hole in the fabric of their existence; it had to be repaired somehow, and it would be, but it would take time.

When they hunted, they noticed her absence the most, because Mame had been the fastest, most indefatigable huntress. They noticed the lack, but the pack managed, the younger female taking over Mame's place, moving up to the beta position, repairing a thread at a time.

The brittle November air invigorated the wolves, and the deep snow kept them on the move, seeking game, perhaps an aging cow elk who'd weakened and fallen prey to the first winter storm.

Star led the pack this bitter-cold Thanksgiving morning. Silverfoot lagged behind, scurrying onto the crest of a scree field, drawing in a lungful of frigid air, testing it. When the pack moved ahead, he raised his muzzle and howled, a drawn-out mournful song, as if he were calling out to others of his kind. Instinct told him to do this, although he hadn't any idea there were no wolves within hearing, hadn't been for two human generations. Receiving no reply, he leapt from his perch on the scree and followed the pack.

Of all the wolves, the pups were the most invigorated. They followed their mother closely, but nonetheless cavorted in the fluffy, dry snow, sticking their noses into it, rolling, nipping at one another. Every so often, Star turned and yipped at her errant offspring, calling them to heel.

One of the young males whom the humans had named Blackie for his dark coat, nuzzled the new beta female. She was slim and small and pale gray, called Ashes by the human caretakers. She had liked Blackie, but now his position in the pack was beneath hers, and when he tried to attract her attention, she snapped at him.

Blackie turned away, tail between his legs, and took his disappointment out on one of the pups, growling, showing his teeth, making the pup cower properly.

Silverfoot caught up to his pack and took the lead, moving toward the forested land below. Then, at the edge of the trees, he stopped and turned to Star, who stood with one big front paw raised, sniffing the air. Silverfoot approached, nuzzled her neck, and they both rose on their hind legs, chest to chest, paws on each other's shoulders. Their noses touched.

But there wasn't time to indulge in affection, and soon the pack was racing into the forest, on the hunt for which they were so superbly equipped: jaws that could crush fifteen hundred pounds per square inch, forty-two glistening teeth, incredible quickness and stamina, a strong social structure in which each member moved in perfect synchrony.

The pack ran, its collective breath smoking over the surface of the ground, and where they went, the cries of the coyotes were suspended.

The wolves moved in a line, swift and beautiful and terrible, and the wind eddied about them cautiously, in awe.

CHAPTER TEN

BRIGITTE FELT as if she were going on her first date. She went through her clothes, wishing she'd brought more of her things from Denver. But how could she have known she'd be invited to Thanksgiving dinner with the whole Slater clan? And how could she have known how much she'd care what they thought of her?

Dumb, she mused, pulling a skirt out of the tiny closet. What did it matter, really? Her wardrobe just hadn't entered into her calculations, and besides, Brigitte didn't usually pay a lot of attention to her clothes. Still, she tried on a couple of outfits before she was satisfied. A rose-colored sweater, long and oversize, over a black broomstick skirt. Boots. Was it the right touch, not too dressy, not too casual? Maybe they'd all be dressed formally, or maybe they'd all be in jeans. No, not for Thanksgiving, she told herself. She did her face, even put on lipstick, which she hardly ever wore, then fussed with her hair. Of course, the whole reason she cut it short was so she didn't have to fuss with it—but this was a special occasion.

It was insane how much some things had come to matter to Brigitte since she'd met Steve: how she looked, what he thought of her, what his girls and his family thought of her. She knew she was a fool, acting on pure emotion like a child, worse. But, darn, she couldn't help it.

She leaned close to the mirror over the sink and wiped away a smudge of lipstick, then fluffed her hair on one side. She knew she was a real jerk for deceiving Steve. It'd been on the tip of her tongue a hundred times to tell him who she really was. It had taken all her willpower not to blurt it out whenever she was with him, such as yesterday at lunch. All of her instincts urged her to tell him the truth, but she couldn't—not yet. And she felt sick about it, because Brigitte couldn't have a relationship without trust. Trust on both sides. If Steve found out she'd lied to him— well, she could imagine his reaction. And he'd be absolutely justified.

If Steve were innocent, she'd screwed up any possibility of a relationship. And if he were guilty, *he'd* screwed it up. Besides, maybe she really didn't want a lasting relationship. Look what had happened to her mom. Look what had happened to Brigitte and her sister. Abandoned. All of them. Maybe she couldn't trust any man at all. Maybe it was always better to keep a safe distance.

So why was she fussing over her clothes, for God's sake?

She glanced at her watch. It was time to go. Maybe she should have taken Steve up on his offer to drive her, so that she wouldn't have to walk into his house all alone, smack into the middle of a family gathering.

Just do it, she thought. *You idiot.*

It was a cold, overcast day, threatening more snow. The ground was covered with white, although it would probably melt when the sun came out. Up in the mountains, though, Vail to the east, Aspen to the west, the ski areas were opening today. There was plenty of snow at the resorts already because of their higher elevations.

As Brigitte drove, she looked up at the peaks, at their pristine whiteness, hidden here and there by heavy, low-lying clouds. The pack was up there, safe, she hoped.

Don't come down here, she told them mentally. *Don't come near these bloodthirsty ranchers.*

When she entered Steve's house, she noticed it smelled heavenly, of turkey roasting and pie and gravy and fresh rolls. It was noisy, too, with women's voices, and small children squealing. It was very different from when she'd been there before, and the kitchen had been taken over by women.

"You must be Brigitte," the older woman said. "I'm Ruth, Steve's mother, and this is his sister, Naomi. We're so glad you could come."

Naomi wiped her hand on her apron and held it out. "Nice to meet you. We've heard a lot about you."

"You have?" Brigitte smiled wryly. "Good or bad?"

"Good. All good," Naomi said, laughing. "By the way, the men are watching football. Go on in and say hello."

Steve got up quickly. "Hey, I didn't hear you come in." He stepped close to her, and for a moment she thought he was going to give her a kiss, but apparently he thought better of it. He took her hand instead and led her to his brother-in-law. "Brigitte Hartman, Jason Tucker."

Jason was slim and blond in striking contrast to Naomi's dark good looks. He pumped Brigitte's hand. "Welcome to the family," he said, making her blush. He talked as if she were engaged to Steve, for goodness' sake.

In the corner of the living room, two little boys were playing with toy cars on their hands and knees.

"That's Timmy and Johnny," Steve said. "My nephews. Cute, huh?"

"Adorable," Brigitte agreed. "And well behaved, too."

"Give 'em a chance," Jason replied.

Steve still held her hand; Brigitte wondered whether to disengage herself from his grasp, but Jason didn't seem to notice. Did Steve often invite strange women to family dinners? No, she thought he'd told her, he hadn't kissed anyone since his wife. And, despite herself, she'd believed him.

"Look," she said quietly, "I'll go help in the kitchen. You watch the game with Jason."

"No, you're my guest, Brigitte. You want to watch the game with us?"

"Steve…" She rolled her eyes at him.

"I see what you mean." He gave her hand a squeeze. "You sure?"

"Uh-huh."

She turned to leave, but she heard him say, "Brigitte?"

"Yes?"

"You look real pretty."

She swelled inside with a singular happiness. "Thanks," she said, and as she left the room, she couldn't believe how Steve could affect her like that, how he could say a word, just a word, or give her a look, and everything she'd come to Sweetwater for flew right out of her head.

Jeannie and Heather were in the kitchen. The younger girl beamed cheerfully and said, "Hi, Brigitte," but Heather kept a careful distance. Brigitte wondered if Heather's aunt and grandmother knew the whole story about Heather and her. If not, they might wonder at the girl's subtle hostility.

Soon she was supplied with an apron, at work laying rolls out on a baking sheet, listening to the women chatter. Jeannie and Heather were setting the dining room table.

"Nine places," Ruth said. "That's right, isn't it?"

"Yes, Grandma."

"Be careful of the crystal!"

Naomi asked her questions, where she was from and so on. It seemed she did know the story about Heather. "That was a great way to handle her," she said. "We all owe you a big thanks, Brigitte." Naomi was testing the turkey leg to see if it was done. "You know, we worry about Steve and the girls. He does his best, but it was tough when Leslie died, really a bad time."

"I've worried for three years," Ruth said. She smiled at

Brigitte. "And I'm really glad to see he's taken up with someone at last."

"Well, I'm not sure he's 'taken up with me,'" Brigitte said, uncomfortable. These were nice people, and she was deceiving all of them. "I think we're just friends."

"Friends," Naomi said, hiding a smile. "Well, that's good. Steve needs friends."

"He's lonely," Ruth said. "He needs someone…"

"Shush, Mom," Naomi interrupted. "You'll scare Brigitte away." Then she added, "And don't mind Heather. It's been rough on her. She was at such a vulnerable age when Leslie died. She's not going to accept another woman around her dad so easily, even if you are just friends."

"I'm not going to push her," Brigitte said. "And I'm trying not to threaten her. I can understand how hard it must have been." She handed a bowl of green beans to Naomi. "Okay, what else?"

Steve stuck his head in the kitchen. "Need any help? Everything okay?"

"We're dandy. Just keep the boys busy," Naomi said. "Another half hour, Steve."

"Are they working you too hard?" he asked Brigitte.

"Hard labor," she replied drolly.

"Go on, Steve," Ruth said. "We're getting along fine."

Brigitte asked a few questions of her own and found out that Jason had a farm implement dealership and that Naomi was his bookkeeper. Ruth lived with them and watched her grandsons while Naomi was at work.

"But you lived here," Brigitte said. "Steve told me the house was built by his great-grandfather."

"I came here when I married Pete. 1950. Such a long time ago. And now I hardly know the place. Leslie redid it. The kitchen's so much nicer, though."

"Your family has roots in this valley, doesn't it?" Brigitte asked.

"Oh, yes, we go back a ways. This land was settled by Slaters before Colorado was a state."

"And the other ranchers around here, do they go back that far?"

"Mostly. You know, no one starts out nowadays to buy a ranch. The work's too hard and there's no money in it. Small ranches aren't financially feasible. You have to be born to it. You have to love it." She sighed. "Not many young folk want to do it these days."

"I was raised on this ranch," Naomi said, "and to tell the truth, I'm just as happy to live in town now. But I sure do have lots of fond memories."

Brigitte took some dirty dishes to the sink and rinsed them. "I suppose you heard about the wolf that was killed the other day."

"Oh, yes, we heard about it. It was on CNN and all the network news shows," Ruth said, shaking her head.

"And Steve told us," Naomi added.

"I don't know what to think," Brigitte said. "I mean, being new here. I've heard both sides, and I don't know..."

"It's a tough problem," Naomi said. She sat down at the kitchen table to rest for a minute. "I'm of two minds about it myself."

"I remember hearing wolves howl back when I first moved here," Ruth said, "but in those days the government paid a bounty on them. They had an eradication program. Funny how things change."

"Do you know the Garretts?" Brigitte asked. "Oh, sure you do."

"Macho jerks," Naomi said. She made a face.

"I've met Chris," Brigitte said, "and he talks like he'd kill all the wolves if he could. It almost sounded as if he was bragging that he *did* kill that one."

"Loudmouth," Naomi said. "He's all talk. He'd never

go to all the trouble to track and kill a wolf in this weather. But he'd sure brag about it, all right.''

"Ben may be a rough kind of man, but he's not stupid. He wouldn't go so far as to break the law," Ruth said. "Although I wouldn't put it past him to egg someone else on to do it."

Brigitte's heart sank. The Garretts didn't look like such perfect suspects after all if Naomi and Ruth were right.

"Hmm. I wondered about Chris," Brigitte said. "He was pretty angry."

"It's a sensitive subject, that's for sure. People feel strongly about it. You hate to see any of your stock killed by some animal when you've got enough other troubles."

"Everyone's still talking about who killed that wolf," Brigitte said, "and no one seems to know. Or do you think they really do know but won't come out and say it?"

Naomi shrugged. "Oh, somebody knows, all right, or they will pretty soon. You can't keep that kind of secret in a small town like this. Frankly, I can't even guess who it could be. One of the quiet ones, I bet. What do you think, Mom?"

"I hate to think it was someone I know. Maybe one of the youngsters, for a lark. Oh, I don't know."

One of the quiet ones, Brigitte thought. Like Steve. Quiet and self-contained, with the kind of inner strength that leads a man to do what he thinks is necessary to protect himself and his family. A proud man. Dear God.

Brigitte bent over the sink, busying herself, washing the pots and pans that had piled up, not wanting to reveal the feelings that must be showing on her face. She had to get herself together; this was Thanksgiving, a happy time, a holiday.

"Oh, let that stuff go until after dinner," Ruth said.

"I don't mind," Brigitte replied. "Honestly. I like to be busy."

She had herself under control by the time they all sat down at the table. Steve carved the turkey, his brows drawn together in concentration. Brigitte could study him to her heart's content, for once—everyone was watching him. She let her gaze rest on the smooth line of his jaw, the way it narrowed below his ear. His mouth, remarkably sensitive in that strong face. His straight nose. His neck, the cords that stood out in the column of his neck, his muscular throat. His dark, dark eyes that rested on a person with a kind of power, with so much feeling in their depths.

He looked up once and smiled, and his face lit up like a boy's. "I'm having a heck of a time with this leg," he said.

Jason made an off-color remark in return, and everyone laughed. Brigitte felt the warmth of the family surround her; it was so very easy to like these people. She had occasional flashes of self-hatred for her deception, but she ignored them. She could indulge in that later. Alone.

They had turkey and corn bread stuffing. Cranberry sauce and green-bean casserole, rolls, sweet potatoes. The two little boys made a mess. Timmy cried, but only once. He ended up sitting on Naomi's lap and eating from her plate until he fell asleep, leaning back against her, eyelashes resting like fans on his flushed cheeks.

"You want me to put him to bed?" Jason asked.

"No, just leave him here. At least he's quiet," Naomi said.

Then there was pumpkin pie and coffee and the groans of people who'd eaten too much. Just like at home, Brigitte thought. And she had to wonder what she would have done tonight if she hadn't been invited to the Slaters'. It would have been awfully lonely.

"What a wonderful meal," she said. "I enjoyed it so much. It was good of you to have me."

Steve gazed at her caressingly, a man replete with food, surrounded by his family. "Our pleasure."

"Can I be excused?" Heather asked. "I promised to call Nancy."

"Sure, go ahead. But don't talk too long. You need to help with the dishes," Steve said.

"I'm so full, I need a nap before I drive home," Jason said. "Too bad we brought two cars. I need someone to keep me awake."

"Take Mom," Naomi said. "I've got the boys to keep me on my toes."

"You know they'll fall asleep, Naomi," her mother said.

Family stuff. Details, kids, cars, people who cared about one another, people who were married and loved one another. A poignant ache grew inside Brigitte. How nice, she thought, to be a part of a family like this. Easy, too easy.

Jason and Steve talked about some piece of equipment Steve needed—his brother-in-law sold him machinery wholesale, of course. And Jason received a whole steer every year—he only had to get it butchered. The barter system.

They all pitched in to do the dishes, although they had to send Jeannie upstairs to get Heather off the phone.

Brigitte loaded the dishwasher, handling china that must have been Leslie's. A wedding present, perhaps. She put the plates and saucers and cups in the racks very carefully, trying to decipher Leslie from her choice of china. Silly, but she still tried. Pastel flowers on white, traditional but with a hint of whimsy. Was she right? Maybe someday she could ask Steve. She'd like to. She'd like very much to know what kind of wife he'd chosen. It might give her some insight into him.

By seven o'clock the dishes were done and Steve's family was packing up, getting ready to drive home.

"I'm glad it isn't snowing tonight," Ruth said. "Goodbye, girls. Be good. Heather, I want to know all about your dress when it comes. Call me. Take pictures."

"Okay, Grandma."

"And, Jeannie, sweetheart, keep up your good grades." She gave both girls kisses. "I miss you two." She turned to her son. "You feed those girls well now—they're growing. I put some of the turkey in the freezer in packages. It's marked. Call me soon."

"We'll get together at Christmas, Mom. It's only a month away. I'll see you then."

Jason shook hands with Steve; Naomi hugged him. "See you in a month." She was carrying one boy, Jason had the other.

"It was good to meet you all," Brigitte said, standing next to Steve as if she were the lady of the house.

Ruth leaned close to her. "It's great to see my Steve with a...friend. I worry so about him and the girls."

"Mom," Naomi said, hitching Timmy up on her hip.

"I'm coming. Goodbye, my darlings, see you soon."

The house was so quiet then, with Heather and Jeannie upstairs, the children gone, the toys cleared away. There was only a single empty wineglass on the coffee table. Brigitte picked it up automatically and took it into the kitchen. Steve followed her, and when she turned around after putting it in the dishwasher, he was very close.

"They all thought you were terrific," he said.

"Oh, so it was a test."

"No, that's not what I meant."

"Sure it was."

"No, Brigitte, what I meant was, I think you're great."

She looked up at him. He did mean it. He was straightforward, no games. It frightened her a little. Her sassy tongue, her flippancy, didn't work with him—he saw right through it or chose to ignore it, and she was left with no defenses.

"Your family is wonderful," she said softly.

"Never mind them. Come here." He pulled her close

and searched her face. "Tell me if I do something Neanderthal, okay? I swear I'll stop. I'm new to this game, Brigitte. I could use some coaching."

She laughed shakily. "It's a deal. But, Steve, I hope... gosh, I don't know how to say this. I mean, I'm not...I'm afraid you think..."

He put a finger on her lips. "Afraid you're in too deep, is that it? A widower with kids, a family, a ranch. Hey, I know. I just like being with you. Nothing serious, okay? No promises."

"Okay," she breathed. "No promises."

He bent his head to kiss her there in the middle of the dimly lit kitchen. His mouth was sweet on hers, his lips soft, his whiskers rough. She could smell his scent, feel his hands on her back. Her body molded to his with perfection, his hardness complemented her softness, his curves fit into hers. She couldn't think, she could only drink in the sensations and melt inside in a warm torrent of need.

He drew back and stared down at her. "Brigitte Hartman," he said quietly. "Just appeared out of nowhere, a fairy princess, like magic."

"I'm no fairy princess," she said soberly. "Far from it."

He released her and took her hand, leading her to the couch in the living room. He put some more wood in the fireplace, poked at it, squatting on his haunches. Brigitte's eyes feasted on his back, which was stretching the fabric of his shirt, on his pants pulling tight across his buttocks, on the muscles of his shoulders flexing. Her hands itched to stroke his skin, to reach under his shirt and run her fingers over his flat belly, down his flanks, up over his back and shoulders....

He rose and sat down next to her. "This is nice," he said.

"Mmm." Her face felt hot.

He rested his arm on the back of the couch, his fingers

idly playing with strands of her hair. "You're awful quiet," he said.

"Just digesting all that food." She turned to face him. "I should be going."

"It's still early. Stay awhile."

"A little while...."

He was silent for a minute, then he said, "There's something about you.... I don't know. I told you yesterday.... Some kind of reluctance. You said there was no guy, but I don't believe it. I wish you'd tell me, Brigitte."

She regarded him gravely for a time, then said, "Okay, I'll tell you. It's a man. I'm madly in love with...Chris Garrett."

He drew back, shocked for a moment. Then he recovered. "You're joking." It wasn't quite a question.

"Maybe I am, maybe I'm not," she teased.

"Not funny," he said.

"Jealous?"

"Like hell I am."

She grinned. "Gotcha." There, things were back on a lighter footing.

"He's younger than you are," Steve said.

"So? Hey, buddy, that's an insult. Verging on Neanderthal."

"What is this with Chris? You dance with him. What else do you do with him?"

"Nothing much. I saw him a few days ago. I was driving around and he was fixing a fence. We talked some."

"Yeah? About what?"

"What else? The wolf."

"The damn wolf."

"He sounded as if he was the one who shot it, Steve, really hard-nosed. I haven't told anybody but..."

"Chris didn't do it," Steve said.

"How do you know?" she asked. *You know because you did it,* she thought.

"I just know. Hey, it's not your problem."

"It's everybody's problem."

"How in hell did we get on this subject?" Steve asked, irritated.

"I heard…" Brigitte splayed the fingers of one hand and stared at them. "I heard that the shooter baited the wolves with a dead deer."

"Where'd you hear that?"

"I forget. Just talk."

"You believe it?"

She shrugged. "I also heard that maybe that same person is responsible for all the cattle killings."

"Oh, for God's sake, Brigitte."

"It makes a great excuse to kill off the pack."

"You're fixated on this thing. Why can't you just believe the wolves are doing what they do best, killing herd animals?"

She looked into the fire, seeing the flames leaping and writhing, seeing in them the green fire of almond-shaped eyes, wolf eyes. "I don't know," she whispered.

"There's no conspiracy here," he said. "It's simple. Wolves kill to eat. Someone got ticked off and shot one, then he got scared because it's against the law and hasn't come forward. That's all there is to it."

"Oh? What if it happens again? Another wolf killed, then another?"

He looked at her curiously then. "Just why do you care so darn much?"

Oh, God, she'd gone too far. Stupid. She gave a little laugh. "Sorry, I get carried away. I just love animals so much."

"Cattle are animals."

"I know…I just…"

He regarded her soberly for a long time. "What're you hiding, Brigitte?"

"Hiding? Me? For goodness' sake, Steve, what could I be hiding?"

"I don't know. That's why I asked."

"Nothing. I'm not hiding anything. Whatever made you think that?"

"Gut instinct."

"Well, your gut's wrong. I'm a simple girl."

"So you say."

Her nerves twanged, her heart pounded. When she tried to swallow, her mouth was dry. She felt like a cornered rabbit.

"Why didn't you ever get married?" he finally asked.

At least she didn't have to lie about the answer to that question. "I almost did once, back in college, but I was too young and I didn't want to settle down, so it didn't work out."

"Do you still feel that way?"

"I'm not too young anymore," she replied pertly.

"About the settling-down part."

"I told you once, I don't know. No one's asked me."

"What if somebody did ask you?"

"Steve…"

"Some generic person, some nice guy."

"How can I answer that?" she said.

"Okay, never mind. I'll change the subject."

"Good."

"What did you study in college?"

"Well, that *is* a change," she said lightly, her mind racing. Wildlife biology was not a feasible answer. "English literature," she said.

"Uh-huh, so you're a secretary."

"What can an English major do? And my spelling's great."

"Brothers or sisters? Parents alive?"

"I have one sister, and her kids. My mother's in Montana. My father...I told you, he left a long time ago. I don't know where he is. And my Social Security number is..."

"All right."

"Do I pass?"

"Brigitte..."

"You said nothing serious, no promises."

"Yeah, I did."

"I like you, Steve. I like you a lot, but we just met. I hardly know you."

"Wrong. You know everything there is to know about me. I'm an open book. The problem here is, I hardly know you.

"Is that a problem?"

"Sure is."

She was sitting with her hands clasped between her knees, her shoulders hunched. She couldn't look at him, because if she did, she'd blurt out the truth, and she couldn't do that.

"I guess I'm not ready for commitment," she finally said, her voice low.

He was silent next to her, his arm withdrawn now, but she could feel his eyes on her, the weight of his gaze. He was hurt, puzzled, put off. She didn't blame him.

"Uh, Brigitte, would it be too much of a commitment for you to go to the Cattlemen's Association Christmas dance with me?"

She turned her gaze to him and nodded solemnly. "I guess I could handle that."

He smiled. "It's a start, anyway."

"I've got to go," she said, rising.

"I hate to send you off like this. I knew I should have picked you up."

"Don't be silly. I'm a big girl."

''Not so big.'' He put a hand out to touch her cheek, pulled her close, his hand reaching around to the back of her neck.

She leaned into him, closing her eyes. It felt so good to be in his arms, to feel him against her. He stroked her hair back with his other hand. She felt his lips on her forehead, then on her nose, and she turned her face up and his lips came down on hers, leaving her limp with longing.

She had to steel herself to break his embrace, and when she did she felt as if she were lost, bereft of everything she needed and wanted. She drew back, away from him, her breath catching in her chest. She tried to laugh, but it was choked.

''What's wrong?'' he asked.

She shook her head. ''Nothing.''

''I care about you, Brigitte,'' he said.

''No,'' she whispered, ''don't.''

He was watching her thoughtfully, his eyes black, searing her skin. ''Okay,'' he said.

''I've got to go.''

He helped her on with her coat. ''You're all right driving home?''

''Of course.''

''Thanks for coming today.''

''I enjoyed it.'' What a ridiculous, stilted conversation.

''I'll call you,'' he said. ''Or I'll stop by Locals Corner.''

''Sure.''

Then she was outside, the cold air slapping her in the face. She got into her car, started it, turned and headed out to the road. Her mind raced crazily all the way home. How had she gotten herself in this predicament? Falling in love with Steve Slater. Impossible. What had gotten into her?

She was treacherous, a liar. How could she do it? Go to his house, eat his food, kiss him, pretend to be someone she wasn't, living a lie. And he knew it, felt it, but neither one of them could stop what was happening between them. This terrible wonderful thing that existed without their consent, as if it had a life of its own.

How could this be happening?

Brigitte drove, seeing the road through a film of tears. She looked up at the dark, looming mountains and she wondered where the pack was right now. Were they safe? Well fed? Warm?

And then suddenly she was struck by another thought, one far worse than all the rest: If Steve were the guilty one, then by giving in to her feelings for him, by even being with him, she was betraying not only Steve and herself, but the wolf pack, too.

CHAPTER ELEVEN

JIM GARRETT, Ben's middle son, arrived back from his trip to Denver a week after Thanksgiving. He was grinning as he parked his father's Jeep Wagoneer in front of the ranch house. He was ready to burst at the seams with pride. He'd done it. In less than twenty-four hours he'd found out all they needed to know about Brigitte Hartman.

Ben looked up from his dinner plate when Jim marched into the dining room. "That was a short trip," he said.

Jim sat in his regular spot, unable to wipe the grin from his face. God, but he felt proud of himself.

"Would you like some dinner?" Audrey asked.

"Yeah, sure," he said.

"Well?" Chris asked. "Did you find out anything?"

"Did I ever," Jim said, taking the plate from Audrey.

"Go on," Ben said.

"In a nutshell, she's Fish and Wildlife."

"I knew it," Chris said.

"She's a field biologist," Jim went on. "She even worked with the pack they let loose up here last year."

"Goddamn!" Ben muttered. "They sent a spy! The goddamn government sent that woman up here to spy! They're paranoid. They still think there's some imaginary guy up here killing stock. I can't believe it!"

"What are we going to do about this woman?" Jim asked, his gaze meeting his father's.

"What's to do?" Ben said. "Let her snoop all she wants.

She's not going to find out a thing. There's nothing to find."

Chris was shaking his head in disgust. "I knew there was something about her."

"Yeah," Jim was saying, "it was a snap finding out who she was. I looked her up in the phone book, drove by her place. It's a little suburban apartment. I tried asking a neighbor, but she wouldn't tell me anything, so I sat in the motel room and started making some calls. Hell, I coulda done it from here."

"So who'd you call?"

"I tried the newspapers first, the *Denver Post* and *Rocky Mountain News,* then I tried some of the local magazines. I even called Sinapu, those crazies who're trying to put wolves everywhere in Colorado. I tried the state Fish and Game Commission. Then I tried Fish and Wildlife, asked for Brigitte Hartman. The idiot on the phone said she was on assignment." Jim laughed. "Wouldn't you think everyone in the office would be careful screening her calls? Anyway, I said I was a reporter and I needed her title for this follow-up article I was researching on the dead wolf incident. The woman on the line told me everything, right down to the fact that little Miss Hartman had been with the wolves right from the beginning of the reintroduction."

"I feel like calling that son of a gun Mac McCarthy right now," Ben said hotly. "How dare he send that woman up here!"

And then Audrey cleared her throat. "Ben, honey," she said, "what if...well, what if one of the ranchers really is killing the livestock and blaming the wolves?"

All four men looked at her, and then Jim burst out laughing. "Oh, sure," he said, "and just who's doing it? Me?"

EARLY the following morning Brigitte got the long-awaited call from Mac. The autopsy report on Auntie Mame was in, and so was the one on the latest dead animal.

"I think we're about to break this wide open," Mac said. "First of all, the examiner found blond hairs this time—human hairs—on both carcasses. Secondly, and you'll love this, wool fibers from a sheepskin coat were found on the wolf's carcass. Lots of them. Now, we know when Hal picked her up he was wearing a down parka. And the man who found her claims he was wearing a canvas barn jacket...."

"Oh, my Lord," Brigitte said, an image flashing in her mind. "Chris Garrett was wearing a sheepskin jacket the afternoon I stopped to talk to him up on his ranch. I can see it as clear as day."

"Garrett," Mac said. "Hmm. He's the old patriarch who's so outspoken at the meetings. Wanted to fight me. It was his heifer we just found the sheepskin fibers on. Hasn't he had a couple of animals killed now?"

"Sure has."

"But why would he kill his own?"

"Off the top of my head," Brigitte said, "I can think of about a dozen reasons. The first one's painfully obvious—no one would think he'd kill his own livestock. And, Mac, the Garretts are all blond!"

"Well, I'll be," Mac said.

"Exactly."

"They can't be the only blondes in that valley, though."

She thought about that. There was Brad Milligan; he was fair-skinned with very light brown hair, light enough to be called blond, she realized. But Steve—it couldn't be him. And she'd never seen him in sheepskin. Never.

"Brigitte?" Mac was saying.

"Oh, just thinking. Sorry. There may be a couple of others. I can certainly narrow it down now."

"You know," Mac said, "we could go public with this.

It's not irrefutable proof, but I think it's enough to shut some of those ranchers up.''

But Brigitte frowned. "I don't know, Mac. By going public, we might just get their backs up even more. I'd sure like to pin this on one of them. Leave no doubt.''

"And how are you going to do that? Get someone to confess?''

"Maybe," she said. "Maybe that's exactly what I'll have to do. Let me think about it. Let's sit on this for a few more days. I'd like to be a hundred percent sure before we throw those autopsy reports in their faces.''

"If you think you can nail it down, go for it. But be careful, Brigitte. I mean, don't go pushing so hard, you drive someone over the line. Okay?''

"Okay.''

"Whoever did this can't be playing with a full deck. You take care and call me day or night.''

"I will, Mac, I will," she said, but when she got off the phone, the only thought left in her head was that Steve couldn't be the one. And now, maybe now, she could tell him who she really was. He'd understand. Of course he would.

But by the time she got to work that Friday morning, her thoughts had done a hundred-and-eighty-degree turnaround. She couldn't possibly tell Steve the truth yet. First of all, he was and always would be a rancher, and he'd never in a million years forgive her. But secondly, and it killed her to have to admit it, Steve wasn't really in the clear yet. None of the ranchers were. For all she knew, they were all involved. What she had to do, couldn't put off any longer, was start pushing. She'd start with Chris Garrett, too. Hadn't he always been number one on her list?

It was a hard day at work. Slow. Too much time to think. She felt as if they were just a breath away from solving the case, and yet they still needed concrete proof. Blond hairs and sheepskin fibers were not going to convince the community or the media that humans were positively behind the cattle killings.

The dance, Brigitte thought early that afternoon. The Cattlemen's Association Christmas dance. One week away. If she hadn't come up with proof by then, every rancher in the valley was going to be there. Maybe all she needed to do was confront Chris or his father with the facts. Even if it wasn't them, they had to know who it was. One of them would open his big mouth and either deny involvement or try to pin the killings on the real culprit. It was her best shot. It was time she took it.

And as Brigitte realized that, she also had to come to grips with another realization. By playing her hand, she'd give herself away to Steve. There'd be no way out then.

She rang up a gas sale on the register and felt like laughing hysterically. She'd spun this web, and now she was stuck in it. No way out.

It was after Brigitte's afternoon break that Bess put her hands on her ample hips and cocked her head. "You keep frowning like that, honey, and you'll have a road map of wrinkles on your face before you know it."

"What?" Brigitte said.

"Something's bothering you. Has been for days. If you want to talk about it, I'm a good listener. Keep a mean secret, too."

Brigitte had been feeding a fresh tape into the credit-card machine. She straightened, then slowly faced her boss.

"Well, let's hear it," Bess prompted.

"I...I don't know," Brigitte began.

"Come on. Spit it out."

Brigitte sighed heavily, then lifted her gaze to meet Bess's. "Suppose there was something..." She paused. "Well, suppose there was something very important you needed to tell someone, and by telling him, you'd ruin everything. I mean, he'd hate you.''

"Now there's a riddle," Bess said dryly. "Want to elaborate?"

Brigitte closed her eyes, breathed, then opened them. "I don't know how to put it."

"You're saying you need to tell Steve something? Right? Something about you, personally. And you think he'll hate you."

"That's it exactly," Brigitte admitted.

"Hmm," Bess said, thinking. "Is it about another man, honey? I mean, don't tell me you're married or something."

"It's nothing like that."

Bess was loading soda cans into dividers in the cooler. She stopped and turned back to Brigitte. "Well, I don't know what your secret is, but to be honest, I always thought it was sort of weird, a smart girl like you all of a sudden showing up in Sweetwater." And then Bess laughed. "You're not an escaped prisoner or something, are you?"

Brigitte couldn't help smiling. "No, Bess, I'm not."

"But there sure is something."

Brigitte nodded.

"You're not going to tell me."

"I can't. Someday I will. But I can't right now."

"Hmm," Bess said again. "Well, to get back to your question then, I'd say the longer you put off telling Steve your secret, the worse it'll be. Might as well let things come to a head."

"Oh, boy."

"You're pretty fond of him, aren't you?"

"Yes."

"Then tell him whatever you have to. If what you have between you is real, things will work out."

"I hope you're right" was all Brigitte could say.

It was nearly quitting time when Jeannie and a couple of her school friends came into the store. They bought pop and candy and then asked if they could wait inside till one of the girls' mothers got there to give them all a ride home.

"Sure you can," Brigitte told them, going back to work. But it wasn't long before she noticed Jeannie staring at her. The young girl looked as if she had more on her mind than waiting for her ride.

Brigitte walked over to her and her friends. She cocked her head. "Why do I get the feeling you want to ask me something?" she said to Jeannie.

The girls giggled and nudged one another. "Go on, Jeannie, ask her," one of them urged. "Go on."

"Yes, why don't you?" Brigitte prompted.

"Well," Jeannie began, and she giggled again, embarrassed. "I was, like, wondering... You see, Dad was supposed to take us Christmas shopping in Glenwood Springs. He said we could go tomorrow."

"And?"

"Well, he can't now. He's got a sick steer and the vet's coming. We'll have to wait until next weekend, and by then it'll almost be Christmas."

Brigitte hid a smile. "Hmm," she said. "I guess you need someone to drive you tomorrow."

Jeannie grinned and looked at her feet. "Could you? Could you do it?"

"I'd be happy to," Brigitte said. "We have to see if it's okay with your dad, though."

"He said it was!" she announced.

"Oh, and when was that?"

"This morning. He said if I asked and you said it was okay, we could go with you."

"I see."

"Can we, then?"

"I'll pick you up at nine," Brigitte said, "and Heather can come, too, if she wants."

"Cool!" Jeannie said. "We'll take Dad's credit card."

All that night Brigitte thought about seeing Steve. She desperately wanted to follow Bess's advice and tell him the truth. But she was being torn apart inside. Steve *could* be involved in this whole mess with the wolf pack. But just as important to Brigitte was her fear of putting too much faith in any man. She wanted so badly to trust Steve, to believe what her eyes told her. She didn't dare, though.

She got to the ranch at nine sharp the next morning, expecting to see him, longing to. But only the girls were there; Steve was already up in the fields with the vet.

"But he knows we're going," Jeannie was quick to say.

Heather went, too, and Brigitte surmised that a shopping trip was simply too good a deal to pass up, no matter how the teenager felt about her.

The drive to Glenwood Springs took a little over an hour. It was a great old Western town, full of history. And, more recently, a bargain spot for winter tourists who couldn't afford the price tags at neighboring Vail or Aspen.

They passed by the site of Doc Holliday's grave and the saloon still bearing his name. Across the Colorado River was the huge hot sulfur springs pool, and both girls crinkled their noses at the pungent aroma. "Phew," Jeannie said. "It always stinks, but it's a lot of fun to swim there. Dad takes us in the summer sometimes."

"He says that European princes and stuff used to come here a hundred years ago to get cured of things," Heather put in from the back seat.

Brigitte had spent a couple weeks in Glenwood Springs almost three years ago when USFWS was seeking the ideal location to release wolves back in to the Colorado high country. "Your dad's correct," she said, turning off the interstate toward downtown. "And wasn't Theodore Roosevelt here once?"

"He came to hunt," Heather said.

"I hate hunting," Jeannie said. "And you should hear some of these creeps at school. There's these two guys in Heather's class? They told everyone they killed Auntie Mame."

"Is that right?" Brigitte said, not believing her ears.

"The mall's out in West Glenwood," Heather said, pointing. "You gotta turn here."

"Mmm," Brigitte said, putting on her directional signal. "Tell me more about those boys."

It was Heather who spoke up. "They're full of it. Everybody knows that."

"But they said they killed the wolf and left her on the road?"

"Yeah," Jeannie said. "But Dad says that's baloney. He says two boys couldn't have done it."

"Your dad's probably right," Brigitte said, and then she couldn't help wondering if that was because he already knew who was to blame.

The talk turned to shopping and the crowds and how great the decorated streets looked. "Christmas is so cool," Jeannie said, staring out the window as they parked. "I want a snowboard this year. Dad says I can ski Sunlight because my friend's mom is going to drive us every weekend. She's got the coolest snowboard."

"I like skiing," Heather said. "Real skiing, like on two skis."

"I'm a snowboarder, you know, a shredder," Jeannie said with great pride.

The mall was beautifully decorated, lights and fake snowflakes strung from every available space. There were dozens of decorated trees up and down the center aisles, elves and Santas and reindeer in doorways, a big sleigh, filled with beautifully wrapped gifts, in a courtyard. In the background, Christmas carols played, and the air was laced with the scent of apple cider and sweet spices. A line of tots waited to sit on Santa Claus's lap near the sleigh.

"Jeannie's going to sit on Santa's knee," Heather teased.

Jeannie stuck out her tongue.

"Okay, girls," Brigitte said as they stood in the middle of the mall. "Where do we start? Do you have a list?"

There was no list, but both girls had a good idea of what they wanted to get everyone.

"Let's sit and get a hot chocolate and make a plan," Brigitte suggested.

Over hot chocolate Brigitte learned that Steve had told the girls they could each spend a hundred dollars on friends and family. Not a large sum, but surely adequate. Of course, each girl wanted to get earrings and bracelets for girlfriends, toys for cousins Johnny and Timmy. Heather was going to get her grandmother a scarf, and Jeannie had thought of a big, warm pair of slippers.

"The rabbit ones," she announced, a mustache of hot chocolate on her upper lip, "with the big pink ears."

"They're silly," Heather said.

But Jeannie held her own. "I can get Grandma whatever I want."

For Naomi and Jason they were going to go in together on a toaster.

"And we're getting Dad a cellular phone," Jeannie said.

Brigitte raised her brows.

"We saved our baby-sitting money all year," Heather explained nonchalantly.

"They're on sale," Jeannie told her. "We saw an ad in the mall flyer."

"Wow," Brigitte said, "that's a great gift. But who's going to pay the monthly bill?"

"Dad is," Heather stated.

"Oh," Brigitte said, and they all laughed.

"What about your shopping?" Jeannie asked.

Brigitte took a breath. "Oh, my. Well, I have an older sister and then there are her kids—they're younger than you—and there's my mom…"

"Where's she?" Jeannie asked.

"Montana. She lives close to my sister."

"Where's your father?" Heather asked.

Brigitte let out a breath. "My father left us when I was very young. I really don't know where he is."

"Do you care?" Heather went on.

Brigitte knew she couldn't lie, not to this young, guarded teenager. "I tell myself I don't give a hoot. But I guess that deep down inside it hurts. I try never to think about it. I suppose a shrink would say I'm in denial." She met and held Heather's gaze before the girl slid her eyes away.

"Anyway," she said, brightening, "that's ancient history. I refuse to be on a bummer when I'm surrounded by all these pretty things. Let's get to that shopping."

"Are we going to have lunch, too?" Jeannie asked.

"I think we should stuff our faces," Brigitte said. "It's Christmas, isn't it? We can all diet afterward."

She never would have believed how much fun it was shopping with two young girls. Through their eyes she saw everything anew. Jeannie squinted at an all-red Christmas tree: red lights, red balls, red ribbons. "Look how cool that is!" the young girl announced, and Brigitte squinted, too. It *was* beautiful.

They must have gone into two dozen shops, seen everything in them and bought several presents before Jeannie said she was starving. So they found a table in the food court, and Brigitte gave each girl money to go to the food stand of her choice, then all meet back at the table.

Brigitte had Chinese lo mein and an ice tea, and Jeannie

showed up with two slices of pizza and a Coke. Heather had a taco, a burrito and a milk shake.

"Ooh, yuck," Jeannie said. "No one eats a milk shake with Mexican."

Heather leered at her. "I'm going to drink it, stupid."

With packages under their feet and on the empty chair beside them, they ate until they were full. Then Jeannie wanted a milk shake, too, so they waited for her to buy one. It was fun watching all the people, and because it was Saturday, there were hundreds of them.

Then they went back to shopping. Brigitte really impressed the girls when she produced a ten-percent discount coupon from the dregs of her wallet and they were able to use it on Steve's cellular phone. The real trick she taught them was to get their gifts wrapped for free whenever possible.

Heather was impressed until Jeannie looked suddenly glum and said, "Mom always did all the wrapping at home."

"Oh," Brigitte said. "Well, I'm not a great wrapper like I bet your mom was, so I have to take advantage of the freebies. I wish I could wrap nice presents, though."

The girls helped Brigitte pick out a pair of leather gloves and a pretty plaid wool scarf for her mother. "I'll have to get all this in the mail pronto or it won't get to Montana for Christmas," Brigitte said.

"Are you going to be in Sweetwater for Christmas?" Heather asked matter-of-factly.

Brigitte sighed. "I don't know yet."

"You live in Denver, don't you?"

"Well, yes. My stay in Sweetwater has been a kind of sabbatical."

"What's that?" Jeannie asked as they walked down the mall, arms loaded.

"It's kind of a break from your usual life. Someday I'll

tell you all about my real life.'' And then she carefully switched the subject. She could never, ever lie to these girls. It was bad enough that she'd been so evasive and untruthful with their father.

By three o'clock they were done in. And in any case, no one could carry another sack without making an extra trip to the car.

"What do you say?" Brigitte asked. "Have we done enough for one day?"

"Ugh, yes," Heather said. "My arms are killing me."

"My feet hurt," Jeannie said.

"Mine, too," Brigitte was saying when she spotted the dress in the store window and eyed it.

"That's so cool," Jeannie said.

"Isn't it?" Brigitte agreed.

"But where would you wear it?" Heather asked.

Oh, gosh, Brigitte thought. "Well," she began, "your father kind of asked me to the Cattlemen's Association Christmas dance next weekend."

"Oh," Heather said suspiciously.

"Neat!" Jeannie chirped.

Brigitte tried a different tack with Heather. "Do you mind my going with him?"

"Why should I care?"

"You have a right, you know."

Heather considered that, then she shrugged. "It's okay, I guess."

"Well, should I at least look at the price, girls?"

"Oh, yes, let's!" Jeannie said.

The dress was midnight blue lace, with a perfectly plain round neck and long sleeves, fitted waist and flared skirt, but all that graceful, swirling lace... It was expensive, though. And where would she ever wear it again?

"Do the women really dress up for the Christmas dance?" Brigitte asked the girls.

"Mom did," Heather said, the first time she'd ever mentioned her mother like that, easily and of her own free will.

"Oh, come on. Try it on," Jeannie said.

Brigitte emerged from the dressing room, looking uncertain. "Well?" she asked hesitantly. Then she looked down at her feet. "Forget the white socks. I mean, with heels, what do you think?"

"Oh," Jeannie breathed, "it's cool."

Brigitte looked at Heather. "Well?"

"It's all right. It's real nice, I guess. Dad'll like it," she added with a hint of sarcasm.

"I don't know," Brigitte said, determined to ignore Heather's remark. "I'd need shoes, too."

As it turned out, because it was so close to Christmas, the saleslady let her have the dress and shoes at a discount. Brigitte walked out of the store, the girls in tow, and felt both wildly giddy and, at the same time, guilty as sin. So much for confessing all to Steve before the dance.

And then, on the ride home, Heather asked Brigitte the most disturbing question she'd been confronted with in a long, long time. The girl turned to her and, point-blank, said, "Do you love my dad?"

Oh my God, Brigitte thought. "I don't know how to answer that," she said. "I'm…very fond of Steve."

"Has he asked you to marry him?" Heather asked coolly.

"Oh, good grief," Brigitte said aloud. "No, no, he hasn't. And even if your dad ever did ask a woman to marry him, I'll bet he'd ask you girls first."

"No way," Jeannie said. "Dad never talks about icky stuff."

"He will about something that important," Brigitte said.

"Bet not," Jeannie said. "When Heather got her period…"

"Oh, shut up," Heather said.

But Jeannie didn't care. "Dad was so embarrassed." She laughed. "And Heather had to buy her own Tampax at the store, and—"

"That stuff's hard for a man," Brigitte said, cutting her off. "Well, some men. I had my mom, so it was different. But I can imagine what it must be like for a man alone...." And they talked about growing up and female things practically the whole way home.

Steve was there when they arrived, and with the dogs running around their feet, they unloaded the car. When the girls were finally upstairs, no doubt eyeing their treasures, Brigitte stood in the kitchen alone with him.

"That was good of you to take them today," Steve said, staring down at her, his eyes warm, the color of sable.

"My pleasure. I got almost all my shopping done, too."

"Where will you spend Christmas?" he asked, and he leaned against the counter and folded his arms across his chest, pinioning her with his gaze.

Brigitte sighed and bit her lower lip. "I... Steve, I..." she began, but the phone rang. The next thing she knew Steve was talking to someone about cattle, and she edged toward the door.

He put up a hand, said, "Hold on a sec" into the phone and then asked her to stay.

"I can't," she mouthed, smiling apologetically, and she turned to the door.

He looked disappointed. "I'll call," he said, and Brigitte was gone, sucking in the cold evening air. Running, running away, she thought. *Chicken.*

CHAPTER TWELVE

THE WEEK that followed the shopping expedition was curiously long. Brigitte only saw Steve for a few minutes, and that was because he stopped at the store to gas up his truck.

His conversation was stilted. "I'll call you tonight," he said, and he handed her his credit card. "I'm sorry, but it's been a really hectic few days. Getting ready for winter, you know."

"Sure," she said, as if it meant nothing, as if the last days hadn't dragged by miserably, while Steve had filled her thoughts, his imprint stamped indelibly on her mind. Even now her heart was beating wildly.

"We still on for Saturday night?" he was asking. "The dance?"

"Oh, right, sure."

"Good. Maybe you could come out for dinner. Wednesday? Thursday?"

"That would be nice," she fumbled. *Nice.*

"Well, okay," he said, and he settled his hat on his head, gave her a quick smile and headed out.

Dinner, she thought a dozen times that day. Wednesday or Thursday, he'd said. How many hours away was that? She wondered if she could bear the passing of time.

As it turned out, they never did have that dinner. First Bess came down with the flu and was laid up for almost three days, so Brigitte worked double shifts. Then, when she did have a free evening, she spent it with Kathy Ramsey.

That had been a fluke. Kathy had stopped by the store on Thursday to finally meet Brigitte and thank her for the call about the shoplifting incident with her daughter Nancy. Then they just got to talking, hitting it off, really, and Kathy's family was in Grand Junction for a couple of days, and somehow they decided to have dinner together.

"That would be fun," Brigitte said, and they planned to meet at the local steak house at seven.

It was a pleasant evening, both of them enjoying the outing. "I can't tell you how long it's been since I got out for an evening by myself," Kathy said over coffee.

Brigitte nodded. She was enjoying it, too, missing her friends in Denver and her social life there.

Kathy told her all about the high school Christmas dance, which had been held last Saturday night. "Oh, the girls looked so cute, I almost cried. All dressed up like real young ladies. Nancy and Heather had to get dressed together, of course. You should have heard the giggling."

"I remember those days," Brigitte said. "How did Heather look? She was still waiting for her new dress, last I heard."

"She looked beautiful," Kathy said. "It was emerald green, and you know her coloring. Nancy so fair and Heather so dark, and those cute young boys." She rolled her eyes. "Adorable."

"So the evening was a success?"

"Oh, it certainly was."

"That's good. You know, Steve wasn't going to let Heather go at first."

"He's a bit overprotective, but I can't blame the guy. It's tough." She gave Brigitte a look. "You and Steve Slater…?"

"Oh, goodness," Brigitte said, flustered. "We're just friends."

"Friends," Kathy said. "Okay."

It seemed a good time to change the subject. She felt a little guilty, because she knew she was going to slip in at least a few questions about the cattle killings. She liked Kathy Ramsey and she was enjoying the evening, but this was just too good an opportunity to let pass.

She eased into the conversation carefully. "You know, I would have thought we'd meet before this," Brigitte said. "I went to that big Cattlemen's Association meeting a couple of weeks ago, and I'll bet you were there, too."

And so they discussed the meeting and all the media hype, and then finally Brigitte said, "Brad Milligan's a strange sort, isn't he? I mean, he seems like a ticking bomb at times."

"Oh, Brad? I guess so. He sits on things and then lets off steam. He's harmless, though. Kind of a milksop, really."

"That's funny," Brigitte said. "When people around here talk about one of the ranchers maybe being responsible for the cattle getting killed..."

Predictably, Kathy raised a brow.

"Anyway, if such a thing were true, well, I would have thought he was the type."

But Kathy laughed. "Not in a million years. You know, I went to high school with Brad. We even dated some. I'm telling you, Brad would never stick his neck out. He's only president of the association this year because it was his turn. There are only seven or eight ranching families here, and the men all sort of take turns."

"Hmm," Brigitte said, and once again she was forced to think that the Garretts were the only logical suspects.

On Friday she checked out the story she'd gotten from Heather and Jeannie about some schoolboys who claimed they'd shot the wolf.

It was a delicate situation. She met with a Mr. Hanling, the school principal, on the pretext of looking the place over for her sister, who might or might not be thinking about moving to the valley.

After a short tour and discussion, she said to him, "I heard a very disturbing rumor about a couple of the boys. They claimed they shot that wolf a few weeks back. I'd hate to think that was true."

But the principal only waved off her concerns. "That little rumor has already been handled," he assured her. "I spoke to the boys myself. It was purely bragging, trying to show off for a group of girls. The second they were confronted, they admitted it. I assure you, they were very embarrassed."

"Well, that's good to know," Brigitte said.

She got Mac's call that same evening, a call that alarmed her until she gave it some thought. "He claimed he was a reporter doing a follow-up article on the dead wolf incident. Millie did give him some information, including the fact that you were involved from the onset...."

"Millie used my name?"

"Well, dammit, she can't remember now if she said it or if he did."

"And what was his name?"

Mac grumbled something under his breath.

"What?"

"I said, she didn't get his name."

"Darn."

"Hey, we can't blame her. She's had a hundred calls from media types since Auntie Mame was shot."

Brigitte twirled the phone cord in her fingers and sighed. "Okay, it's not her fault. And besides, it's a real slim chance that it was someone from the valley."

"I'm sure you're right," Mac said. "I only told you about her slip-up because I thought I should. I'm not worried."

"Let's just hope no one up here reads an article with my name in it."

"So far no one in the office has seen a thing."

"Good," Brigitte said, dismissing the whole matter as she went on to tell Mac that it was looking more and more as if the Garretts were responsible for not only the dead cattle, but Auntie Mame's death, as well. "I'm going to the big Christmas dance tomorrow night," she said. "Maybe I can weasel something out of one of them. I'm sure going to try."

"Hey," Mac said, "why not ask that Chris Garrett character if you can get a wool sample from his sheepskin jacket?" He laughed.

And so it was Saturday morning before she and Steve actually had a chance to talk again. Bess was well and working, and it wasn't going to be long before she had to let her go for the slow winter season. Which was fine with Brigitte. One less thing she had to feel guilty about when she left the valley. Now, if only she knew what to do about Steve.

When he telephoned her at the cabin, she almost told him who she really was. Almost. But somehow the words stuck in her throat, and besides, she thought, she didn't want to blow the evening. Not just because she was going to try to talk to the Garretts. It was so very much more. She was desperate to be with Steve. She craved his touch, the sight of him, the way he gazed at her with such feeling. She wanted to savor every last second with him before she told him the truth.

After the dance, she promised herself. *I'll tell him then.*

"Pick you up at seven-thirty?" he was saying.

"Seven-thirty. I'll be ready."

"I hear you have a new dress."

"Oh…right. The girls."

"I can hardly wait to see you in it."

"I hope I don't disappoint you."

"You could never do that," he said, and a knife of guilt and longing plunged into her belly.

By seven-thirty she was more than ready, having spent two hours preening. She'd fussed with her hair, her makeup, her hosiery, changing from tan panty hose to black to tan again. She couldn't imagine having ever spent such a long time getting ready for a man. But this was Steve, and despite all the alarms sounding in her head, she'd never felt this way about a man before.

She heard his tires crunch on the gravel in the parking lot and pulled aside the drape. His girls were in the truck, and she remembered Steve was going to drop them at friends' houses in town.

She waited for him to knock. Then, trying not to seem too anxious, she opened the door. She wasn't wearing her coat yet, and she did a little curtsey and a three-hundred-sixty-degree turn.

"Well?" she asked. "What do you think?" It was crazy how very much it mattered.

Steve just stared at her, his face expressionless.

"Oh, come on. Is it me?" she tried again.

"You look…beautiful," he said.

"Thanks. You do, too."

Steve did look great. He was dressed up Western-style, in snakeskin boots, dark slacks, a white Western-cut shirt with bolo tie under a tweed wool sport coat. And he was wearing a dress Stetson, one she'd never seen before. He couldn't have looked more handsome.

When he escorted her to the truck, Brigitte's perfume filled the crowded cab.

Jeannie, in her usual upbeat manner, exclaimed, "You smell so pretty!" Heather only muttered grudgingly, "The dress looks nice."

They dropped the girls at the homes where they were

spending the night, and Steve told them what time to be ready to go home tomorrow. "And don't keep me waiting," he reminded them.

Finally she was alone with him. He pulled out of Heather's friend's drive, his arm stretched out on the seat back as he steered in reverse. Brigitte feasted her eyes on him and drew in his scent. She felt light-headed, giddy with pleasure. The ulterior motive she had for going to this dance was the farthest thing from her mind.

"I missed you this week," he said, putting the truck in first gear.

"And I missed you," she admitted. *God,* she thought. *Why am I torturing myself?* It could never work between them. Never.

The parking lot of the Elks Lodge was jammed, everyone arriving at once. They walked side by side to the entrance and then went in with the crowd.

"Oh, wow!" Brigitte said, seeing all the Christmas decorations. "Someone went to an awful lot of trouble."

"I'll guarantee it was the Ladies' Auxiliary," Steve said. "Leslie used to…" But then he caught himself. "Sorry."

Brigitte put a hand on his coat sleeve. "There's nothing to be sorry about, Steve. You were married, happily married, and she died. You *should* have memories. All your life you should have happy memories. If you didn't, I wouldn't think very much of you."

He said nothing, only looked ill at ease, and then he nodded.

They filed into the big room that was connected to the main dining room and bar area. Dinner was to be served first, then the tables would be cleared, opening up the big dance floor. A band was all set up and ready to go in the corner of the lodge room.

Everyone milled around, finding friends and tables, and Steve automatically took Brigitte's hand as they threaded their way through the crowd. She followed close behind, and she ached for it to always be like this: good cheer, the warmth of the holidays and her hand in his. She felt a little like Cinderella. All dressed for the ball, everything so beautiful, a man by her side who was the stuff of dreams—but it was going to end. Maybe not at midnight. But soon enough.

They had dinner with three other couples. Two of them Brigitte knew—the Ramseys and the Milligans. The third couple was a husband and wife named Kapochek. He was the manager of the local co-op. Evidently she stayed home with their two small children.

"Hi," Kathy Ramsey said as they got settled in their seats. "Two dinners together in a week. This is a first for me. Maybe my kids are finally getting to an age where I can have a life again."

The table conversation centered around Christmas, of course, and what everyone was getting their kids. Dinner was a choice of prime rib or Alaskan salmon. Brigitte had the fish, Steve the prime rib, and they traded entrées halfway through the meal. Everything was excellent.

It was over dessert that Kathy leaned toward Brigitte and whispered, "You look fabulous. New dress?"

Brigitte nodded and smiled and felt her face grow warm. Steve, who'd no doubt heard Kathy's comment, pretended he hadn't.

After dessert they had coffee. Brad Milligan's wife was the first to mention the wolf pack. "Thank God no dead cattle turned up this week," she said. "I'd hate to have Christmas spoiled. Is everyone else as sick as I am of seeing Sweetwater in the news?"

"Damn sick and tired of it," Kathy's husband said.

"Maybe the wolf pack took off for greener pastures," someone said, and they all laughed.

"Fat chance," Brad Milligan returned.

Of the two hundred or more people at the party, Brigitte realized she must have recognized half. People were friendly, too, saying hello, including her in their conversations with Steve when they waited near the bar area for the music to begin playing. Everyone commented on her dress and said how beautiful she looked. They were open, warm, unguarded, and she realized that this brand of easy familiarity was only possible in a small town. She experienced a stab of guilt for all her less-than-cordial thoughts about these people and their narrow-mindedness. They were only protecting what was theirs, their way of life, their traditions.

The music started at nine. Brigitte cocked her head at Steve. "Do you dance?"

"Sure," he said.

"You and Leslie used to dance?"

"Uh-huh," he said, "but mostly before the girls were born. It was hard to find baby-sitters afterward."

"And expensive," she added.

"That, too.

"Shall we?" he said, and he took her hand again and led her toward the floor. "I used to be pretty decent," he said, "but I'm probably rusty. If I step on your toes, just squeal."

Steve didn't step on her toes. Through dance after dance of popular music from the past thirty years—country-western, rock and roll, slow-and-easy tunes—he led her around the crowded floor. They took breaks only when the band did, and Brigitte thought she could do this forever, but only in Steve's arms. There'd never be another night like this.

"Don't you get tired?" Bess asked when they were all standing together during one of the breaks. Then she looked from Brigitte to Steve and back. "Oh, I guess not," she said with a big grin.

They danced to the "Tennessee Waltz" when the band started up again, and Steve held her close to him, her breasts pressed to his chest, their hips moving together in a flowing rhythm. She could feel him, every muscle and sinew, as they moved, and the back of her neck grew damp. Once, he kissed her and brushed his lips along her collarbone, and she went limp with desire.

And then Chris Garrett cut in.

"Sure," Steve said, albeit reluctantly, when Chris tapped him on the shoulder.

She was in Chris's arms, feeling lost, as if being carried out to sea, away from the safe harbor of Steve's arms.

"You sure look good tonight," Chris said against her hair.

"Thanks," she mumbled.

"Got plans for later?"

"Yes, but not with you."

"You're breaking my heart," he whispered.

"Hmm," she said, thinking. Wasn't she going to confront this man? She'd waited for this opportunity, told herself this was why she'd come to the party with Steve, why she hadn't confessed to him. But now...now she simply couldn't bring herself to confront anyone. All she could do was search for Steve in the throng. Steve, so achingly handsome, so straightforward and open—or so she needed to believe.

"Hey, how long are you going to be around here, anyway? Bess can't need you much longer," Chris said in her ear.

"For a while," Brigitte said.

"And then what? Back to Denver?"

The music changed to something more lively, and Chris had to loosen his hold on her.

"I do live in Denver," she said.

"And this was just a what, a break from the hustle and bustle of the city?"

"Something like that."

"Nice town, Sweetwater," he said, "Be hard to leave here."

"Yes, it will."

"But you probably have a real job you have to get back to."

"Uh-huh."

"A good job."

"It's a living."

Chris twirled her and then brought her up against his chest. "But Steve'll miss you, won't he?"

"You'd have to ask Steve that."

"Oh, I think he'll miss you. Everyone in town's talking about it."

"How interesting," she said coolly. "What's the point of the third degree, Chris?"

"No point. I just kind of liked you myself, but you've disappointed me."

"Well, I'm very sorry to hear that," she said.

"Of course we could…" he was saying when Steve finally cut back in. Chris smiled and turned her over to him with an old-fashioned, mocking bow.

"Phew," Brigitte said. "That man could do with a little less ego."

"How's that?" Steve asked. "I thought you liked him."

"Oh, nothing," she said, just happy to be in his arms again. And it wasn't till the band finished for the evening that she truly berated herself for not even asking Chris Garrett a single question about her suspicions. How could she have let the perfect opportunity slip through her fingers? She'd had him right where she wanted, trapped in her arms, and all she'd thought about was getting back to Steve. She was obsessed. Couldn't even do her job.

No one left immediately after the band packed it in. Instead, everyone congregated around the bar for a last brandy or soda or beer. It had been too lovely an evening to just say goodbye.

Steve handed her a tall soda and lime and they stepped away from the bar. "You know," he said, "I missed you last week."

"So you said." She took a long drink, then looked up.

"I thought you needed some space."

"Steve," she began, "maybe we both need some space."

He laughed. "Speak for yourself. I'm not afraid of commitment."

Oh, Lord, she thought.

"Cat got your tongue?"

"Yes," Brigitte admitted, "I..." But she never finished, because Bess and her husband stopped to say good-night, and then everybody seemed to be leaving amidst calls of, "Merry Christmas!" and "Hope I see you before New Year's!"

Then Steve was getting their coats and they were outside, the bitter-cold December air making them hurry to the truck.

Steve held her door for her and then went around to the driver's side and got in, turning on the motor, flipping the heat lever to high.

"Cold," he said.

"Yes." She hugged her coat around her.

He let the engine warm for a few minutes, then turned to her, and she knew in that heartbeat what was coming.

"I want you to come home with me," he said softly.

Oh, God, she thought, and she closed her eyes and tried to take an even breath. She had to tell him no. All along she'd known this moment was going to come. She'd prepared herself. There was no other choice.

He reached out and touched her chin with his fingers, carefully, bringing her face around to his. "Brigitte? Did you hear me?"

She swallowed. "Yes."

"Yes you heard or yes you'll come home with me?"

"Yes to both," she whispered.

CHAPTER THIRTEEN

THE WOLVES MADE their own kind of music. One would start, usually Star, then Silverfoot would chime in, then Uncle Joe, Blackie, Ashes, then the three pups, their high voices laughable against the chorus of deep-throated ululations.

They had already sung that night, and now they were silent. Hunting. They raced across the frozen surface of the snow, tireless shadows in perfect darkness because it was a new moon. Their noses led them; they had no need for moonlight.

An old cow elk was injured, a wound on her leg, and she had struggled in the snow all day, trying to keep up with the herd. The wolves knew all about her even before they'd reached the herd's resting place. They had scented her age, sex, size, the blood on her leg, the smell of sweat and fear. They knew everything they needed to know, and they fanned out, seeking the old cow, totally ignoring the rest of the herd.

Ashes the huntress came into her own. She circled the elk, got behind her, herded the animal away from the rest, ran, snapping and panting, pushing the ailing cow. Then Blackie took over when Ashes was winded, then Star. The three pups watched and joined in when the cow floundered in a drift and they were safe from her deadly hooves. They were still learning the art of the kill—they'd need another few years to perfect it, then they'd go off to form their own pack.

Silverfoot took over the chase, his tongue lolling between glistening teeth, and he was the first to leap in for the kill. It was over quickly, the old cow giving up without a struggle. It was her time, and she knew it.

They ate, and when the pack was satisfied, they lay in the trampled snow for a time, licking their paws daintily. The female pup played with a piece of elk hide, then carried it in her teeth to Uncle Joe and laid it in front of him. He licked her muzzle in thanks.

Then, finally, they left their kill and trotted back to their home burrow under a fallen tree. They would never return to this kill—that was a rule of safety they would never break. But tomorrow night they would sing and hunt again.

STEVE KNEW he wanted Brigitte. He'd known it for weeks. All day he'd planned his seduction, growing hot and cold in turn. It had been a very long time since he'd done this sort of thing, and he didn't undertake it lightly.

He had her consent now, and as he led her into his dark, empty house, he could hardly think rationally. He wanted her, wanted to feel her skin, see every inch of her unencumbered by clothes, nothing between them. He wanted to bury himself in her, lose himself as he hadn't been lost in a very long time.

He flicked on the kitchen light and watched Brigitte shrug out of her coat. He loved the way she moved; every tiny gesture was as poignant as a kiss. His longing for her was so powerful, he felt ill.

She was uncomfortable, he could tell. No one-night stands for Brigitte; she took this seriously, too.

"Are you going to leave your coat on?" she asked, breaking the tense silence between them.

He looked down, gave a short laugh and pulled his coat off, throwing it over the back of a chair. "Okay?"

"Uh-huh."

He stepped close to her and held her eyes with his. Her chest rose and fell; her lips were parted.

"Oh, Brigitte," he said, and he pulled her to him and kissed her with an urgency from which there was no retreating.

He breathed her scent deep into himself as if he were drowning, and he shuddered and withdrew from her to find some level of control.

"Steve," came her voice, a thread of sound.

He looked down, saw her clear blue eyes glazed with desire. His head dipped again.

"No, wait, Steve. Please."

"What?" he whispered, his lips brushing her ear, her neck.

"We have to talk."

"Are you changing your mind?" he asked. "Brigitte?"

She turned her face away, her expression changing, but he was far past the point where he could decipher its subtleties.

"Oh, no, but…"

He kissed her again, felt her relax into his arms, boneless and oddly weightless, and the air around them pulsed in rhythm with the rise and fall of their breathing.

He broke free. "Are you okay with this?"

She nodded, then rested her head on his chest.

"Come on." He took her hand and started toward the stairs, and she followed, silent.

He didn't bother turning the light on in his bedroom. He held her and tasted her mouth again. He felt her tug his shirt out of his pants, felt her small, warm hands on his skin. He drew in his breath sharply.

She was pulling her dress down over her shoulders, her waist. It puddled at her ankles, and she stepped out of it, kicked off her shoes. Moonlight spilled in through the window and washed over her. He drank her in like a man parched by a drought with cool, clear water before him.

He sat down on the edge of his bed and tugged at his boots.

"Damn boots," he muttered.

"Let me." She straddled his foot and pulled off each boot in turn, tossed them aside, then stood in front of him in her bra and panties, white scraps on her skin.

"Come here," he said hoarsely, and held his arms out.

They fell together across the bed, a soft collision of bodies. Mouth to mouth, chest to chest, straining to fit closer. He was dizzy, filled with a sweet pain.

He groaned when she reached for his belt buckle, his zipper, and he got out of his pants, pulled off his socks, his shorts, all these details, prolonging the agony.

She lay next to him and ran her fingers down his ribs. "You're thin," she said, surprised. "You look heavier.... I thought..."

"Disappointed?" He kissed her nose, slipped a bra strap off her shoulder.

"No, no."

Her touch was unbearable. He brushed a nipple and felt it harden with an answering twitch in his belly, his groin.

He unhooked her bra, and it fell away. Her breasts were small and firm and very pale. He caressed one, then the other, his hands on her skin. It was so soft, like satin. He bent his head to kiss each nipple, trailed his tongue across her skin, then took a nipple in his mouth. He heard her moan, and his groin tightened with exquisite pain.

"Brigitte," he breathed.

She arched up to meet him and closed her eyes.

He pushed her panties down, gently stroked the mound of her womanhood, the inside of her thighs. She quivered and sucked in her breath. When she reached out and closed her fingers on him, he felt that she had possession of him wholly and utterly.

"Quick," she whispered. "Oh, Steve, hurry."

When he entered her, he felt her heat. She swelled around him and rose and fell with him until a burning surge lapped slowly throughout his body. He broke out in a sweat and rose over her again and again, holding himself in check, his breath coming too fast.

Their eyes were locked in rising urgency as their bodies moved quicker and quicker. He saw at last the surprise in her face, heard the cry in her throat as she arched against him, and then he let himself release into her, a long explosion that came from his core, a shuddering flood into her that jolted his body, then surged like a tide into every part of his being.

He only became aware of reality when she moved under him much later.

"Are you asleep?" came her voice in his ear.

"No, more like unconscious." He raised himself on his elbows, bent to kiss her.

She was smiling when he lifted his head again. He could see the white of her teeth. She drew a hand out from between them and ran a finger along his lips. "Not bad for being out of practice," she murmured.

"It's like riding a bike, they say. You never forget." He nuzzled her neck, the hollow at the base of her throat, the sensitive place where her neck met her shoulders. She twitched.

"Ticklish?"

"Mmm."

"Should we get under the covers?" he asked.

"Maybe. Are you cold?"

"No.

"Brigitte…" He hesitated.

"Uh-huh?"

"No regrets."

She smiled a secret woman's smile. "No regrets."

"You're beautiful," he said.

"No, I'm not, but I like hearing it," she said lazily.

"You're a terrific person."

Silence. He felt her move a little beneath him. Then, her voice barely audible, she said, "You don't know me."

"Ah, wrong. I know you."

They fell asleep in each other's arms. Steve woke once in the middle of the night and marveled that this beautiful, wonderful woman was in his bed. He wondered once if he was being disloyal to Leslie's memory. But he knew he wasn't. He'd mourned his wife, and she'd want him to love again. She'd want a mother for her daughters.

He regarded Brigitte for a time in the dark, with the familiar night noises of his house around him, and he knew he was in love.

Damn.

When he awoke again it was light out, and Brigitte was gone. He experienced a moment of panic, but then he heard the shower. He lay with his arms behind his head, looking up at the ceiling. He felt young, so young. The kids were gone, a woman was in his shower, the sheets still warm and full of her scent. Oh, yeah, he was in love. The question remained: Did Brigitte love him in return?

He roused himself and padded naked into the bathroom. It was full of steam. "Hey," he said, pulling aside the shower curtain. "It's me."

She looked startled for a split second, then she smiled. Her body was wet, her short hair slicked back with water. In the daylight he could see her better, every angle and hollow, every curve.

"Mind if I join you?" he asked.

They kissed with the warm water sluicing over them, and she hooked one leg around his knee, her hands sliding over his wet flesh. He couldn't get enough of her, the abandon of her loving, her sense of humor, a foil for his too-serious ways.

And they made love there in the shower; he took her quickly and wildly until she cried out and he shuddered into her. Again.

"You're killing me," he gasped.

"I wouldn't do that," she whispered.

"I'm not so young anymore."

"You could have fooled me."

"Ah, Brigitte, this has been some night."

"The water's going cold."

"Yeah, and I have chores to do. I have to pick up the kids."

She fixed him breakfast, puttering around the kitchen, asking him where things were. She wore an old bathrobe of his with nothing under it, her feet bare. He couldn't take his eyes off her. Slender, high-arched feet, curving ankles and calves. He could feel her body under his hands.

"What're you looking at?" she asked once, poised with a spatula in her hand.

"You."

"You're making me self-conscious."

"I can't help it."

"I can't think, Steve. Stop it."

He rose and went to her, put his arms around her, and she leaned back against his embrace.

"You've bewitched me," he said, looking down at her, laughing. "You're a sorceress."

She laughed, too, her eyes blue as the sky, crinkling at the corners. She shook her head.

"I want you to stay here," he said.

"I can't." Abruptly she was serious. "You know I can't. You've got kids, and I..."

"You what?" he asked softly, holding her.

"I... You said no promises, Steve. Remember?"

"I remember."

"Look, we really have to sit down and talk. This morning." Her eyes searched his, sober and assessing.

He let her go. "Sure, whenever. About anything." He frowned. "Something wrong, Brigitte?"

She turned back to the stove and flipped a pancake. "Damn, I burned it."

"Don't worry. The dogs'll eat it. Brigitte..."

But before she could answer, Steve heard someone honking a horn outside: Ben Garrett's signal. What in hell was he doing here?

"I'll go out and see what's up," he said. "Then we'll talk."

She gave him a long, lingering look, her eyes so full of feeling—love, he hoped—then the corners of her mouth turned up in that sweet, pert smile of hers. "Go ahead. I'll fix the rest of these."

"Back in a minute," he said, and he gave her a quick kiss and a grin and went out to see Ben.

"Hey there," Steve said, crossing the driveway, snow crunching under his boots. "What's up, Ben?"

"Is that Hartman woman inside?" Ben asked, leaning on his elbow on the open window of his truck.

Steve was taken aback. "What the hell kind of question is that?"

"Is she?"

"You mean Brigitte, right?"

"Yeah, Brigitte."

"Yes, Ben, she's here, but what business is it of yours?" Steve folded his arms and watched Ben closely.

"It's my business, it's everybody's business."

"What in God's name are you talking about?"

"Your friend Brigitte isn't who she'd like you to believe."

''Are you crazy, Ben?''

''Listen, Steve, I've been sitting on this for a week or more. Then I saw you with her last night. I could tell you were...close. So I figured I'd better tell you.'' Ben pushed his hat back, exposing a strip of baby-white forehead. ''Damn, Steve, I don't like to do this. I'm sorry, but you've got to know.''

''Spit it out, Garrett.''

''Brigitte Hartman is an employee of the U.S. Fish and Wildlife office in Denver. She's a wildlife biologist specializing in wolves. She's...''

''You're a goddamn liar.''

''No, I'm not, Steve. Jim went to Denver and asked around. Found out where she lived, spoke to her neighbors, even called her office.''

Steve felt the shock so deeply, his hands and feet went cold. Everything fell into place with a vicious click: her evasions, her strange behavior, her interest in the wolves, her reluctance, her sudden wanting to talk.

''Hey, it wasn't just you,'' Ben was saying. ''She deceived the whole town. Came up here to spy on us, and picked on you, I guess, because you're single. Hey, I don't know—''

''Okay, Ben,'' Steve interrupted. ''Thanks.'' His voice was cold and flat.

''Sorry I had to be the one to tell you.''

''Yeah.''

''Now, listen, we've got to do something about her,'' Ben said. ''We can't just let 'em get away with this.''

Steve's head came up sharply. ''I'll handle it, Ben. It's my problem. I'll take care of it. You don't do a damn thing.''

Ben held up a hand. ''Okay, fine. I'll leave it to you. But I'll tell you, Steve, those goddamn feds can't get away with this stuff.''

"Leave it alone, Ben."

"Yeah, okay. Take it easy, Steve." Ben started his truck and turned the wheel. "See you later."

Steve stood there watching the truck disappear down the driveway. He didn't feel the cold; he didn't feel anything but the pain of the truth and a stone in his gut where happiness had been five minutes earlier.

BRIGITTE HAD a stack of pancakes ready for Steve. She figured she'd let him eat in peace and then tell him everything. And if he never spoke to her again, so be it—she'd asked for it. Maybe, though, he'd understand. Just maybe.

She tried very hard to tell herself she'd get over him. She'd gotten over men before. Steve was just another guy in an infrequent string of men in her life.

Brigitte wiped off the stove top and told herself all those things. But in her heart she knew she was lying to herself. If Steve spurned her, she'd die a thousand deaths.

When Steve finally reappeared, he picked up his coffee mug and stood there for a minute, staring into it, not saying anything.

"So who was it?" she asked.

"Ben Garrett."

She piled a plate with pancakes. "What did he want this early on a Sunday morning?"

"Ah, nothing much. Some cattle that, uh, wandered off."

"Oh." She put the plate on the kitchen table. "Sit down. Here's breakfast."

He looked at her, a quick, flashing glance, as if he'd just realized she was there. "I'm not hungry," he said. "'Scuse me. I've got some things…" And he strode out of the kitchen, disappearing upstairs.

Brigitte was bewildered. Not hungry? He'd just said he was starved. She looked at the pile of pancakes and frowned. What had happened? Had Ben told him something to upset him? But why couldn't he tell her about it?

She nibbled at a pancake, sitting alone at the kitchen table, worried, not sure what to do. Maybe she should go upstairs and confront him, ask him what was wrong. But they were so new to each other, the relationship so fragile. She couldn't push herself on Steve.

It could be, she thought, that his behavior was due to his sudden realization of what he'd done. Perhaps he felt guilty, making love to another woman in Leslie's house. Surely he was worried about his girls and how they'd react to a relationship. Perhaps it was just that so many things had hit him all at once. She could understand that. Steve came with a lot of baggage, and he took his responsibilities very seriously. That was one of the things she loved about him.

She tidied up the kitchen, put foil over the plate of pancakes. Maybe he'd eat them later; probably the dogs would get them.

Indecisive, she hung around the kitchen a bit, reading the notes on the refrigerator door: dentist appointment, veterinarian expecting new VS inoculations, volleyball game Monday after school. Still no Steve.

Eventually she climbed the stairs and went into the bedroom. He wasn't there. She peeked out into the hall and saw that the door to his office was closed. Should she knock? What was going on?

She got dressed—Christmas party clothes on a cold December morning. Her panty hose were torn, so she stuffed them into her purse. They must have ripped when they were... Her mind went back to the night before and his hands on her, his mouth, his body, so lean and hard that she'd been surprised. She'd been able to feel every rib, running her fingers along the grooves, making him shiver. And the sharp jutting of his hip bones, with the fine, baby-smooth skin in their hollows.

She'd been held in thrall, and she could remember what had gone through her mind: There was nothing in the world except this time and this place and this man, and there was no room, no reason to consider right or wrong.

It could be that she'd made a very big mistake.

She straightened the bed, smoothing the rumpled sheets with her hands, recalling what they'd done there, and her heart clenched when she thought of it.

She'd been ready to tell him everything—it'd been on the tip of her tongue, but fate had intervened, and now the moment had passed and the mood was all wrong. Steve was upset by something and wouldn't, couldn't listen to her. The time wasn't right. She'd wait.

She was tucking the sheets in when he appeared abruptly in the doorway. His glance stabbed at her.

"You don't have to do that," he said.

"I don't mind."

"I have to pick up the girls."

"Okay, I'm ready." She paused, then blurted out, "What's wrong? What did Ben say?"

"I told you, nothing much. Not your problem." He was suddenly remote.

"Steve…"

"I have to get the girls now," he repeated.

She was stung. She gathered up her purse and followed him downstairs. "I left the pancakes for you," she said.

"Okay, thanks."

He was pulling on his coat, his back to her. She felt ashamed, as if she'd done something wrong—but what? And there was nothing to do but follow him out to his truck, climb in and sit there, watching the road in front of them. She glanced at his profile occasionally; it was set and hard, and her heart ached for him. Why couldn't he tell her what was wrong?

When they got to her cabin he stopped the truck.

"Thanks for the ride," she said inanely. "I had a wonderful time last night." She put a hand on his arm. "Steve...I..."

Suddenly he turned toward her in a swift, jerky movement and pulled her to him without a word. His mouth covered hers in a rough, deep kiss, his tongue probing, his arms like bands of steel, leaving her breathless, flushed. Then he let her go so quickly, she fell back against the seat.

"I've got to get the girls," he said hoarsely.

"Yes, okay." She opened the truck door and climbed out. "Steve..." she began.

"I'll call you," he interrupted. "Gotta go."

She slammed the door shut and watched him drive away. Something had happened; she wasn't sure exactly what. But she knew that she was in love with Steve, despite her best intentions, her job, her responsibilities, her terrible doubts. Nothing mattered. But overshadowing everything was her need to tell him the truth. She had to.

Oh, God, she thought, they were so good together, but there was so much holding them apart. Could they make it work?

She went inside, feeling terribly alone, troubled and singularly afraid. But not once did it occur to her in all her tortured pondering that her cover was blown.

CHAPTER FOURTEEN

HE'D SAID he was going to call, but he hadn't. Three days, no, four now, and he hadn't phoned or stopped by Locals Corner. Brigitte hadn't felt this way since her father had left his family, abandoned them. There was an ache inside her, an insidious pain. And yet she couldn't believe Steve was cut from the same cloth. There was nothing similar about them. Her father never should have been a family man. But Steve fit the role through and through. So what was she afraid of?

And then she thought: maybe the girls had put up a fuss, Heather especially. Maybe he needed to back off for a while. But he could have called.

"Oh, for goodness' sake, phone him," Bess told her. "Stop mooning around."

"I'm not mooning."

"You sure are. Call him."

"Maybe tonight," Brigitte said, lying. She wasn't going to call him, because she didn't want to know if he'd used her and dumped her. She couldn't face it.

Sweetwater was a small town, but if someone wanted to make himself scarce, it wasn't hard, and Steve was nowhere to be seen.

A million scenarios ran through her mind. Brigitte calling him, Steve saying, "Sorry, I've just been so busy. I was going to call you tonight." His voice low and intimate. Or running into him in the street or the grocery store. And he'd smile and give her a quick kiss, their eyes would meet…and hold.

One scenario ran through her mind, but she banished it as impossible. He'd found out who she really was. But he couldn't have, and besides, if by some far-fetched chance he had, wouldn't he have confronted her, angry—furious, in fact? Sure he would have. Frankly, she would have preferred that. This way, she could only assume he didn't return her feelings. He hadn't said anything about love, after all.

Her hand went to the phone a dozen times a day, but she never made the call. She couldn't.

She was scheduled for a three-day weekend off. She was only working four days a week now, and it'd be less after Christmas, Bess had said.

"I may go back to Denver after Christmas, anyway," she'd told Bess.

"Let me know," Bess had replied, shaking her head. "But why don't you call him?"

Brigitte left for Denver Friday morning. She had to get away from Sweetwater. She didn't tell Bess and she didn't tell the manager of the cabins. She just left.

Back in her own apartment, she flopped down on her couch and went through her mail. Bills, bills, Christmas cards, more bills.

She did some laundry and tried to eat lunch—canned soup, because there wasn't anything in her fridge except sour milk, a withered carrot and yogurt with green mold on it.

She'd never felt so alone in her life.

By two o'clock she'd cleared off her desk and was as antsy as the devil. Half an hour later she was walking into the office of the U.S. Fish and Wildlife Service.

Everyone said hi, smiled, wished her Merry Christmas. Nice, familiar faces, people to whom she didn't have to lie.

Maybe she'd just stay here and go back to work, pick up her old life.

Mac was surprised to see her. "Any news?" he asked.

"No, not really. I needed a break, that's all. I checked out the rumor about the high school boys, but it was nothing but bragging. And I'm pretty sure it isn't Brad Milligan."

"So Ben Garrett's our man," Mac said.

"Looks like, but I don't have any real proof. Should we ask everyone who's blond to donate some hairs, then have the FBI lab do a DNA analysis on them?"

Mac laughed humorlessly. "Donate? It'd take years in court to force them."

She sighed. "I know."

"Well, at least there aren't any more dead wolves."

"Probably only because the snow's too deep in the mountains now. Wait till spring." She ran her hand through her hair, and her bangs stood up in tufts.

"Look, Brigitte, forget all this for the weekend. The Christmas party is tonight. It's at Dale's Seafood Bar. Come and have some fun."

"Maybe," she said, trying to smile. It wasn't like her to be so down.

She called her mother that evening, and they had a long talk. She hid her sadness, not wanting to burden her mom. Besides, what on earth could her mother do about it?

"Well, there are still some ranchers up here belly-aching about the wolves in Yellowstone, but it's worked out pretty well," her mother said. "Soon as they start in about stock being killed, they get a check in the mail from the fund set up, and they keep their mouths shut."

"That's good, Mom. It'll work out in Colorado, too, but it may take some time." Like forever.

"You just keep doing what you think is right, Brigitte."

What you think is right. She hung up and thought about

that. The reintroduction was right, she was sure of that, but was her ill-conceived plan of spying right? Was deceiving Steve right?

She got dressed up and went to the office party. No sense staying home alone and moping.

The room at Dale's was decorated with Christmas wreaths and red and green crepe paper and balloons. There was a sprig of mistletoe hung over the doorway, and some of the guys insisted on kissing every female who walked under it.

Mac was dressed up like Santa Claus, but Brigitte could tell who he was because of the way his ears stuck out. "Glad you made it," he boomed. "Merry Christmas!"

Almost everyone drank too much, got too loud. Brigitte had a couple of drinks, and the alcohol succeeded in bolstering her mood. She knew it was only temporary, but she'd take anything she could get.

Hal Franklin and his wife were there, and so was Millie. Most of the office staff were there, too, with spouses or significant others. Only a few were single, like Brigitte, but she refused to think about that.

Eric Hanson, the lab technician, the one who'd done the cow autopsies, was one of the single men, and he'd had too much to drink.

"Give me a kiss," he said, pulling her to a spot under the mistletoe.

"Come on, Eric."

"Nope, you don't get away until I get a kiss. It's Christmas, for God's sake."

Dutifully Brigitte gave him a peck on the cheek.

"No, not like that. C'mon, where's that fire!" He grabbed her and bent her over backward and gave her a sloppy, rum-scented kiss. Everyone applauded.

Brigitte tried to laugh it off, but the feeling of Eric's mouth on hers was offensive. What was wrong with her?

Last summer she'd thought Eric was great, a possible date even. Now everyone but Steve was wrong.

There was a sumptuous buffet and champagne and funny little presents. Mac stood up at his place after dinner and gave a short speech, his Santa beard lopsided, then he handed out the Christmas bonuses. The atmosphere was all light and cheery, everyone happy, looking forward to the holiday, to family visits, kids home from school, turkey dinners and Christmas trees and presents. It all seemed irrelevant to Brigitte, though, the holiday cheer and all these people who were partying so hard.

Miles away in Sweetwater, Steve was... What was he doing? Eating dinner with the girls? Was he thinking of her? Did he care?

And farther up in the mountains was the wolf pack, warm in their thick fur coats, hunting, romping. Safe, she prayed.

But Brigitte played the role, smiling and joking, wishing everyone Merry Christmas, answering a thousand questions.

"Yes, it's a nice town. Small but friendly. I've been working in a minimart... No, I'm not sure when I'll be done up there. After Christmas. Maybe sooner... I haven't got a clue who did it. No one seems to."

The next day Brigitte drove downtown. She still had a couple of Christmas presents to buy, for Jeannie and Heather, which she hadn't been able to do when they'd been with her. She drove past the state capitol and imagined it at night with all the thousands and thousands of Christmas lights outlining the entire building. The whole city was festooned with decorations; the streets were full of shoppers.

It was cold and clear, and there was only a little leftover snow in shadowed places. Denver rarely had a white Christmas, but everyone always hoped it would happen. Weathermen on television vied with one another to forecast the odds of snow. Of course, up in the mountains it was different, and Brigitte wondered if it were snowing there.

She parked at the Tabor Center and walked along the Sixteenth Street Mall, with its shuttle buses and festive atmosphere and Christmas carols piped out onto the streets.

She racked her brain, trying to come up with small gifts for the girls, just mementos, nothing Steve could object to. Even if he never spoke to her again, she wanted to let the girls know she cared. She had some ideas, because she'd seen what they'd liked on their last shopping trip.

Finally she chose a gift pack of stylish socks for Jeannie, and agonized over a set of lotions and bubble bath in a fragrance bar for Heather. She finally decided on citrus.

Sunday morning dawned gray, with bleak skies. The forecast was for snow showers. Brigitte sipped coffee and stared out at the granite sky that backlit the jagged snow-capped mountains just to the west of Denver. Clouds blew in, obscuring a peak, then trailing on to hide another, tattered ghosts traveling on the west wind.

She sat in her apartment, surrounded by familiar things, looking out over familiar landscape, and everything in her was drawn back to Sweetwater.

STEVE COULDN'T help it; he stopped by Locals Corner on Sunday morning. It had been a week, and he'd avoided town like the plague, unable to face Brigitte, to see her in her new role as a spy for the feds. He knew he should have been able to confront her with her perfidy, but he couldn't. He called himself a coward, and lots of other names, too, but he kept returning to "stupid." He should have figured it out without Ben Garrett having to tell him. What a fool he was, suckered by a woman, seduced and betrayed. An old, old story.

He'd carried on myriad conversations with Brigitte over the last week, all in his head. In those conversations he was in turn furious, coldly superior, ironic, offhand, hard. In his heart he was sore, pathetically wounded. Even the girls noticed.

"Dad, where's Brigitte?" Jeannie asked all week. "Can't she come over?"

"She's busy," he always replied.

Even Heather mentioned her. "Did you like her dress, Dad? We helped her pick it out."

"It was very nice," he answered. Nice. It had been beautiful, prim and sexy at the same time, the blue reflected in her eyes, the skirt swirling about her legs.

Heather cocked her head and regarded him. "Did you have a fight?"

"What would we fight about?" he said, irritated. "We hardly know each other."

But Heather gave him a knowing look. "Well, then, how come you haven't called her?"

"I'm busy, kiddo."

He pulled up at the gas tanks in front of Locals Corner and got out to fill his truck. He was nervous. What if she were inside? What if he had to talk to her, face-to-face? She must be wondering why he hadn't called her all week. Maybe she was mad and would give him the cold shoulder. Maybe she'd ask why he hadn't called, and he'd have to come up with an answer. None of it mattered, though, not even what she'd done. He couldn't wait any longer; he had to see her.

"Hey there, stranger," Bess said when he went in to pay. She must have noted his furtive glances around the store, because she said, "Brigitte's not here."

He tried to appear casual. "Oh. Day off?"

"She's been off since Friday, and to tell the truth, I haven't seen her."

He grunted something in answer, paid for his gas and

started to leave. At the door, Bess's voice stopped him short. "Don't you think you two better have a chat?"

He didn't answer, went right out the door, the bell dinging behind him, and drove away. At the edge of town he did a quick U-turn, spurting gravel from under his wheels, and drove straight back to Brigitte's cabin. The door was locked, her car gone. He inquired about her at the office and was told that she'd left on Friday but that she hadn't checked out.

"When will she be back?" he asked.

Nobody knew.

He drove out to the ranch frustrated, hurting like hell. A part of him despised her for being a lying sneak—the rest of him ached for her. And now he couldn't even find her.

Where was she? Why hadn't she told anyone where she was going?

He was turning into his own driveway when the thought hit him like a sledgehammer. Could something have happened to her? It occurred to him that if the Garretts knew about her, everyone else did, too. Sure, Ben had said he'd let Steve handle her, but could the Garretts—or someone else—have gotten tired of waiting, done something on their own? Threatened her, chased her away?

Once again he swung the wheel of the truck around and drove straight to the Garretts' ranch. Knocking on the door, he thought of what he was going to say, and when Audrey let him in, he asked brusquely where Ben was.

"In the office," she said. "Is there…?"

But he was already striding across the floor, pulling open the door.

"Well, howdy, Steve," Ben said, surprised, turning in his chair.

"Where's Brigitte?" he blurted out, irrational anger filling him.

"Brigitte?"

"Yeah, you know, the only goddamn Brigitte around here."

"How in blazes would I know where she is?" Ben asked. "Isn't it a lot more likely you'd know that?"

"She's gone," Steve said between clenched teeth.

"Good."

"No one knows where she is."

"Probably hightailed it back to Denver when you told her you knew who she worked for," Ben said, sneering.

"I didn't tell her," Steve said tightly. "She doesn't know."

Ben looked at him, bemused. "I'll be damned," he finally said. "You've got it worse than I figured."

"I don't have any damn thing, Ben. I was going to tell her today, but she's gone."

"Good riddance."

Hot anger filled him. At Ben? At Brigitte? He wasn't sure which. He turned on his heel, then spun back. "And you tell that son of yours to treat my daughter with respect, Ben. Or I'll have his hide!"

Ben grinned. "You are in a state, Slater."

"Oh, for God's sake," Steve said in disgust, striding out of Ben's office.

Chris and Jim were there, coming in for lunch. They both were muddy, looked like they'd been out riding. "Hi, Steve," Chris said. Jim doffed his hat.

But Steve shouldered past them, glowering, silent, and left the Garretts' house.

He drove home too fast, furious at himself, at Ben Garrett, at her. When, if, he got his hands on her, he was going to throttle her, give her what-for. Then the image of her flew into his head—her white skin, her long legs, the silky, hot feel of her under his hands, her face glowing with passion, her smile that made his stomach roll over, her voice that purred like a cat, full of pleasure, his name on her lips.

He swore aloud, mad at himself and her and everyone else. And the worst thing of all, the thing that had him writhing internally, was that he couldn't find her. No one knew where she was. She was gone, had disappeared, leaving no track, so he couldn't even vent his anger on her.

When Steve got home, he called Information in Denver and asked for Brigitte Hartman, wondering whether he was going out of his mind. He tapped his fingers, impatiently waiting for the computerized voice to give him the number, which he scrawled on the pad by the phone.

He stared at the number for a long time; then he dialed it carefully and listened to the phone ring in his ear. There was a click and his heart jumped. An answering machine came on, and her voice: "This is Brigitte. I'm unable to come to the phone, but if you'll leave your number, I'll return your call." Then a beep and silence. He listened for a moment, then put the receiver down.

Where was she, damn it? Where in hell was she?

BRIGITTE ARRIVED back in Sweetwater at six in the evening, and at seven there was a knock on her door. She couldn't imagine who it could be, unless it was Edie Zimmer with some messages for her.

She'd barely turned the knob when her door was pushed open so hard she had to back up a step. She drew in her breath—Steve.

He came in and stood there, looming over her, his brows drawn in a thick black line, a muscle ticking in his jaw. She could feel the anger emanating from him—and something else behind it. It occurred to her briefly that she should be afraid.

Then, before she could say a word, he lashed out at her. "Where in hell have you been?"

She blinked, gathering herself. He looked like a bomb about to go off. "I was in Denver," she said.

He swore at her, his dark eyes flashing, and she thought for a crazy instant that he was going to strike her. But instead he threw his hat on the bed and grabbed her arm, pulling her against his chest. He swore at her again and then groaned. His head came down and his mouth covered hers. He kissed her with a kind of desperate passion, as if she were the last woman and he the last man on earth.

It shocked her at first; then the hot, slow burn began inside her belly. It was Steve kissing her, his hands, his body, his breath inside her, his tongue curling over hers. He wanted her, he was with her, he'd come to her. He was there, and nothing mattered but his closeness, his questing mouth and her terrible, glorious need. No time for questions or reasons. He was there.

They broke apart for a minute, but only long enough for her to pull her heavy sweater over her head, for him to shrug quickly out of his jacket and shirt. Then he was fumbling with her belt, the button on her jeans, the zipper. By then their mouths were clinging, and Brigitte felt the cold wall at her back. Her knees were buckling, and she wrapped one foot around the back of his legs as he reached behind her, his hand snaking down between her underwear and flesh. Little shock waves shot up her belly.

"Oh, Steve," she breathed against his mouth.

They kept right on kissing, even as he unhooked her bra and she shed it like an unwanted skin onto the floor. He put both hands on her breasts, and she moaned. Then his head bent, and he kissed each one, cupping it, whispering against her, "I'm sorry if I hurt you. I'm sorry."

Brigitte held his head to her breasts, felt ripples of excruciating delight as his teeth caressed her nipples. She didn't know how long she could wait. She wound her fingers tightly in his thick, dark hair and moaned again. "Steve, oh, Steve."

He picked her up then and laid her on the bed, stared

down at her as he unbuckled his belt. She shrugged off her pants and underwear, her body trembling, aching. When he, too, was naked, for a long moment he stood above her, drinking her in, his eyes still dark and flashing. Never had she wanted a man this way; never had she known such urgency from deep, deep inside.

He lay on top of her, supporting his weight on his elbows, and she opened to him. He held her gaze and then thrust inside her, and she cried out shamelessly, her whole body gripping him to her. He thrust again and she reached her climax, shocked at the wild abandon of her body. And then he, too, shuddered above her and they kissed, long and deep, their sweat-slicked bodies locked together.

For a long time after their lovemaking neither said a word. Fear boiled up inside her as she remembered the look in his eyes when he pushed his way into the cabin.

He knows. Somehow he knows, she thought. But he couldn't. Impossible. He'd never make love to her if he knew. He'd been angry, sure, but angry that she'd run off to Denver without a word.

Brigitte rolled on her side and put a hand on his chest, her fingers sifting through the dark mat of hair. He was so quiet, spent, his hands behind his head, his stare fixed on the ceiling. Now was the time to tell him everything. Now, when all he had to do was look in her eyes to see how much she loved him. *Do it,* her mind commanded. *Tell him.*

He turned his head toward her. "I didn't…hurt you?" he asked.

"No, of course not."

"Mmm," he said, his gaze holding hers, but there was something there, something hidden in those dark depths.

He kissed her then, and his hands came from behind his head to pull her against him and eventually on top of him.

She laughed lightly. "I'll squash you."

"Never," he said, his mouth moving over hers in a kiss

that deepened, and she could feel him against her thigh, his hardness, and a wave of pleasure rolled inside her.

Steve aroused her with a hand between them, his fingers slipping into her warmth. And then she positioned herself astride him and they were one again, moving in the timeless rhythm of love. He watched her above him, his hands spanning her waist, guiding her, helping her until they were both panting and gasping and he quickly eased her down onto her back again and entered her, pushing to the hilt of her womanhood, again and again until they both cried out.

With Steve still on top of her, she soon drifted into an exhausted, spent sleep. She awoke sometime later. He was next to her, and she smiled a dreamy smile.

At midnight she awoke with a start. Was she alone? She switched on the bedside lamp, peered, blinking, into the light. "Steve?"

There was no answer. She sat up straight, trying to orient herself. But he was gone.

BRIGITTE DROVE OUT to the ranch the following afternoon. Heather and Jeannie's presents sat on the car seat next to her, beautifully wrapped. Even if Steve threw her out after she confessed today, he couldn't begrudge her these small gifts to the girls.

She was going to confess. She would have told him last night—she knew that in her heart—but he'd slipped out. She still couldn't quite comprehend that but decided he hadn't wanted to wake her. There was no other rational explanation. If Steve knew the truth, he never would have made love to her. Twice.

She looked at her watch. It was almost 4:00 p.m. Already the sky was darkening in the east. December twenty-second, she thought. The shortest, darkest day of the year, a perfect day to bare her soul to Steve.

She turned into his long drive and thought she saw lights

on in the house. But when she got there, it was obvious his truck was gone. Well, maybe the girls were home.

She turned the engine off and got out, presents in her arms. Steve's dogs ran up, both barking, their tails wagging. "Down, you two beasts," she said, heading toward the side door that led into the mudroom and kitchen.

Arms full, she knocked and waited and, finally, when there was no reply, she maneuvered the packages so she could turn the knob.

"Hello!" she called out. "Heather! Jeannie! Hello!"

Still no answer. They were all gone, then, probably on errands. She'd wait. If she left now she might never again get up the nerve to tell him. As it was, this had taken her all day, not to mention a push from Bess.

"You told that man your secret yet?" Bess had asked that morning.

"Ah, not yet."

"Well, damnation, honey, you best tell him, because I'm bursting at the seams to find out myself."

"You won't be," Brigitte had muttered darkly.

But Bess had assured her that nothing she could have done or said would change her opinion. "I like you, honey. You're good people."

"We'll see" was Brigitte's grim prediction.

Right now she stood in the kitchen and glanced around. The sink was full of dishes, and two cereal bowls sat on the table with corn flakes glued to their sides. She wanted to take them over to the sink and run water in them, do the dishes. But it wasn't her place.

She shrugged off her parka and decided to put the presents under the tree in the living room. Then she'd wait in there. But once she'd switched on the lights and arranged the gifts beneath the tree, an unforeseen sadness took hold of her. After she told Steve, it was all going to be over. She'd never sit in this cozy room again, never laugh with

Jeannie or wonder what words she could use to comfort Heather. She'd certainly never look into Steve's eyes or feel the hardness of his body against her again. It was all her doing. She could have confided in him from the very start. If she had...

But she hadn't. And now it was too late.

She stood in the middle of the room and stared at the Christmas tree, its lights beginning to blur in her vision. *Fool,* she whispered.

Abruptly Brigitte spun on her heel, ready to flee. She wasn't going to wait here. She'd telephone him tonight. What did it matter if she told him in person or over a telephone line?

And that's when she saw it.

It was thrown over the back of a chair that sat by the door. A sheepskin coat.

Brigitte froze, staring, trying to fit her mind around the actuality of it. A sheepskin coat. But she'd never seen Steve in one. Well, maybe, she surmised, this was someone else's coat. Maybe...

Oh, come on! her mind screamed at her. It was so painfully obvious. The coat was his. He wore that Buck knife. The two big-pawed dogs running around out front were Steve's. Forget the blond hairs. They could have come from anywhere.

Without realizing it, Brigitte had moved to stand over the chair. She reached out hesitantly and touched the coat, feather light.

"Oh, dear God," she breathed. Not Steve. This was all a mistake.

She picked the coat up tentatively, as if it might tell her something, and she saw the two big blotches on the inside of the arm—dark stains. Dark like blood.

A strangled gasp escaped her and she dropped the coat. *Auntie Mame!* her brain cried. *It's Auntie Mame's blood.*

She wanted to run. Every fiber of her ached to race out of the house. But she knew what she had to do.

Steeling herself, fighting the painful thudding of her heart, she went to the kitchen and found a pair of shears in a drawer, a plastic bag in another one. She went back to the living room, took a ragged breath and cut some of the woolly fibers from the inside of the coat, dropping them with shaking hands into the bag. Then she tried to scrape flakes of the dried blood from the inside of the sleeve. It was difficult, but she got a sampling. The edge of the shears left a long, white mark on the tanned hide; she couldn't help that. It ran through her mind that a forensic pathologist might not be able to do a thing with the blood and fibers. On the other hand, surely the wool had been treated or dyed with specific chemicals. Perhaps every manufacturer used his own brands. And if the blood was from a wolf…

She sealed the bag, then stuffed it into her pocket and checked the label on the sheepskin coat before draping it over the chair again. Morelands, made in England, it read.

Oh, please, she cried silently, *don't be a match.*

Brigitte never knew how she got out of the house and into her car. She really only became aware of her surroundings when she was halfway back to Sweetwater. Her thoughts were whirling. *It can't be Steve. No.* Then she'd flush with anger and pain. It was him. He was nothing more than a cowardly liar. *Damn you, Steve.* She needed to get to a phone and talk to Mac.

She drove and thought about the wolf pack and the danger they were in, and how soon, very soon, that danger would end. They had their man now. There couldn't be any doubt left. She wouldn't sit on this, either, not for a second. No way.

But back in her cabin the minutes dragged by, the hours, and she didn't call Mac. She told herself it was too late, she'd wake him. She'd call first thing in the morning, express mail the samples and close this case. She would do it, by God!

But even as Brigitte swore to herself that she was going to bust Steve, she wondered if she could really do it. There were no truths anymore. Maybe there never had been.

CHAPTER FIFTEEN

ON THE EVENING of December twenty-third, the weather forecasters in Denver called for eight to twelve inches of snow to fall overnight in the Flat Tops, even more in the high valleys of Summit County. Each network broadcast a warning. "A big Pacific front is coming our way, folks, and it looks like we'll have a white Christmas, after all. There's a lot of moisture in this one, and if you're traveling in the mountains, drive very carefully. Chains or adequate snow tires will be required over Loveland and Vail passes. The avalanche danger will increase significantly on west-facing slopes…"

The man saw the forecast and smiled to himself. He had the perfect chance—the snow would cover all his tracks. This incident would be the last straw, the wolves coming down this far, killing one more time not three miles from the house.

He waited until it was late, then pulled on his heavy, insulated parka, a hat with earflaps and work gloves. He patted the Buck knife he always carried in a sheath on his belt, then he went out into the storm, leaving the darkened house behind him.

The weather was too bad to use a horse, but he knew his tire tracks would be hidden under the snow, which was starting to stick, laying down a smooth white blanket on every surface. By morning it'd be so deep there wouldn't be a mark left to show where he'd been.

He took the two dogs with him, letting down the truck's

tailgate for them to jump in. He gave each one a pat, and they wriggled happily, not caring that snow covered their coats. "Good boys. We've got work to do tonight," he said.

His headlights tunneled through the thickly falling snow, opening up a path for him in the white wall, then closing behind him into utter darkness. He knew the way, though. It wasn't far to the field he wanted, where the full-grown steers ready for market were kept.

He had to stop the truck and get out to open two gates, and his tires plowed parallel furrows across the still-soft ground, but he knew they'd be covered up long before morning. He grinned.

When he reached the field, his headlights played on the huddled herd, their rough coats protecting them from the snow. They'd give him no trouble, being so used to people. Hell, they'd eat out of your hand—they knew who fed them.

He stopped the truck, kept it idling, lights on. Whistling to the dogs, he got his rope from the truck, shook it out into a loop and went to work.

When he finished, he was sweating. He wiped his knife on the snow and let the dogs go at the carcass for a time, standing there in the silent, dark field. The other cattle had spooked and run at the scent of blood. Snow fell straight down, big, wet flakes, landing with tiny taps on his Stetson brim, on his shoulders, on the trampled ground. It was snowing as if it'd never end; maybe there'd be more than a foot by morning.

Eventually he whistled his dogs into the back of the truck, got in and retraced his way across the fields toward home, the snow still falling hard, like an opaque curtain in front of him, his lights piercing the seemingly impenetrable barrier in twin beams, like eyes glaring through the storm.

This was good, he thought, squinting into the white-out. This was better than good.

BEN GARRETT SKIDDED to a stop in front of his barn, jumped out of his truck and hollered for his sons.

Dave was there, home on Christmas break, Jim was still up at the house and Chris came running from the feed barn at his father's bellows.

"Goddamn it!" Ben shouted. "There's another one dead! Up in the steer pasture!"

"What?" Chris said.

"Another animal down on the snow and half-eaten. Those damn wolves! This does it. I'm through fooling around! Some damn Christmas present this is!" He was red in the face, the veins swelling in his neck.

"Take it easy, Dad," Dave said. "You sure it was wolves?"

"Of course I'm sure! There it was, all torn apart, half-eaten, the snow trampled and bloody. Paw prints. What else could it be?" Ben took his hat off and slapped it against his thigh. "I'm calling Fish and Wildlife again. I don't care if it is Christmas Eve. They can just get their ignorant butts up here!"

"I don't believe this," Chris said.

"You'd better believe it, son," Ben spat out. He strode furiously across the yard to the house, yanking the door open, startling Audrey.

Jim was finishing breakfast.

"You hear that?" Ben yelled. "Another one of our cattle killed by wolves!"

"Oh, no," Audrey said.

"You sure it was wolves?" Jim asked.

"Why do you kids keep asking me that? 'Course I'm sure! Any fool can tell."

Jim went to the kitchen window and looked out. There

was only three inches of new, white snow on everything. "It wasn't covered with snow?" he asked in a flat voice.

"Hell no. The snow stopped early, I guess. A foot, my ass. 'Scuse me, Audrey, honey. Clear as day up there. Paw prints. I'm calling Fish and Wildlife."

"You sure you want to bug them on Christmas Eve? They probably aren't even there," Jim said.

"I'll bug them, all right. Even if I have to track them down at home. I've had enough!" Ben went into his office, furious, slamming the door behind him.

"Oh, dear," Audrey said. "This'll put him in such a mood. It'll ruin Christmas."

"Don't worry, Audrey. I've got an idea," Jim said, and he followed his father into the office.

They came out later and Ben was smiling. "Let's go get the other boys, see what they think."

"Okay, Dad."

They met in the barn, their breath pluming in the cold, the dogs sitting at their feet.

"So I figure I'll get a couple of my pals and we'll just go up there, track 'em and kill 'em," Jim said. "Shoot a deer, maybe. Lure 'em in. All we have to do is wait."

"It'll be cold as heck," Dave said. "And I think it's against the law."

"The law." Ben spat. "I spoke to Mac McCarthy, but he says there's no one working until after Christmas. Office is empty except for him and some bookkeeper. Can't send anyone up here till then. The law isn't a whole lot of help."

"I think it's a great idea, Jim," Chris said. "There's no one gonna fault you once they see what the pack did this time. It's too close for comfort."

"I don't know," Dave said doubtfully. "I think you should wait."

"Until what?" Jim said. "I'm going today. I'm not waiting for anymore goddamn government red tape."

"Atta boy," Ben said proudly. "I'd come, but I'm just too blasted old now. Dave? Chris?"

"Not me," Dave said. "I told you what I think."

"Listen, I'd do it, but I've got this date tonight. Big party. If I miss it, I'm dead meat. You understand," Chris said. "Maybe I can make it in a couple of days if you're still up there."

"Well, Jim can handle it," Ben said. "He'll get rid of those vermin for us."

Jim stood there in the cold and smiled. "I'll take care of 'em all right," he said. "Don't you worry, Dad."

"That's my boy," Ben said, slapping his son on the back. "I always knew you had guts. I'm real proud of you."

Jim smiled again, feeling as if he would burst with joy.

BRIGITTE SAT on the edge of her bed and stared at the plastic bag that lay on the rumpled spread. Everything in her demanded that she tell Mac about it, send it to Denver, maybe even drive it in herself. This was her job. She was paid, and paid well, to do it.

So why didn't she?

The fibers and dried blood samples weren't going to disappear. Either they'd match the evidence found during the autopsy on Auntie Mame or they wouldn't. Either Steve was guilty or he was in the clear. In her heart she'd never believe Steve Slater guilty of such a low deed, but her brain told her otherwise. She was staring at some pretty conclusive evidence.

Why? she cried silently. Why did it have to be Steve?

Brigitte didn't call Mac that Christmas Eve morning. Instead, she bundled up and walked to Locals Corner, where she was scheduled to work a few hours, most likely her last shift there.

It was busy. Bess had people lined up at the register, and

Brigitte tossed her coat in the storeroom and stepped in to help. But it was mindless work, and all she could think about was that bloodstained sheepskin coat.

At noon it slowed down in the store, and they were able to restock shelves and check invoices. "The last hurrah before the off-season," Bess said as she unfolded an invoice and eyed it. "Glad you made it in. It's always like this 'cause I'm closed tomorrow."

"Hmm," Brigitte said, preoccupied.

Bess counted six cases of motor oil stacked by the front door, checked them off on the invoice. "Why don't you spend tomorrow with me and Stan?" she asked. "It's a pretty quiet Christmas for us, but we sure do cook up a feast."

In the background, "Silent Night" played on the radio. Brigitte looked up from the cash register, where she was subtotaling the morning's credit-card receipts. "I can't, Bess," she said. "That's so sweet of you to ask, but I really can't."

"Uh-huh," Bess said. "You spending Christmas at the Slaters'?"

Brigitte felt her heart squeeze, and a sudden image of Steve flashed into her mind—Steve, smiling at her, tugging at the brim of his hat, his dark eyes resting on her. She was beginning to understand the meaning of a broken heart.

"Well, are you?" Bess said, and the image of Steve shattered like a broken glass in her head.

"I...uh, no, I'm not going to the Slaters'," Brigitte said.

"Well, if you don't mind my saying so," Bess went on, "you and Steve have got one helluva strange relationship going."

Brigitte stared at Bess from across the store, and she knew there was no point continuing the lie. Eventually everyone in Sweetwater was going to find out who she really was. And Brigitte wanted Bess to hear it from her own lips.

She took a breath. "Remember a while back when I told you there was something..."

"Do I ever," Bess said tartly. "Don't tell me you're going to spill the beans at last."

Brigitte smiled ruefully.

"Well? Let's hear it," Bess prompted.

And finally she confessed all. It was hard, the words tripping over one another as she spoke. Then a customer came in, browsed, paid for gas and finally left.

"Okay, go on," Bess said, her hands on her hips. "You're with U.S. Fish and Wildlife Service...."

Brigitte sighed. "That's right. And it was my brilliant idea to come up here and find out what was really going on."

"Undercover, so to speak."

"I'm sorry about that. I lied to a lot of people."

Bess shrugged. "If the end justifies the means, who am I to say it was wrong?"

"I don't know if it was wrong," Brigitte continued. "But it was sure wrong of me to get...close to Steve and his girls."

"He doesn't have any idea?"

Brigitte shook her head. "And what's worse is that Steve could very well be behind this whole thing."

"You mean...? Oh, no, Brigitte," Bess said. "That's not possible. Not Steve Slater. No way."

Then she told Bess about the sheepskin coat and the blood, his two big dogs, the knife he carried. "And he advocates getting rid of the pack, Bess. He's as against the reintroduction as anyone here."

"Well, I don't give a rat's butt what evidence you think you have, honey. You're barking up the wrong tree. I'd bet a year's net from the store that Steve's not the one."

Brigitte heard her loud and clear, and everything in her wanted to believe it. Ached to believe it. But the evidence… "I don't know," she finally said. "I'm as confused as I've ever been in my life over this whole thing."

"Get over it, honey. Talk to him. Tell him everything."

But Brigitte was shaking her head. "Someday… I don't know. The first thing I've got to do is have those fiber samples analyzed. Then…"

"You haven't done that?"

"No, I…"

"You don't believe he's guilty."

"I don't want to believe it," Brigitte was saying when the store suddenly seemed to fill up with customers. They never did get back to that conversation, though Brigitte ran Bess's words through her head a dozen times over the next hour. *Steve's not the one.*

Business finally slowed again in the early afternoon, and Brigitte punched out for what was to be her last shift ever. She was eternally grateful to Bess for her understanding and kindness, and they hugged when it was time for Brigitte to go.

"Now, I meant it when I said you're invited to Christmas with me and Stan, honey. If you're here in town, don't you dare spend tomorrow alone in that cabin. Promise?"

"I promise," Brigitte said. "And thanks, Bess. Thanks for being a friend and so understanding about everything."

But Bess only smiled and waved aside her gratitude. "It doesn't matter to me, honey. You're the best clerk I've ever had. If you ever need a job… Well, you're welcome anytime, you know that. And you stay in touch. Hear?"

"I will," Brigitte said, and they hugged again.

She walked back to the Whispering Pines, thinking about Bess's suggestion: *Tell him everything.* Bess was right. She owed Steve that much. Even if he was guilty as sin, she owed him.

She was still mulling that over when she opened her cabin door and a scrap of paper stuck between the door and the frame fluttered to the ground. She picked it up. "Call Mac," it read, and it was underlined twice.

Mac answered immediately. "It's happened again. A dead steer this time. On Garrett's ranch."

"Oh, God."

"It fits the pattern if someone up there's doing it. The time between each killing is getting shorter, just like one of those crazy serial killers."

"When?" she asked.

"Last night sometime. Ben Garrett found it early this morning. Like to have a fit on the phone. And you think it could be him doing it? I'll tell you, he put on a good act."

"I don't know," she said, thinking only of Steve, her gaze fixed on the bag that lay on the dresser now.

"I want you to get up there right away," Mac was saying. "You might see something. I told Garrett I couldn't send anyone up till after Christmas. Which is true. So you go on, get yourself to his place. And you can drop the undercover act if you want. You're out of there in a couple of days anyway, so it doesn't matter. Pull rank on them if you think it'll get results."

"Where did it happen?" she asked.

"Right on Garrett's ranch, real close to home."

"I'll go right now."

"Good luck, Brigitte. And by the way, Merry Christmas."

"Right," she said. "Merry Christmas." *The worst of my life,* she thought.

"Keep in touch."

She put on boots, a warm parka, gloves and a wool hat. Her stomach felt as if there were a ball of lead in it. This was it, she thought. This was the final confrontation.

Whatever she found up there, she wasn't going to lie to anyone anymore. It was time to end this mad charade.

She drove toward the Garretts' ranch, past the turnoff to Steve's place. What would she find up there? Steve's boot prints, his dogs' paw prints, his tire tracks?

She didn't even go to Ben's house, just bypassed it entirely, shifted into four-wheel drive and followed the fresh tire tracks past his barn, along the dirt road that led to his fields. She saw that the gates between fields were still open, which meant Ben had been in such a hurry, he hadn't bothered to get out and close them. The route was easy to follow because there were only three inches of new snow on the ground, and his tire tracks were like a neon sign directing her.

There it was. Ben's tracks ended, and just beyond them was a carcass, the trampled snow tinged pink.

She pulled up, stopped, took a good look at the area, then got out. Walking slowly, head down, she read the story left in the snow. She circled the carcass again, knelt on one knee to brush away the fresh snow, then looked away, across the fields, eyes unfocused, thinking hard.

She rose and felt the knowledge fill her. Her insides twisted with anger and fear and righteous indignation.

Whoever had done this had figured on all the evidence being covered by heavy snow. But he—Steve?—had miscalculated, or rather, the weather forecasters had, and there wasn't nearly enough snow to hide the signs that were so very, very clear.

There were two sets of tire tracks—Ben Garrett's fresh ones from that morning, and underneath them, barely concealed by last night's snow, another set that stopped at the same spot. There were men's footprints, dogs' paw prints—not wolves' huge six-inch pug marks—and a half-chewed carcass. Why hadn't Ben noticed the discrepancies?

Had he just been too damn mad or had he deliberately not mentioned them?

If it had been wolves, if it had been the pack, why weren't there any prints leading down from the mountains?

"Okay," she said out loud. What she had to do now was follow the tire tracks from last night, the half-covered ones, back to their source. If they turned out onto the highway they might be lost, mixed in with new tracks, plowed over. She'd just have to see. *Oh, God,* she thought. *Don't let them lead to Steve's.* But she was so terribly afraid they would.

Her heart pounding like a drum, she studied the old tracks, partly erased by this morning's new ones. Damn it, she'd driven over them herself, not knowing they were there. But they headed back the way she'd come, as clear as day once she knew what to look for.

She got in her Cherokee and turned around, driving back over her own tracks, watching the ground ahead so intently, her eyes watered. A few times she had to stop and get out, search for the old tracks, but she found them every time, and they followed the dirt road right back to the Garretts' barn.

She drove through the last open gate, across a field. They still led her on, two grooves in the sparse snow, the edges smoothed out, crisscrossed by Ben's newer tracks, by her own in places. But nevertheless leading inexorably on, around the corner of the hay barn, past the main barn, across the broad driveway to the place where all the Garretts' trucks were parked. There was Ben's mud-spattered truck, with its crisp new tracks, and there were the blurred tracks, leading to an older blue pickup. One of the Garretts' trucks.

She sat in her car, breathing hard, as if she'd run all the way from the fields. Lowering her head onto the steering wheel, she rested there for a time, her eyes closed, her insides roiling.

It wasn't Steve. That was all she could think. The thought filled her mind as wild relief flooded her. It wasn't Steve, it wasn't Steve, it wasn't Steve.

She lifted her head eventually, and a steely resolve filled her. Okay, it was one of the Garretts, but which one? Were they all in it together or was it only one of them?

It occurred to her to confront Ben right now, but she decided not to. Better to formulate a plan, definitely call Mac. He'd figure something out. Better not to go off half-cocked in her usual impulsive way, the way that'd gotten her into this situation in the first place. *Calm down, be logical,* she told herself. *Think.*

She drove back to town, trying to plan rationally, but all she could think was that it wasn't Steve. The jacket, the blood, there was another explanation for that. There had to be. She owed him an apology. The truth and an apology. And if he hated her, she deserved it.

She drove up to her cabin and parked. She was grinning like a fool, feeling better than she had in weeks. Maybe she'd burned her bridges with Steve, but at least he was innocent and her conscience was clear. Now she had to call Mac.

Merry Christmas, indeed!

She jumped out, thinking about what she had to tell Mac, figuring out how to prove which Garrett it was. Maybe a simple confrontation would work. *"We know one of you did it, and we're going to have to prosecute...."* She strode toward her door, and that was when she became aware of someone sitting on her front step. She stopped short and looked again, and the figure rose and spoke. "I've been waiting... Can I talk to you? I'm sorry, but I didn't know who else to go to or what to do, and Dad'll kill me 'cause

I hitched into town. He doesn't know, but I had to do something, and I waited and waited!''

"Heather," Brigitte breathed, "what on earth?" She unlocked and opened the door and pulled the girl inside. "What's wrong?"

"Everything's wrong!" Heather wailed. "Nobody understands...."

Brigitte pulled her hat and gloves off and threw them on a chair. "You must be frozen. Sit down. Want some hot chocolate?"

"No, no. You have to listen."

"Okay, sure." Brigitte sat down across from the obviously distraught girl. "Tell me what's happened."

Heather's face screwed up as if she were going to cry. "Dave came over this morning and..."

"Dave?"

"Dave Garrett," she sobbed.

"Oh, right."

"He brought me a Christmas present." She drew in a quavering breath. "Then he told me... He said his brother Jim and some of his friends are going up... It was about the dead steer this morning, and they were going up into the mountains to kill the wolves. They took guns and everything, and they..."

"Jim Garrett," Brigitte said.

"Yes, and two friends. They were on the phone all morning planning it, Dave said. All because of the dead steer."

"Oh, my God," Brigitte said, half to herself. She was filled with horror. This was what she'd feared all along—vigilante justice. And it was based on a lie. But of course Jim Garrett knew that—or maybe not. Maybe Ben had sent him to do the bloody deed, deliberately planning it all.

"I didn't know what to do!" Heather cried. "They can't shoot the wolves!"

"No, we can't let them," Brigitte said. "Does Steve… does your dad know?"

She shook her head, tears brimming in her eyes. "He was out feeding the stock. And he hates the wolves anyway. He wouldn't have let me come. He doesn't understand me at all! He doesn't know anything…."

Brigitte leaned forward and very slowly, very carefully, drew the young girl against her side. She gently whispered, "I'm glad you came to me. I'm glad you trust me, honey, and I do understand. Really I do. It will be okay now, I promise."

Heather looked up at her through red-rimmed eyes. "You've got to stop them!" she wailed. "Isn't that your job?"

Brigitte's heart kicked in her chest. "Wh-what?" she stammered.

"Your job. You're a Fish and Wildlife agent, aren't you?"

Brigitte was stunned. "How…how did you know that?"

"I heard Dad. He said it. He was really mad, but I'm not. I think it's good. They're all a bunch of jerks."

"Your father knows?" Brigitte breathed.

"Uh-huh." Heather sniffed.

Dear Lord, he knew. He knew who she was and hadn't said a word to her. And abruptly all the pieces fell into place: Ben Garrett's visit the morning after the dance, and Steve's change in behavior; his not phoning; his leaving her that night. His anger. He'd known all that time.

Brigitte leaned back against the chair and put a hand over her eyes, trying desperately to regain control. She couldn't let Heather see how upset she was—she couldn't involve the girl.

"What are you going to do?" Heather asked plaintively.

Brigitte cleared her throat. "I…I'm not sure. I have to think. Give me a second."

And as her mind whirled, trying to sort out what to do, she wondered what upset her more—the wolves' danger or Steve's knowing the truth about her and not saying a word. Not one single word.

CHAPTER SIXTEEN

By FOUR O'CLOCK Steve was really starting to worry. Heather had been gone the better part of the day, and even Jeannie didn't have any idea where she'd gone.

"Tell me again," Steve said at Jeannie's bedroom door. "She must have said something."

His daughter was sitting cross-legged on her down quilt, a half-wrapped present in front of her. "Jeez, Dad, you've asked me ten times. She didn't say a word. She, like, got her coat and left."

"Left for where? Did a car come, one of her friends or something?"

"No. I told you that. She just left. I guess she walked out to the road."

"You mean to meet someone? To hitchhike? What?"

"Da-a-ad. I don't know. While you were out with the herd, Dave came by and left her a present. After that she just left."

"Did she go with Dave? Maybe he was waiting outside for her."

"No," Jeannie said. "I told you. He drove off before she left."

"I don't get it," Steve muttered. "Where on earth would she go? It's Christmas Eve, for God's sake. Where would she go without telling someone or leaving a note?"

But Jeannie only shrugged and went back to her wrapping.

Steve went downstairs and searched the house for the

fourth time, looking for a note. He was getting more worried by the minute, all sorts of crazy scenarios running like a fast-action film through his head: Heather had run off with Dave; she'd gone hitchhiking to town for last-minute shopping and had been picked up by a maniac; she'd just flat-out run away.

"Damn," he said aloud, none of those things making sense.

It finally occurred to him to call the Garretts and talk to Dave—if Dave and his daughter hadn't run off together, he thought darkly.

He strode into the kitchen and was reaching for the wall phone when he heard tires crunching in the drive. His heart thudded, and he went to the kitchen door and yanked it open. He recognized the vehicle in a split second—it was Brigitte's Cherokee. And there were two people in it.

"Oh, boy," he muttered, recognizing Heather in the passenger seat. Relief flooded him, then hot anger.

The two females got out of the car, and he met them halfway to the house. Both looked upset, but he was so mad at Heather, he barely noticed.

"How could you just take off like that?" he thundered. "Without so much as a note! Goddamn it, young lady, don't you have any idea how worried I was?"

"Steve," Brigitte said softly, "please. Let me explain. Once you hear..."

"I don't want to hear a thing out of you," he said between clenched teeth. But even as he vented his anger on her, Steve felt that betraying tightness in his groin. He hated her right then, but not nearly as much as he hated himself for still wanting her so damn much.

Brigitte was staring at him. She took a deep breath and said, "Steve, I have to talk to you. I don't have time to apologize or explain or anything, but you've got to listen. I need your help."

Steve glared at her. "Go on inside," he said to his daughter without taking his gaze from Brigitte. "Go on, Heather. Now."

"But, Dad, you have to help Brigitte! You..."

"Get inside."

"Dad."

"Now!"

Finally she did, stalking away, her dark eyes brimming with tears.

"That was unnecessary," Brigitte said.

"Don't you presume, you of all people, to tell me what's right or wrong."

"You...hate me," she said in a choked voice. "I know that. And I don't blame you, Steve, but you have to put all that aside and hear me out. It's about the wolf pack...."

"Oh, really?" he said, sarcasm dripping from his voice.

But she waved that aside. "Let me start at the beginning. It was this morning when Ben Garrett telephoned Mac in Denver and..."

"I don't give a damn about any of this."

"Please," she implored. "Just listen." She went on to tell him how Ben had lost another steer, how she'd gone up to the site and followed the tire tracks directly back to the Garrett ranch. Then she'd telephoned Denver.

"You expect me to believe any of this?" he asked.

"Yes, you have to."

"The hell I do. Listen, lady, you'd better leave."

"Wait, Steve..." She swallowed, and he could see she was trying to get a grip on herself. If he let down for a second, he'd be feeling sorry for her.

"There's a lot of evidence," she said. "Boot prints—a man's boot prints around the carcass. Barely covered by the snow. And dog prints. He thought everything would be covered—don't you see?—but it didn't snow as much as it was supposed to."

"So what? Ben was up there."

"He didn't get out of his truck—that's what he told Mac. Steve, believe me, it's true. Someone, one of the Garretts, was killing the cattle. Your cattle, too."

"Bull."

She shook her head, her eyes begging him, those beautiful blue eyes, red-rimmed now, miserable. "And the lab reports. The autopsies showed blond hairs and knife marks on the cattle. We know they weren't killed by wolves. Don't you understand?"

"What I understand is that you lied to me, and I have a real hard time believing anything you say."

"Leave me out of it. Look at the evidence."

"I can't leave you out of it," he shot back.

"Oh, God."

"Thank you for bringing Heather home," he said stiffly.

"Please, Steve, don't make this mistake. One of the Garretts has killed cattle and blamed it on the wolves and then killed a wolf. Those are criminal acts. And now Jim's gone up into the Flat Tops with some friends to hunt down the pack, and we have to stop them," she said desperately.

"We?"

"Yes, you have to help me."

Steve held up a hand. "That's enough," he said. "You just don't get it."

"Dad," Heather called out from the house, "it's the truth. Dave told me. Jim's going up to hunt the pack. He's going to shoot them!"

"Be quiet, Heather," he said.

"Dad."

"Please, Steve…"

"Go back to Denver, Brigitte. Go back to whatever twisted, crazy thing you do. Just get out of my life."

He saw tears spring to her eyes, and she bit her lower lip. "Steve, I…"

He held up his hand again, as if to ward her off. "Just go, Brigitte. You've done enough harm here."

"Please," she said, wiping away her tears with angry bravado. "I'm asking for your help. We have to stop Jim! There isn't time for anyone from Denver to get here, and I can't do this alone."

"Sorry," he said. "I don't aid and abet the enemy."

She looked at him incredulously. "You can't stand by like this and let Jim slaughter the pack. I know you, Steve. You won't let this…"

"Well, I guess you don't know me at all," he said, and then he did the hardest thing he'd done since he'd buried Leslie. He turned on his heel and left Brigitte standing there alone in the gathering dusk. He strode to his door, pulled it open, went in and closed it, shutting her out of his life. Heather and Jeannie were there in the mudroom; both were sobbing. He took a long breath and leaned against the door. *Merry Christmas,* he thought bitterly.

BRIGITTE WAS SHAKING from head to foot by the time she got to the end of Steve's drive. She stopped and gripped the steering wheel, put her forehead on it and cried. She'd lost him. She'd lost Steve and she'd probably lose the wolf pack. By the time Mac sent help from Denver, it was going to be too late.

She could call the local sheriff. But everyone knew he was on the side of the ranchers and resented the federal interference in his county. He wouldn't believe her, not in a million years, and even if he did, he'd delay until it was too late.

She dragged her head up off the wheel and thought for an instant that she could turn around and beg Steve again to help. Maybe he'd calmed down. But she knew in her heart he was never going to help her.

She drew in a quavering breath. It was hopeless. There was no way to stop Jim Garrett.

And then suddenly it came to her. Maybe there was a way. Now that the Garretts had been exposed, maybe they could be stopped. It was worth a try.

She spun the wheel and took off in the opposite direction from town, toward Ben Garrett's spread. If she could put the fear of God into just one of those men—the fear of a huge fine and plenty of jail time—maybe someone over there would see the light.

She drove too fast along the snow-packed country road, almost losing control on a steep, descending curve. She looked at the clock in the car. Oh, God, there were only a couple of hours of daylight left. Somewhere up in the high country those men were tracking the wolf pack, maybe baiting it. Maybe they'd already found it.

But she couldn't afford to think that. She had to believe she could reach them in time. She wasn't absolutely sure of Jim Garrett's guilt, but even if he was the one who'd done all this, she was sure the men with him didn't know. They could be stopped. Once they knew the truth, they couldn't possibly go on with their hunt. All she had to do was reach them in time.

She drove to the Garrett ranch house, practically right to the same spot she'd been that morning. It seemed like years ago.

She got out and steeled herself, went to the front door, lifted her hand and knocked. *Please let this work,* she prayed.

Ben's wife, Audrey, answered the door. She turned white when she saw who was there.

"Is Ben home?" Brigitte asked, holding her gaze.

"He's, ah, well, yes. Sure. Won't you come in? It's Miss Hartman, isn't it?"

Brigitte nodded and stepped inside. From the vestibule

she could see into the living room, a lovely big room with comfortable-looking leather furniture, a Turkish rug, a big stone hearth. A tall Christmas tree sat in a corner, presents all neatly arranged beneath it. Brigitte could smell a holiday ham cooking.

"I'll, ah, get my husband," Audrey said, and she disappeared down a hallway.

Brigitte stood there in her heavy parka and closed her eyes for a moment, gathering herself.

It was only a short time before Ben appeared with Chris and Dave on his heels. He led Brigitte into the living room, offered her a seat, which she declined.

"If you've come here to tell me that Fish and Wildlife is going to send someone to investigate my dead steer, well, young lady, it's too damn late." Ben, too, remained standing, folding his arms across his heavy chest.

"That's not why I'm here," she said, looking from father to son and back. "I'm here because if someone doesn't stop your son from killing the wolves, he'll not only face one huge fine, but I guarantee that the government will put him behind bars for a long, long time."

"Oh, really," Ben said, a muscle working furiously in his jaw. "After I've had valuable animals killed and you've done nothing? You're bluffing, and it isn't working."

Brigitte stared at him. Bluffing? Was it possible Ben Garrett had no idea that someone from this very ranch had killed the cattle? No way.

"Look," she said. "Maybe you don't realize it, but the autopsy reports are in from the last steer killed and the wolf that was left dead on the road. There's no doubt anymore. Humans are responsible."

"Lady, you're nuts."

"Listen, Mr. Garrett, we're talking about a federal crime. I have evidence, empirical evidence that someone on this ranch killed the cattle to blame it on the wolves and that the same person killed the wolf."

Ben laughed harshly. "I saw the dead cattle, Miss Hartman. You can't tell me that...."

"You should've looked closer, then." And she went through the whole list again: the boot prints, the dogs, blond hairs, knife marks, tufts of sheepskin wool from a coat.

"I can't believe that's what my taxes pay for—some nerdy guy in a lab finding blond hairs on a dead wolf," Ben said. "Now, if you don't mind, we have a nice dinner ready for Christmas Eve."

"Mr. Garrett, please." She was growing more desperate by the second. First Steve and now Ben Garrett. Why wouldn't they see the truth? "There were tire tracks leading from the dead steer to your place."

"Sure, I drove up there. So what?"

"No, yours were there, but I saw another set made last night, covered with new snow." She was aware of Audrey, who had been standing behind Ben all the time. The woman made a strangled noise, but Brigitte was so intent on Ben, she didn't pay any attention to her. "Whoever killed that steer thought the tracks would be hidden by snow, but they guessed wrong."

"Dad, should I show her out?" Chris asked.

Brigitte whirled on him. "Did you do it, Chris? You sure talk big enough."

"Holy cow, she's gone off the deep end," Chris said. "Some kind of monthly problem."

"Chris!" Audrey said.

"Which one of you did it?" Brigitte asked. If reason didn't work, maybe confrontation would. She had to do something. Time was running out. "Did you do it, Mr. Garrett? You've mouthed off plenty, too. Tell me if you did. It'll go easier on you."

Ben puffed up his chest and stuck his jaw forward pugnaciously. "You have some goddamn nerve coming into my house, on Christmas Eve no less, and blaming me, Miss City-Slicker Hartman. Lying all these weeks, putting one over on poor Steve."

"Ben," Audrey admonished.

Somehow Brigitte believed Ben. He couldn't be that good an actor. She believed his indignation, and she sure as heck believed his dislike for her.

"Come up with me to your dead steer," she challenged. "I'll show you."

"Good God, woman, the sun's been on the snow all day. You couldn't tell a thing up there anymore. You'd be wasting my time," he said scornfully.

Damn, he was right. "Let's go find Jim, talk to him," she tried. "Maybe he did it."

Chris laughed.

"So it was you," she said, turning to Chris. "I thought so."

"It wasn't me—" Chris chuckled "—though I sure wish it had been. I'd like you after me. Vicious little thing, ain't you? Like one of them pit bulls."

"Shut up, Chris," Ben said.

"So it must be Jim, then," she said. "Did you know? Did you know what he's been doing this whole year, Mr. Garrett?"

"Jim," Chris said scornfully.

"Jim wouldn't do that," Ben said.

"Then why is he up there hunting the wolves?"

"Because they're killing my cattle, that's why!"

"No, they're not, Mr. Garrett," Brigitte said coolly.

"I think you'd better leave," he said.

"Please, I need to find Jim. Won't you help me?" She felt so useless, unable to save the wolves, unable even to convince these men of what was really happening. It was like talking to a stone wall.

"Leave or I'll call the sheriff," Ben said, standing in the middle of his living room.

Brigitte's shoulders slumped. She'd failed. She could try to find Jim on her own, but it'd be hit and miss. "Just tell me where he started from," she said. "I'll find him myself."

"Fat chance," Chris said.

"No," Ben said.

"I'll go anyway. I'll drive around to every trailhead in the area until I find their trucks."

"Good luck," Ben said, and he took her arm to lead her to the door.

"Wait."

Everyone stopped, a frozen tableau in the cheery room. Brigitte looked around, astonished. Audrey.

"Wait," Audrey said again in her soft voice.

"What the hell?" Ben asked.

Audrey looked at her feet. "Listen to her, Ben. What if she's right? What if Jim's up there killing the wolves and they really haven't done what you think? What if the wolves are innocent and Jim's a criminal?"

"What?" Ben asked, nonplussed.

"Shouldn't you try to find out? Ben, honey…"

Ben swore. "Audrey, stay out of this. You don't know what you're talking about."

"Ben, listen. She isn't making this up," Audrey said.

"How do you know she isn't?" Chris asked, but no one paid him the least bit of attention.

"Ben…" Audrey came around in front of him and put a hand on his arm. She stared straight into his eyes and said, "I saw Jim drive away last night. Late. I couldn't sleep. I was taking an aspirin and I…"

"Don't," Ben said hoarsely.

"I have to. You can see that, honey. I saw him drive away in his truck, and I heard him come back."

"No," Ben said.

"Yes," she whispered.

"She's as crazy as the other one, Dad," Chris said.

"No she's not." It was the first time Dave had uttered a word. "I saw Jim, too. Last night. And it's happened before. He slips out late.... The next morning there've been dead cattle. Dad," Dave said, his voice breaking, "I think it's been Jim all along."

Silence filled the room like a living entity. It surrounded all of them, pressing heavily, filled with tension.

"No," Ben said again, but there was doubt in his voice now. "It can't be."

"Let's find out," Brigitte said. "Before it's too late, before he gets into even more trouble. Mr. Garrett...Ben," she tried. "At least tell me where he's gone."

"Dad, don't tell her," Chris said.

"Ben..." Audrey said.

"I have equipment in the back of my car—a flashlight, extra down vest, gloves," Brigitte said, grabbing the initiative. "I'm going up to the Flat Tops, and I'm going to try to find Jim. If you have any idea where he's headed, I need to know. If I can stop him, well, it'll be that much less trouble he's in."

Ben sank into a chair. He looked dazed.

"We need to hurry," Brigitte said.

Ben sat there like a stone. His expression was tortured, and all Brigitte could think was that he really hadn't known. It had been Jim all along, and no one had known.

"I'll do it," Ben finally said in a strained whisper.

"No. Look, Dad, you're too..." Chris began.

Ben swore and rose to his feet, pushing Chris aside. "Jim is my boy, goddamn it, and I'll do what I have to do to help him!"

"Dad, are you sure…?"

But Ben was already heading to get his things.

A half hour later, Brigitte and Ben reached the trailhead where Jim and three of his buddies from town had left their vehicle and gone on foot into the Flat Top Wilderness. Brigitte got out of her Cherokee and lifted the back hatch, reaching for the day pack she always kept with her. Inside it were two water bottles, extra gloves and socks, matches, two candy bars, a down vest and a big flashlight. Ben had also brought along extra mountain gear, and he shrugged on his own pack, his face drawn and tight. She realized they'd barely spoken a word the entire way to the trailhead, Ben only giving directions when absolutely necessary. He was here for one reason only: to keep his son from ruining his entire life.

Brigitte closed the hatch and slipped on her own pack, then looked up at the sky. "In an hour it's going to be pitch-black," she said.

"If they've gone where I think they have," Ben said, "we'll be there in an hour."

Brigitte nodded.

Following the tracks of the four men was a snap. First of all, it had snowed four or five inches at this altitude last night. But secondly, the men had followed a well-known path called South Cliff Trail. If Ben was right, they would run across his son and the others where this trail intersected another one. Supposedly the site was a deer and elk hunter's dream, and Ben, though he didn't say so aloud, must have figured his son would try to lure the wolf pack into the ravine that ran below the two trails. From what Brigitte had gathered at the Garrett ranch, if the men were unsuccessful here, they were equipped to spend a couple of nights and could move on.

Ben was in the lead as they wound their way along a ridge and then began to climb up through a pine forest.

Mostly the going was easy, the trail pretty trampled down by the men ahead of them. Their feet crunched in the newly tracked snow, and their breath came out in heavy white plumes.

"Doing okay?" Brigitte asked Ben, but he only turned for a moment and shot her a dark look, then went on doggedly.

Okay, she thought. *So much for pleasantries.* And the truth was, she was in no mood to talk herself. At any moment she expected to hear gunshots, and it crossed her mind more than once that they might already be too late.

There was something else sitting heavily on her mind as she followed Ben's lead into the high country. Steve. It really was over between them. All her fears had come true. She asked herself a dozen times what would have happened if she'd told him the truth from the beginning. Or, at least, before they'd... But she hadn't. And it was water under the bridge. She'd just have to get over Steve Slater.

It grew dark quickly. The sky turned deeper shades of gray until it was the color of slate. In the west there was a short bloom of magenta and then darkness fell over the mountains.

They switched on their flashlights.

"Shouldn't we be getting near that ravine?" Brigitte asked.

Ben stopped and swung toward her. "We'll be there soon enough," he said. "And I'll tell you something else. You better hope you're right about my son being responsible for the dead cattle. You better pray you're right."

"I'm right, Ben. You heard it from your wife and son, too. But tell you the truth," she said, "I always thought it was you. Chris, maybe, but I'd have put money on it being you."

He grumbled something, took a swig of water from a plastic bottle, then began to head up the trail again.

Brigitte sighed and pulled her wool cap down around her ears and took off after him, her flashlight spearing the cold darkness ahead. Once she stepped on a fallen branch on top of the snow and it cracked loudly in the brittle air. Her heart thudded against her ribs, and she realized how intensely she was dreading that first sound of gunshots in the night. Wolves hunted at dusk. They'd be on the prowl right now. And if those men successfully baited the pack...

Don't think about it, she told herself, and she put one foot in front of the other, her shoulders beginning to hunch against the cold.

CHAPTER SEVENTEEN

STEVE'S DAUGHTERS stood in the middle of the living room, facing him down.

"What do you think I am, some knight on a white horse?" he yelled.

Jeannie flinched, but Heather regarded him mutely, her dark eyes brimming with tears.

"Okay," he said harshly, furious with his kids and with Brigitte—with himself, too. "Okay. Ruin Christmas. I'll go to the Garretts' and see what I can find out. Satisfied?"

Heather nodded somberly.

"I don't know when in hell I'll be home. Merry Christmas!" he muttered, and he grabbed his coat and hat, snatched up the truck keys and stomped out. *Unbelievable,* he thought. *Ungoddamn believable.*

Steve started the truck and spun the tires on the snow, careening down the driveway. "Damn her," he said aloud. "Damn her." Causing all this trouble. With her big blue innocent eyes and those pink curving lips that looked so sweet. Lies. Everything they uttered was lies.

He pulled up at the Garretts' and went to the door. He felt like a fool and a traitor, and he had no idea what he was going to say.

Audrey answered the door; she looked as if she'd been crying. What in the devil was going on with these women?

"Ben here?" he asked, staring at her.

"No, he isn't," she replied. "He's gone." She sniffed, blew her nose.

"On Christmas Eve?"

"He's gone," she repeated. "He's not here."

"Mind if I ask where he is?"

Chris Garrett came up behind his stepmother then. "He went with that woman of yours," Chris said. "He's up in the mountain somewhere looking for Jim."

Steve felt a new rush of anger. "First off, Chris, she isn't my woman, and second, why in blazes did Ben go with her?"

And then Dave appeared from the living room. "They're trying to stop Jim from shooting the wolves."

Steve was thunderstruck. "Your father is helping Brigitte?"

"Yeah, he is." Dave nodded.

Audrey looked up soberly. "I told him he had to. He's got to stop Jim from getting in even deeper."

Steve stared past the Garrett clan, thinking. Brigitte had begged him to help, and when he'd refused, she'd done the next logical thing—gone to the source. And somehow she'd convinced Ben to go with her.

"Where'd they go?" Steve asked. "You know? What direction?"

"South Cliff Trail," Audrey said. "I heard Ben say so."

A sense of urgency gripped Steve. Brigitte up there in the dark, bitter-cold mountains, alone with Ben Garrett and Jim and his trigger-happy pals. "Listen," he said, "Audrey, please call my kids and tell them where I'm going. Call the sheriff, too. Tell him what's going on. I'll try to find them."

"Oh, thank you," Audrey said fervently, and she gripped his hands.

"Take it easy now," he said. "They'll be fine." He sounded far more assured then he felt. "And, hey, Merry Christmas."

"Yeah, right," Chris said. "Merry goddamn Christmas."

Steve drove to the trailhead, following dark, winding country roads that were utterly deserted on this holiday evening. Everyone was home or visiting relations, indulging in a big dinner, egg nog, fruitcake and Christmas cookies. And here he was, out on a wild-goose chase, after a woman he'd sworn never to speak to again.

She'd managed to upset his kids, him, his entire life. She'd shown up in Sweetwater—a fairy princess, he'd called her. Oh, that was a laugh. And here he was, worried as hell, chasing after her on Christmas Eve.

He found the trailhead; it wasn't hard, because parked right there were Brigitte's Cherokee, Jim's truck and another vehicle that must have belonged to one of Jim's friends.

He got out of his truck and began rummaging in the tool container, where he kept a bunch of gear in case he ever got stuck. It would come in handy now: a good flashlight, an extra down vest, gloves, an old wool hat.

He lifted his shotgun off the rack of the cab and filled his pockets with shells. He hoped the snow wasn't too deep, but, then, the trail must be half-packed down by now.

He was ready. He stood there for a minute, looking up at the dark mountains. Brigitte was up there somewhere—feisty, pretty Brigitte who'd loved him and lied to him.

He wished he knew what lay ahead; he wished he knew to what lengths Jim and his pals would go if they'd already found the wolves. And just how would Brigitte react if she discovered that precious pack of wolves butchered?

He started up the trail, his flashlight beam playing on the snow where it was trampled in a straight line leading up. He didn't feel the cold, didn't see the stars, didn't notice his breath frosting as he began the climb. He had to find

Brigitte—that was the only thought his mind could hold. Ben might have agreed to bring her up here on the pretext of finding Jim, but the reality was that Brigitte could be in just as much peril as her beloved wolves.

That was when he heard it. He stopped dead in his tracks, listening, straining to hear. Nothing. Then the sound echoed down the mountainside again. It was very faint but unmistakable—the distant, long ululation of a single wolf, rising and falling on the night air.

For a long time Steve stood in the cold isolation of the wilderness, listening, the tiny hairs on his neck rising.

"DAMN," Ben said, stopping and breathing hard. "They aren't here."

Brigitte looked around, playing her flashlight over the snow, the black trees that overhung the clearing. "This is where you thought they'd be?"

"Yeah." He put his hands on his knees and bent over, panting.

"Are you all right?" she asked.

"Yeah, sure I am. Just a little winded."

She walked around the perimeter of the clearing, shining the flashlight on the ground. "This is the way they went," she said. "I can see their footprints."

"They went up onto that ridge to see if there were any elk in the next valley," Ben said.

"How do you know?"

"Because it figures. The wolves follow the herds, right? And if they want to locate the pack—" he paused to breathe "—they'll shoot a deer and leave it for the wolves to find. Get them to come to you."

Brigitte wanted to hurry, but Ben needed a few minutes' rest. They'd gone as fast as they could, though it wasn't fast enough for Brigitte.

"Okay," Ben said, straightening, "let's move on."

But as desperate as she was to reach Jim and his buddies in time, she hesitated. "You need to rest a bit more."

Ben snorted. "Thought you only cared about those damn predators," he said.

"That's not fair, Ben."

"Since when have you been playing fair?" he shot back.

Brigitte couldn't say a thing.

They headed off again finally, following the tracks upward to where the ridge overlooked another valley. It was dark, and she couldn't see very well, but there were faint sounds carried on the night air—voices, human voices, vague wisps of sound that came in snatches on the night breeze.

Every fiber of Brigitte wanted to rush to those men, stop them before it was too late. But Ben... He was done in, unable to catch his breath even when they rested. Now there was a gradual downhill slope to negotiate. If he slipped, fell...

"Take my hand," she said, reaching for him, but Ben shook off her gesture.

"Careful, then," she urged, her own boots slipping on the loose snow as they descended.

Brigitte paused on a level spot and waited for Ben. It was then that she noticed the moon was about to rise. She could see the glow that lit up the sky to the east, but a mountain hid it from view. The sky was like velvet, so deep and black, studded with a universe of stars. It would have been beautiful if she'd had the leisure to stop and study it.

She could hear Ben behind her, huffing and puffing. He was exhausted. She was really beginning to worry about him. What if he couldn't make it? What if he collapsed out here?

They reached the valley floor and kept following the tracks, which led toward a stand of tall spruce. Brigitte could hear voices clearly now.

"Jim," Ben called out when they were a hundred feet from the trees. "Hey, Jim-boy, it's me!"

There was silence, then a shadow broke away from the trees and moved toward them.

Maybe they were in time, Brigitte thought, because if they'd killed the wolves, they wouldn't still be here.

"Dad?" came a disembodied voice.

"Yes; it's me!" Ben forged ahead quickly.

Brigitte was right behind him when they met Jim. "What are you doing up here?" he asked. "Who's with you? Is that Audrey?"

Ben was gasping now. "No, not Audrey..."

"It's Brigitte Hartman," she said, and she heard him swear.

"What'd you bring her up here for, Dad? What's the matter with you?" he said, angry, disbelieving.

"I'm here in an official capacity," Brigitte said. "Your father was concerned about you breaking the law, so he led me here."

"What in hell?" Jim said furiously.

Ben tried to say something, but he was too out of breath.

"Let's get him someplace he can rest," Brigitte suggested.

"Yeah, sure, okay. Dad, are you nuts?" Jim put his father's arm around his neck and helped him into the clearing under the trees, which were so thick, the ground beneath them was dry.

There were three men sitting there around a Coleman lantern, each with a rifle or shotgun across his knees. One of them called out to Jim. "What's going on? Who's with you?"

"My dad," Jim said, letting Ben down slowly onto the ground, where the older man sat slumped over, still breathing in great gasps. "And this chick from Fish and Wildlife."

All three men jumped to their feet, shouting, cursing, demanding explanations. "Goddamn it, Garrett, what's the matter with you?" "Stupidest thing I ever saw!" "Gonna arrest us all for something crazy!"

"Quiet," came Ben's voice, and finally they heard him and stopped their yelling.

"I brought her up here…because there's proof that someone—" he took a deep breath "—killed the cattle. It wasn't…the wolves."

More shouting and cursing. Brigitte shrank back into the shadows, listening. Oh, she'd been brave enough coming up here to save the wolves, but now that she was alone in the middle of the mountains with four furious strong men, well, her courage was ebbing. Tombstone courage, they called it out West, the kind of dumb, unthinking, impetuous foolhardiness that gets you planted six feet deep. She cursed her impulsiveness. She should have called the sheriff. She should have… But it was too late. Now all she could do was try to get out of this mess in one piece. She shivered.

"What in the devil are we going to do with her?" one of the men asked.

"Someone can watch her while we take care of business," another suggested.

"Then she'll only turn us in when we get back!"

More cursing, arguments.

"You're making so much noise the pack'll be in Timbuktu by morning!" one yelled.

Jim held up a hand. "Okay, okay. Cool it, guys. We have to think. The moon'll be up soon, and then we've got to get into position. Leave her here—tied up, maybe."

"No," Ben croaked. "Son, you're in enough trouble as it is. Give it up. Let's go home. It's over."

"Trouble? What kind of trouble?" one of them asked. "Protecting our cattle?"

''I'm only doing what you wanted, Dad,'' Jim said in a high voice. ''I'm doing what you wanted, and now you say I shouldn't? Are you nuts?''

Ben held up a hand. ''Son, come here. Listen. We know the cattle were never killed by wolves. And that wolf that was left dead on the road...''

''Great shot, that was,'' Jim bragged. ''Wasn't it, Dad? Got her with one clean heart shot, two hundred yards.''

''Oh; God, Jim-boy,'' Ben said, his voice immeasurably sad. ''It *was* you, wasn't it?''

Brigitte's heart banged against her rib cage.

The moon showed above the shoulder of the mountain now, the curve of a silver disc. It was remarkably bright, and Brigitte could see the shadows cast across the snow beyond the spruce trees. She wondered if the wolves would come, dark wraiths against the snow, and if they came, would bullets meet them, blasting them into oblivion?

''Yeah, it was me,'' Jim was saying. ''And it was a good plan—get rid of those lousy wolves like you wanted. That's what you said, wasn't it, Dad?''

''Jim-boy, I'm sorry. I didn't know, I swear. I don't like the wolves shoved down our throats, but to do what you did...''

''You killed those calves?'' one of Jim's friends asked in a low, dangerous voice.

''I had to!'' Jim yelled. ''Don't you see I had to? Don't you? It was the only way!''

''Jim, calm down,'' Ben said. ''It's gonna be okay. Let's go home now. Come on, Audrey's waiting. She's worried. It's Christmas Eve.''

''No! I'm not going back until I do what I came for. Go on, all of you. Cowards, stupid gutless cowards! Go on, go home.''

He's gone crazy, Brigitte thought, and a frisson of fear rippled down her spine.

Ben stood up shakily and put his hand on his son's arm. "Jim, come on, boy."

But Jim knocked his father aside with the barrel of his gun in a quick, convulsive movement, screaming at him, and Ben fell to his knees.

Two of Jim's friends ran to Ben. One went to Jim, saying, "Give me the gun, Jim. Okay, it's time to give it up. It's me, Tommy. Now hand it over." But Jim cursed viciously and swept his friend's hand away, yelling, babbling.

Brigitte ran to help Ben, too. He had a nasty gash on his temple, and he was pale, as ashen as the moonlight. One of Jim's friends made a snowball and held it to the wounded spot. She knelt by Ben and asked, "Are you all right?"

He didn't answer, and they got him into a comfortable position, lying on a sleeping bag, covered by another. His eyes were closed, his breathing faint.

"Is he okay?" Brigitte asked one of the men. She was close to panic; she'd forced Ben to come up here.

But he didn't answer because Jim was ranting, standing in the middle of the moonlit clearing, holding his rifle braced against his hip, pointing at them. "You're all cowards! I'll do it myself, I'll get them. Soon as the moon's up."

Tommy was backing away, scared. And Jim was pretty frightening, his face all screwed up, his body so tense, he looked as if he were about to blow apart. His finger was on the trigger of the gun....

Ben stirred and opened his eyes. He mumbled something.

"Thank God," Brigitte breathed. "Ben, are you okay?"

"Yeah, yeah, okay. Jim?"

"He's gone bananas," one of the men said.

"Dear God."

"Can you try to reason with him?" Brigitte asked the man.

"Can you?" he retorted.

They crouched there, huddled around Ben. Tommy was trying to talk Jim down, but it only seemed to make him crazier. He kept swinging his rifle, sweeping it back and forth, covering them. He could pull the trigger at any time, by mistake if not on purpose. And he kept raving, talking. "Dad wanted it. No one else did it. Chris too damn cowardly. Dave a damn tree-hugger."

Brigitte was held by morbid fascination of the man who was so far out of control. She could see his gloved finger on the trigger; she could almost hear the blast, feel the bullet slam into her. She couldn't look away.

Ben was groaning, trying to rise, while the others were pushing him back onto the sleeping bag. Brigitte was kneeling there, shivering, staring at Jim. The clearing resounded with his voice, his terrible, anguished voice. She could see the hole in his gun barrel, like a dark, evil eye.

The moon came out then, freed from the mountain that had blocked it. Huge and silver, it hung improbably in the sky, casting light on everyone, on everything, every tree branch and rock, glaring off the snow, lighting the group of humans and the one who stood in the center of the clearing, yelling and swaying and swinging the gun back and forth, back and forth.

Suddenly a voice came out of the night. A low voice, but it stopped all of them in their tracks; even Jim paused, swinging the gun toward the sound.

"That's enough there, Jim," the voice said in a calm, measured tone.

Everyone's head turned toward the voice. Everyone saw the man step out of the shadow of a spruce tree into the moonlit clearing. Everyone saw his shotgun in his hands, ready.

"Steve," Brigitte breathed.

Utter silence fell over the scene: Jim whirled, his gun

ready, trained on Steve. His eyes were wild and his chest rose and fell with his panicky breathing.

"Put it down, Jim," Steve said. "That's it. It's over."

And then, from beyond the clearing, up above them somewhere on the craggy shoulders of the mountains, came the mournful, drawn-out howl of a wolf. It reverberated in the bitter night, terrible and awe inspiring. It rose like a dirge from the earth to the heavens, a warbling hymn that celebrated its own existence on this eve of Christmas, and Brigitte could see how it held every person there in thrall. She closed her eyes, the unearthly sound reaching deep, deep into her soul.

CHAPTER EIGHTEEN

THE WOLF'S WAIL died away slowly, trailing off into an echo. No one moved, no one said a word, not even Jim. Steve kept his gun ready, his heart pounding slow and steady, alert for any move.

Jim had gone crazy, that's the only explanation Steve could come up with for the ranting he'd heard. And Ben was hurt, and Brigitte...she was all right. She was fine.

He stood there in the moonlight and tried to come up with a plan to defuse the situation. Jim could do anything—on a moment's notice he could charge or start shooting.

Brigitte spoke first, breaking the silence. "Steve," she said, "thank heavens you came."

He switched his gaze from Jim to her, and in the glow of moonlight their eyes met and locked, all those unspoken words racing between them. He sensed her fear, her relief, her gratitude, her love, and he was inexpressibly glad he'd come.

Quickly he shifted his attention back to Jim. "Come on, Jim, put the gun down," he said. "No one's going to shoot anything up here tonight."

Jim shook his head, muttering something. Steve could see sweat shining on his face.

"Put it down, Jim," Tommy said. "Take it easy now. No one's going to hurt you."

"Jim-boy," Ben said weakly, "stop this. Stop it. It's over."

But Jim made a violent motion with his weapon and backed away toward the nearest spruce tree. "I'm getting out of here," he cried. "I'll find the wolves! Don't follow me."

"Please, Jim," Brigitte said, taking a step toward him, holding out her hand, "don't make this worse. Your father's hurt."

"Brigitte," Steve warned urgently.

But it was too late. Jim snatched her hand and dragged her close to him, using her as a shield.

"No, Jim, no!" Ben cried.

Steve swore under his breath. He stepped toward Jim, talking the whole time, calmly, reasonably. He never let his shotgun down, but he couldn't use it—he'd hit Brigitte. "Okay, Jim, everything's cool. Listen, we need your help to get your dad back down to the trucks. You don't want to hurt anybody, Jim, we know that. Just relax and lay that rifle down."

"No!" Jim screamed. Then he started backing away into the darkness under the huge spreading branches of the trees.

All Steve could see was the pale oval of Brigitte's face, her eyes wide, fixed on his, beseeching him to save her.

Tommy caught Steve's eye, made a small gesture, then started talking. "Hey, Jimmy, come on. We're all friends here. Maybe we should help you. Okay if I get my gun?" And he moved away, off to the side, hoping to distract Jim.

Steve stepped closer. Just a few feet and he could pull Brigitte to safety, wrestle Jim down. He had to do something, but the last thing on earth he wanted was to shoot somebody. Only if Brigitte's life was at stake, he thought. Only then.

The whole scene was a nightmare, lit by the moon from above, the lantern from the ground. A shadow box of crouched men, a woman held against a crazed outlaw, another man with a gun, one on the ground. Curses and Jim's hoarse breathing filled the air as eyes gleamed with fear and veins pumped with adrenaline.

What happened next was so utterly bizarre that Steve never quite believed it. A sound came from behind one of the big trees, and it silenced everybody as if a switch had been thrown. A sound, an unearthly, alien sound that was very close.

"What?" someone whispered, quickly shushed by someone else. They all listened, straining to hear.

There it was again, that low, penetrating sound. A snarl, a throaty rumble. *My God,* Steve thought, *it couldn't be...*

"A wolf," Brigitte whispered.

Jim lurched toward the sound, dragging Brigitte with him. His gun barrel swung around, pointing into the darkness. It came again, that menacing, feral voice. And then a pair of burning orbs appeared in the darkness, reflecting from the lantern light, a pair of almond-shaped, golden eyes, then another set—and another. Steve blinked, not believing his own eyes. He heard someone gasp, and then everything moved in very fast motion.

Jim cried out, the gun barrel shaking in his hand, and Steve lunged toward him, grabbed the barrel with one hand and yanked it out of Jim's grasp, pulling Brigitte behind him with the other.

"Oh, my God," he heard Brigitte say in a shaking voice.

Then the three others surrounded Jim, and Steve stood there, holding both guns, his breath coming too fast, the sour taste of fear in his mouth.

Tommy took the guns from him. "Thanks," he said.

"Grateful for your help," Steve acknowledged in turn, then Brigitte was standing in front of him, though he wasn't sure how she'd gotten there or when he'd let her go.

"Thank you," she said, but her look spoke eloquently of so much more.

"Damn fool," he mumbled.

"You or me?" she asked softly.

"Both of us."

"I'm sorry I lied to you," she said, but he cut her off.

"Later," he said. "We can both make our apologies later."

"Okay, deal." She put her arms around him, laid her head on his chest and stayed there for a long time. Then she raised her head and said to him, "You saw them, didn't you?"

They looked at each other and knew that was all either of them could ever admit.

IT WAS A LONG HAUL back to the trucks. The moon lit their way, and Jim's friends helped support Ben on the trek back down to the trailhead.

Jim himself was oddly quiet and passive. Once he'd been subdued, all the fight went out of him. For the whole way down he walked close to Ben.

No one talked much. Occasionally someone would say, "Watch this rock" or "It's slippery here" or "It must be near midnight, can't see my watch." Once Tommy said, "Some Christmas this turned out to be. Well, at least my wife'll be glad to see me home in the morning to open presents." There were murmured replies, a caustic "Merry Christmas!"

Ben seemed to be all right, although he was very tired. He walked out slowly, painfully, with help, and he said nothing—not to Jim, not to anyone.

When they finally reached the trailhead, Brigitte was so relieved, so exhausted, so cold and hungry, she couldn't think straight.

But Steve and Jim's friends organized themselves quickly—Brigitte would drive Ben home in her Cherokee, the rest would accompany Steve as he drove Jim. Just in case, leaving one vehicle to be picked up later.

Steve suggested they take Ben to the hospital, but the older man roused himself and refused. "I'm okay, just tired. I'm not going to any hospital. Just leave me be."

"Are you okay driving?" Steve asked Brigitte.

"Sure, just tired."

"Be careful, okay?"

She followed his taillights along the winding road. The ride seemed to take forever, and Ben was totally silent. He sat slumped next to her, looking straight ahead.

"I'm really sorry about Jim," she said once, but she got no answer and gave up.

They finally arrived at the Garrett house, and they found quite a reception committee. The sheriff was there with a deputy, waiting. Audrey and the other Garrett sons ran out when they heard Steve's arrival. There was a lot of talk, some angry exchanges. Audrey cried and led Ben in, shaking off everyone who wanted to talk to him.

It was confusing to Brigitte—all the lights and noise and people milling around. She was so tired.... The sheriff asked her a few questions; he was furious at being called out on Christmas Eve for something he said the feds should have taken care of.

"Young lady, you've caused a lot of trouble in Sweetwater," he told her.

Steve had to explain the whole thing over again. Jim Garrett sat in the sheriff's car, saying nothing, seemingly unaware of all the tumult around him. His brother Chris tried to talk to him but gave up, shrugging. "He won't talk," he said.

Finally the sheriff drove away with Jim. They were going to put him in protective custody until they could get hold of a judge. One by one Jim's friends drove off, the Garrett boys went inside and Steve and Brigitte were left alone. She was sitting in the passenger seat of her Jeep, her head against the headrest, feeling as drained as she'd ever been in her life.

Steve walked over, put a hand on the roof of the vehicle and leaned down. He looked at her for a minute, saying nothing. Then he asked, "How you doing?"

"I'm okay," she replied.

The moon silvered the landscape, but his face was in shadow. "Some evening," he said.

"Uh-huh." She waited, her heart pounding slowly and steadily. She felt, she knew, something had to happen between them now.

"It's Christmas morning," he finally said.

"Yes."

"Brigitte…" He paused, as if rethinking what he was going to say. "You were brave up there."

"I was scared to death."

He put a hand out and tipped her chin up. "Come home with me," he said softly.

"Now?"

"Yes, now."

"But…"

"It's Christmas. You shouldn't be alone. Come home with me."

She looked up at him and studied his face—the strong black eyebrows, the flat plane of his cheek, the sculpted jaw, all that she loved and wanted.

"Yes," she breathed. "But, Steve, are you sure? Are you… You were so angry…."

"Never mind all that. Leave it for some other time, okay?"

"Okay." She wondered what he was thinking. A million questions chased themselves around in her head. Had he forgiven her? What did he feel? What would happen? But it was not the time, and she was too tired. He was only being polite, a gentleman. She couldn't allow herself to take his offer any further than that.

She followed him home and parked beside him on the familiar driveway. The lights in the house were on.

"Damn kids are still up," he said.

"They're worried."

The girls were asleep, huddled together on the living room couch under a blanket, the television set on. Steve bent over them and woke them up gently.

Heather rubbed her eyes, then sat up abruptly. "Dad!"

"Hey, kiddo, Merry Christmas," he said.

"What happened? What…?" She saw Brigitte and stopped.

"Everything's okay," he said. "We found them. The wolves are fine and it's all over."

"Oh, Dad…"

"Yeah, I know."

Jeannie sat up, owl-eyed, half-asleep. "Daddy?"

"What, honey?"

"Is it time to open the presents yet?"

"No." He laughed. "It's not quite morning yet. Go on upstairs and go back to sleep."

"Dad…?" Heather was looking at Brigitte.

"Brigitte's real tired, kids. It's been a rough night, so I asked her to come home with me. She's going to celebrate Christmas with us."

"Can she come to Aunt Naomi's with us?" Jeannie asked.

Steve gave Brigitte a searching look.

"I don't know," she replied. "Let's talk about it to-morrow."

"Go on upstairs," Steve said. "It's late." He smiled. "You better go to bed real quick so Santa Claus can come."

"Right, Dad," Heather said, rolling her eyes.

Heather got up off the couch, pulling the blanket around her shoulders. She started toward the stairs, then she stopped and turned to Brigitte, her dark eyes very serious. "I'm sorry I was mean to you…you know…"

Brigitte knew. "Thanks, Heather."

The girl ducked her head, embarrassed. "It's okay if you and Dad…" Her voice trailed off.

"That's nice of you," Brigitte said just as seriously. "I appreciate your saying that." But she knew the likelihood of anything happening between Steve and herself was pretty remote at this point. She'd seen to that, hadn't she?

Finally they were alone. Brigitte sank down onto the couch and sighed.

"God, I'm beat," Steve said. "But I've got to put the rest of the presents under the tree."

"Want some help?" she asked.

"Sure."

They were like a married couple, Brigitte thought. Sadness gripped her, and she became very quiet.

"Something wrong?" Steve asked.

She gave him a quick look and tried to smile. "No. I'm just tired, you know."

"You can, ah, sleep in the guest room," he said.

"Thanks."

"If you want to."

"I think it's better, don't you?"

"Yeah, sure. Whatever you want."

I want you, she cried silently. But she could never say that aloud.

She gestured with a hand. "Maybe I should just drive home. Maybe…"

"No," he said, his eyes searching hers. "It's too late."

"Mmm."

"Brigitte…"

She looked at him questioningly.

"We'll talk tomorrow."

"Sure," she said, trying for levity.

"When our heads are clear."

"Absolutely." She nodded.

"You're asleep on your feet," he said.

"Practically."

"Good night, then. Merry Christmas," he said quietly.

"Merry Christmas," she repeated. They stood there in the half-light of his living room, and she was so terribly aware of him and so achingly afraid that nothing she could ever do would make amends for the way she'd lied to him.

As tired as Brigitte was, she didn't fall asleep immediately. Her mind was filled with questions—Steve, his daughters, Jim Garrett and what would happen to him, Mac's reaction to the whole affair. Too much, too much. Her brain was on overload.

She lay there in the downstairs guest room and knew that Steve was just above her; she could see his room in her mind's eye—the bed, the dresser, his clothes thrown over a chair, Steve in the bed, alone. She saw every curve of his body, the muscles that sheathed his arms and shoulders, the lean look of him, the black hair that covered his chest and thinned down to a line over his flat belly.

He was there, so close. She wondered what tomorrow held—no, today, she thought. Christmas Day. A time for family and happiness, good food. A day for gifts of love.

Brigitte fell asleep finally, alone in the guest room, and she dreamed of golden eyes shining in the darkness, dozens of pairs of glowing embers, and they were all focused on her, but she wasn't afraid. Somehow, even in her sleep, she knew the wolves were her friends.

CHAPTER NINETEEN

No one was exactly up at dawn to open presents on Christmas morning. When Brigitte finally rolled over and looked at the clock, it was almost 9:00 a.m.

She scrubbed a hand through her hair, sat up on the side of the bed and yawned. Then she looked down at herself, at her underwear, and over at the pile of dirty clothes she'd tossed on the chair by the door. Swell.

She showered and used the new toothbrush and toothpaste in the medicine cabinet and was about ready to drag on her dirty clothes when there was a knock on the bathroom door.

She opened it a crack.

"Hi," Heather said, standing there with a pair of folded jeans and an Irish knit sweater in her arms. "Dad got these out of the attic. They were Mom's."

"Are you sure it's okay?" Brigitte asked.

Heather smiled. "We're all sure."

By the time she was dressed, her hair pushed into damp spikes, everyone was waiting for her in the living room.

"It's about time," Jeannie said brightly. "I was going to start opening presents, but Heather and Dad wouldn't let me. Can I start now?"

"It's okay with me," Brigitte said, and she caught Steve's gaze from where he stood near the fireplace. He nodded at her, a neutral gesture. "Thanks for the clothes," she mouthed, and again he nodded.

While the girls tore open their presents, Brigitte sat and

watched with a cup of coffee in her hands. She was acutely aware of everything. Jeannie, or maybe Heather, had put Christmas music in the CD player and Steve had started a cozy fire. The tree, of course, was lit, and the colorful balls reflected myriad hues while a bar of December sunlight spilled in through a window. Naomi had given Heather a scented candle, and she'd already lit it and set it on the coffee table. The whole room smelled of Christmas spices: pine and nutmeg and cinnamon and oranges. There was joy and laughter in the house and lots of hugs and kisses for Dad.

"Oh, I love this!" Heather exclaimed, holding up an oversize black cable-knit sweater. And when Brigitte looked at Steve with approval, he only shrugged, embarrassed.

He was embarrassed, too, when the girls kept bringing him gifts to open and then waited on pins and needles to see his reaction. He had gotten socks and a belt and a new barn jacket from his mother. Heather gave him a pair of work gloves, and then there was the big moment when he opened the cellular phone.

"Oh, no," he groaned. "I was the last holdout in the valley. You aren't going to make me…?"

"Oh, yes, we are," Jeannie said, her hands on her hips. "And you have to pay the monthly bill."

Steve groaned again and then snatched her hand and dragged her over to give her a kiss. "Okay, okay," he said. "I guess I'll just have to be a man of the nineties."

Everyone laughed.

There were little gifts for Brigitte, too. Jeannie and Heather had gotten her a ski cap and mittens, baby blue. "They match your eyes," Jeannie announced. "Don't they match her eyes, Dad?"

Brigitte smiled and blushed.

"Yes, they do," Steve said from his easy chair, but she could read nothing in his expression.

And there were her gifts to the girls. It was almost as if they were an ordinary family. But, of course, they weren't.

It wasn't long at all before the entire living room floor was littered with gold and silver and red paper, yards of ribbon and bows, boxes lying askew with crumpled tissue paper hanging out. Then there were the stockings. Steve had stuffed them with practical items. Heather dumped hers on the floor and grinned. "Oh, wow, Dad. Like how clever. Let's see. Toothpaste, toothbrush, cotton balls, soap, dental floss. Now that's cool."

Steve just smiled.

"I got a hairbrush set in mine," Jeannie announced, "and candy. You didn't get candy."

Heather stuck her tongue out. "Dad knows I don't want to be fat like you."

Jeannie whirled around to Brigitte. "Am I fat?"

Brigitte laughed. "You're as thin as a rail, pumpkin."

It was a very special Christmas morning. After all the presents were opened and the paper burning in the hearth, Brigitte helped Steve cook breakfast. She put strips of bacon in the iron skillet and felt terribly ill at ease—eventually they were going to have to talk. They couldn't go on like this, both pretending.

Steve was busy mixing pancake batter when she turned to him and took a deep breath, not even knowing where to begin. "Steve," she said, "I'd really like to…"

But just then Heather came in. "Dad, can I drive over to Dave's? It's Christmas, and there won't be a single car on the road. Please?"

Steve caught Brigitte's gaze before turning to Heather. "It's not that," he said. "I just think that maybe today's not a good time to—"

But Heather cut him off. "I just talked to him, Dad, and everything's okay."

Steve raised a doubtful brow.

"No, really," she went on. "Dave said his dad's feeling better, and Jim's even home, and..."

"Huh?" Steve said.

"They got a lawyer or something. And Dave says he may be crazy. They have to get him... What's the word?"

"Evaluated?" Steve said.

"That's it. Dave said they were up all night talking."

Steve was shaking his head. "Look, I still don't think it's proper for you to go rushing over there. And on Christmas. It's a family day."

Heather looked as if she were ready to stomp a foot. "Just one lousy hour. I'll be home in plenty of time to go to Aunt Naomi's. Please?"

Brigitte was keeping her hands busy, trying not to interfere. Hadn't she interfered enough?

Then Steve let out a low whistle. "All right. We eat breakfast first, though, as a family. Then one hour. That's it. And you're to drive very carefully."

"I'll be on the ranch roads, Dad."

"You'll be on the county road for at least a half mile," he said, taking plates out of the cupboard.

And so it went all through the big Christmas breakfast. Normal family stuff. Brigitte ate and thought about Jim being at home, and she guessed that was okay. He wasn't going to run off or anything. And, really, he did need professional help. She could just imagine all the hullabaloo the media was going to create over the next few weeks. She'd even bet the Garretts were already being inundated with phone calls begging for interviews, even on Christmas Day.

She ate and avoided eye contact with Steve and realized she had to call Mac and update him. And her mom and sister, to say Merry Christmas. Her gifts were still back at the cabin, too, unopened. Should she just pile them in her car with everything else and head back to Denver? Maybe even this afternoon?

But she wasn't going to leave Sweetwater before she and Steve had a long talk. She had to know it was okay with him, that he understood now why she'd lied about who she was. He didn't have to forgive her. He only had to say he understood. As for the other things between them... That was all over. Love couldn't survive a betrayal like this.

She did the dishes and knew she had to talk to the girls, too. Over these last weeks an important bond had formed between them. She wasn't going to break that. Denver wasn't all that far away, after all. Maybe they could visit once in a while—for weekends. Shop. Go to ball games. Whatever. Steve would let them. Sure he would.

Heather was racing out the door when Brigitte realized she might be gone by the time Steve's daughter returned from the Garretts'. She grabbed her parka and ran out after her, catching her with the key in the ignition of Steve's truck.

"Oh, no. Don't tell me Dad's changed his mind," Heather groused.

But Brigitte reassured her that he hadn't. "I wanted to talk to you," she said. "I may not be here when you get home, and it's just that, well, I have to get back to my real life. I plan to leave tomorrow."

Heather cocked her head. "But I thought..."

"I can imagine what you thought. But your dad and I... Well, this is hard. All I can say is that I wasn't honest with him about who I really was, and that kind of spoiled everything."

Heather was staring at her.

"You see, well, relationships have to be based on honesty, and I..."

"Do you love my dad?" Heather blurted out.

"Well, I... Yes. I do." *Oh, God,* she thought.

"Does he love you?"

"I don't know. He may have, honey. But now... I broke a trust."

Heather mulled that over. "But I don't really understand. Why can't you make up?"

"It's not as simple as that." Brigitte stood in the cold December morning and tried her best to explain. "It's that trust and, well, my life in Denver, my job."

"But you could work in the mountains," Heather said. "Why do you have to live in Denver?"

Brigitte hugged the parka around her shoulders and thought about that. "I don't have to, I guess. It's simply the way it is for now."

"It's the way you want it, you mean," Heather said, frowning. "You don't want to stay here or you would."

"I...I wish it were that easy," she replied. "I really don't know how to put it into words. I blew it here. I blew it with your dad, anyway. I only wanted you to know that I care about you. I care a lot."

Heather was very quiet.

"I'm hoping we'll still be friends. I'm hoping that you and Jeannie will come to Denver and visit. There's so much we can do together. I feel as if...we're family, somehow. I don't want to lose that. What do you think?"

Heather looked at the steering wheel, then out the window. "I'd like to go to Denver. I mean, without Dad. He hates the malls and all that. I guess it would be neat if we could come see you."

"Then it's a deal." Brigitte smiled and leaned in the window and gave her a hug, which she accepted.

It was harder to talk to Jeannie, who really didn't understand at all. She cried and clung to Brigitte and didn't settle down until Brigitte promised she could come to Denver for a weekend in January. Now all she had to do was convince Steve.

After talking to Jeannie, she went downstairs to find him. He was out in the barn, working even though it was Christmas Day. The life of a rancher. A good life, really, an honest life. If she'd learned nothing else by coming to Sweetwater, she'd learned that she was wrong about small-town folks. They worked hard, cared for their families and, yes, protected their property fiercely. She'd always thought that lifestyle was provincial and narrow-minded. But now she'd come to realize it had its own validity. It was a wholesome, caring way to live. She'd been so bitter after her dad had left, so miserable and afraid, that she'd come to distrust men and relationships. His betrayal had colored her thinking for so long it was hard even now to tell fact from fiction. The one thing she had learned was that Steve Slater never had been and never would be anything like her father.

Steve was restacking bales of hay when she walked into the big, cold barn. The dogs ran up to greet her, then went back to Steve's side.

"That was a nice Christmas," she said, hands in her parka pockets. "Thank you, Steve. Thank you for having me. I know it wasn't easy."

He kept right on working, only glanced at her and wrestled another bale of hay onto the stack. "The girls liked having you here," he said, puffing with the exertion.

"Hmm," she muttered, aware that he'd said nothing about his own feelings. What had she expected? She shrugged that off and put a smile on her lips. "I'm afraid I may have presumed a lot when I said goodbye to them, Steve. I, ah, asked them to come and see me in Denver. I hope you don't…"

"I don't mind," he said, avoiding eye contact. "They both like you."

"Well," Brigitte said, steeling herself, "that brings me

to another subject. I think we have to talk, Steve. I've got to go soon, and I'm not leaving till we…well, talk. Okay?''

He let out a low breath and finally stopped stacking bales. ''I'm not much for words,'' he said. ''You know that.''

''I'd like to try. Maybe if we went for a walk…?''

He stood there for a long moment and then finally nodded. ''All right, Brigitte.''

Side by side, dogs running ahead, they strolled down the fence line, the crusted snow crunching beneath their boots. In the gently sloping fields, the cattle nosed aside the snow and grazed, and high above them—somewhere—Brigitte could picture the wolf pack cavorting under the pale winter sun, sniffing the brittle air for the scent of deer or elk.

She mused aloud. ''You realize,'' she said, ''that the pack won't be bringing down any livestock. They never did.''

Steve nodded, then he, too, glanced up toward the Flat Tops. ''I was wrong about that. Dead wrong. We all were.''

Brigitte let his words settle between them, then she said, ''Jim's going to have to pay a price for what he did. I wonder if people here realize that.''

''We're not stupid,'' Steve said, avoiding her gaze. ''We were all taken in by him. Bunch of damn fools.''

''And by me, too,'' she ventured.

''Mmm,'' he said.

''But do you understand now why I had to do it?''

''In a way,'' he allowed. ''But you could have trusted me.''

''And I should have. Hindsight is always twenty-twenty. I'd give anything to turn back the clock. You'll never know how bad I feel. I lied to you. I lied to everyone.''

He shrugged. ''It was your job. I understand that. I only wish you'd told me.''

''You'll never forgive me,'' she stated. Then she stopped

and put a hand on his arm. "There's something else, Steve. I…I came over to leave the girls their presents under the tree and… Oh, God, this is hard. But I saw your jacket. A sheepskin jacket. And there was blood on it and I thought…I thought…"

"That it was me."

She dropped her gaze to the ground.

"Yes," she whispered. "After the autopsy report about sheepskin fibers and the dog prints all over the snow…"

"It *was* blood on the jacket," Steve said. "Blood from a calf that got hung up in the fence."

Brigitte nodded. Then she took a deep breath. "I didn't tell Mac. I knew I should have, but I couldn't. I couldn't stand to think it was you. I…I liked you too much."

"I see" was all he said.

So she went on. What did it matter now? "Everything between us was real. I told myself every day that I was going to come clean with you. I almost told you several times."

"So why didn't you?"

She looked up and met his dark eyes, so solemn now, and her gaze again dropped to the ground. "I think maybe I was afraid that you'd…you'd understand or something, and then I'd be… Well, I wouldn't have had any excuses for… This is really difficult. But, I guess, I would have had to let my feelings for you come out, and then, well, it would have meant…"

"Making a commitment."

"Yes," she said softly.

"Look," he said, "I know I was under suspicion. I understand that. I know you were doing your job. But if you'd looked past all that… What I'm saying is that I think you've confused me with your father, with his leaving you, I know that. You could have trusted me, Brigitte. You should have seen that."

Then she gave a sad, short laugh. "I blew it."

"Yes," he said very quietly, "you did."

They walked back toward the ranch after that, slowly, not saying a whole lot. Brigitte was lost in her thoughts, her heart sore. Everything she'd said—everything Steve had said—was so painfully honest. All along she'd avoided his acceptance, the love he'd so willingly given, by pretending that if she told him the truth he'd hate her. The actual truth was that she'd known in her heart he'd forgive her. And she'd have had to accept his love.

Oh, Lord, she thought. She'd ruined everything. Everything.

Back at the house she collected the gifts from the girls and then found Steve. Jeannie was with him in the kitchen, helping to put together the things they were taking with them for Christmas dinner with the family in New Castle.

"Well," Brigitte said with false enthusiasm, "that was a wonderful morning. I've got to get going, though. Lots of calls to make, you know."

"Sure," Steve said.

"Can you come to New Castle with us?" Jeannie asked.

"No, sweetie," Brigitte said, standing there, facing them, "I really can't."

Jeannie frowned. Then suddenly she smiled. "But we're coming to Denver, aren't we? And we can go shopping."

"It's a promise." She simply could not meet Steve's eyes.

Then Jeannie rushed over to her and gave her a hug. "Please don't go," she said against Brigitte's parka. "Please, Daddy, tell her she can't!"

It was the hardest leavetaking Brigitte had ever known. Ever would know. But somehow she left the Slater ranch. She got into her car and drove off without another word to Steve, and the snow-packed ribbon of road before her was a blur.

STEVE DROVE to his sister's house in frozen silence. He was going through the motions, nothing more. He kept trying to relive the walk he'd taken with Brigitte and the things they'd said—and hadn't said—and recall the way the weak December light had struck her hair, her face, her eyes.

He knew he was torturing himself, the same way he'd done when he'd buried Leslie. Reliving the last moments together. Over and over. Wondering if there was something he could have said or done. Something that could have forever altered the terrible outcome. He really didn't care anymore that Brigitte was with USFWS. He secretly admired her education and beliefs, her dedication. He could forgive her all that easily, though he sure wasn't about to forgive her for not trusting him enough to tell the truth. And as far as her making a commitment in a relationship, she wasn't ready. She'd probably never be ready, he figured. Not for him and not for anyone else. How in hell had he fallen in love with someone so unattainable?

The notion almost made him laugh out loud. Then abruptly he wished he could get his hands on that no-account father of hers. He'd wring the man's neck for doing this to her.

Only once on the drive to New Castle did one of the girls say anything about Brigitte. It was Heather. "I think you're both really stupid," she said from the passenger seat.

And Steve said, "One more word, young lady, just one more word and we're turning around." The tone in his voice left no room for argument.

Christmas dinner at Naomi's was miserable for him. First everyone had to know all about Jim Garrett and the dead cattle. Then Jeannie told the family about Brigitte and how she'd saved the wolf pack with Steve and how she was really a Fish and Wildlife biologist.

Naomi, naturally, wouldn't let go of it. "Well, I think that's great. She really showed you ranchers, didn't she?"

"She showed us, all right," Steve said darkly. "She also tricked us."

But Naomi shrugged that off. "If she hadn't come to Sweetwater undercover like she did, Jim Garrett would still be up there killing cattle. I guess you're just suffering from some wounded male pride there, brother."

The talk just kept going, about the cattle and the wolves and how maybe USFWS would now release a new pack in the San Juan Mountains of southwestern Colorado.

"I bet Brigitte gets to work with the wolves," Jeannie said. "When I grow up I want to be just like her."

Naomi caught Steve's eyes and laughed. Steve merely groaned.

Then Ruth started in. "I really did think you two hit it off. Is the problem that her job makes her travel? Gosh, I would think you could work that out. Nowadays it's so common. And I'll bet she makes a darn good salary."

"Can we talk about something else?" Steve begged.

But there was nothing else to say. The drive home was tiresome, and Steve realized he'd barely slept a wink the night before. It hadn't been the adrenaline. It was more that he hadn't been able to get the image of Brigitte out of his head. He couldn't get her out of his thoughts now, either, and he felt sick with the need for her.

It was before the turnoff on Interstate 70 that Heather put in her last two cents' worth on the subject. "Don't get mad, Dad, but you know Brigitte's leaving tomorrow. If you're going to, like, do anything…"

"Well, I'm damn well not going to do anything about it. Now stow it, will you?"

"Sure, Dad," she said, and Steve drove on into the night—Christmas night—and knew in his heart he was making the biggest mistake of his life.

DESPITE IT BEING the most miserable day in her life, Brigitte had to admit to a couple of bright moments.

After she'd left Steve's and cried the whole way into town, she'd collected herself enough to stop by Bess and Stan Cantrell's to say goodbye. She hadn't expected a gushing welcome but had gotten one nonetheless. She'd left with a big hug and kiss from Bess and promises to stay in touch.

"Go get 'em," Bess had said, giving her a heartening smile.

And then Brigitte had made a last stop. She'd driven out to the Ramseys', wanting very much to say goodbye to Kathy and apologize for not telling her the truth. They'd become friends, after all.

Kathy had surprised her. "I always knew you were somebody. And I'm really proud of you. We were all fooled by that Jim Garrett, and I hope you throw the book at him. He had no right to deceive us like that. No right at all. I only wish you could stay. I thought maybe you and Steve... Well, you know. It would have been so good for the girls, too. I guess he's pissed, huh?"

Brigitte had summoned up a smile. "You could say that."

"Men are such babies."

They'd hugged and said goodbye and even made a lunch date for January when Kathy was going to be in Denver, college-hunting with her oldest. Brigitte had arrived back at her cabin feeling a little better. And then she'd stood in the doorway and looked at the bed and remembered Steve had known all about her then. Everything. And yet he'd still made love to her. Maybe, she thought, maybe there was a ray of hope....

But there wasn't. People didn't get second chances. Not with the heart. If love ever knocked again, if she ever got over Steve, that was, she'd grab the gift and hold on for dear life.

It grew dark and she switched on her lights and packed her clothes. When she was finished she called her mother and sister in Montana and wished them Merry Christmas and told them all about her adventures in Sweetwater, without mentioning Steve Slater. Even the sound of his name was enough to make her choke up.

Steve, she thought. Oh, God, how she was going to miss him.

She tried telephoning Mac but got his recorder at home, so she left a message. "I'll be in the office by noon. Looking forward to the mountains of paperwork. Ugh. And the press. Double ugh. See you then."

She sat on the side of the bed and sighed, wondering why the heck she didn't toss her stuff in the Cherokee and drive back to Denver tonight. There was nothing keeping her in Sweetwater. Only painful memories. Only a masochist would stay. So she decided she'd go ahead and leave. It was Christmas, after all. She should be with friends, especially now. It was the holiday season—you were supposed to be joyful. She checked the bathroom for personal items, looked in the closet once more, in the dresser drawers. She'd erase herself from this place as if she'd never ever been here.

She had one large suitcase and a small bag full of odds and ends. That was it. Lord, she sure hadn't brought much. She pulled on her coat, looked around the room one last time and bent over for the strap of the small bag.

There was a knock at the door.

Brigitte straightened.

The knock came again, then the voice. "Brigitte, are you there? Open the door, Brigitte."

Her heart fluttered in her chest like a wild thing. For an

instant she was frozen, then she rushed to the door and wrenched it open.

It was really Steve. It was really him standing there in her doorway. She gasped and stepped back, and he reached forward and took the bag out of her hand, setting it down. She hadn't even known she was holding it. She just stared at him.

"We didn't finish talking," he said, his face in shadows, all straight, serious planes.

"What?" she said idiotically.

"We never finished talking."

"Oh."

"And I was going to ask you something. If I don't ask, I'll be kicking myself in the butt for the rest of my life."

"Oh," she said again, her knees suddenly weak.

"Brigitte," he said, "you know I'm not real good with words. But I was wondering, would you stay here? I mean, with me. We'd get married, of course."

Brigitte thought her head was going to burst. She leaned against the wall of the cabin, put a hand on her forehead and said, "Yes."

"What?" Steve said.

"Yes. I said yes," she whispered. "I love you."

A smile broke out on his face. "You do? You will? I mean, you don't have to quit work or anything. I want you to have your work. Even those wolves of yours. Whatever you want."

"I want you. I want you and the girls and a whole long life together. And maybe a baby, too."

"As many as you want," he said, and he took a step toward her, put his hands on her cheeks and leaned close. "Brigitte," he breathed, "if I hadn't come here tonight... Well, would you have really left? Were we both so stubborn we were going to throw this away?"

She brushed his lips with hers. "I might have made it to the interstate."

He kissed her hungrily. "That far?" he whispered.

"Mmm," she said, "probably not."

FAR ABOVE the Sweetwater valley, Star moved slowly, stealthily, through the black forest until she came to a rock outcropping that was bathed in moonlight. Behind her the pack waited, and Silverfoot kept watch, his ears swiveling to the sounds of the night. Star knew no fear in the cold shadows. She turned and viewed her pack and, satisfied, raised her muzzle to the moon and howled, the timeless, lyrical eulogy of the wolf. Before her, the thick, life-giving forest spread. At last, like the woman far below in the valley, she'd found a home.

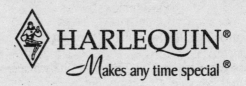

HARLEQUIN®
Makes any time special ®

	Upbeat, All-American Romances
HARLEQUIN® *Duets*™	Romantic Comedy
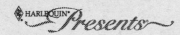	Historical, Romantic Adventure
HARLEQUIN® **INTRIGUE**	Romantic Suspense
Harlequin Romance®	Capturing the World You Dream Of
HARLEQUIN® *Presents*	Seduction and passion guaranteed
HARLEQUIN® *Super*ROMANCE®	Emotional, Exciting, Unexpected
	Sassy, Sexy, Seductive!

HDIR2

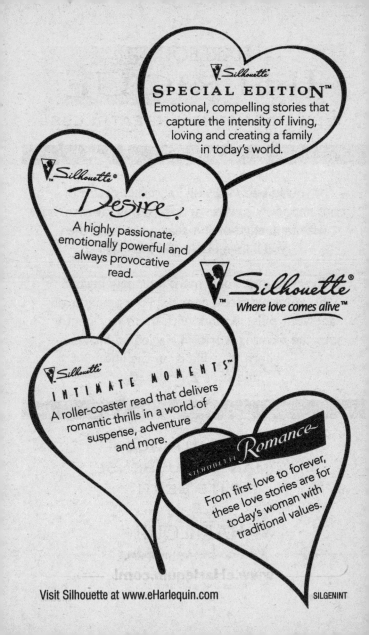

SPECIAL EDITION™
Emotional, compelling stories that capture the intensity of living, loving and creating a family in today's world.

Desire®
A highly passionate, emotionally powerful and always provocative read.

Silhouette®
Where love comes alive™

INTIMATE MOMENTS™
A roller-coaster read that delivers romantic thrills in a world of suspense, adventure and more.

Romance
From first love to forever, these love stories are for today's woman with traditional values.

Visit Silhouette at www.eHarlequin.com

SILGENINT

SILHOUETTE *Romance*™

Escape to a place where a kiss is still a kiss...
Feel the breathless connection...
Fall in love as though it were
the very first time...
Experience the power of love!

Come to where favorite authors—such as
Diana Palmer, Stella Bagwell,
Marie Ferrarella and many more—
deliver heart-warming romance and genuine
emotion, time after time after time....

Silhouette Romance—
stories straight from the heart!

Silhouette®
Where love comes alive™